CATALYST

CATALYST

A TALE OF THE BARQUE CATS

ANNE McCAFFREY

ELIZABETH ANN SCARBOROUGH

DEL REY

BALLANTINE BOOKS · NEW YORK

Copyright © 2010 by Anne McCaffrey and Elizabeth Ann Scarborough

Published in the United States by Del Rey, an imprint of The Random House Publishing Group, a division of Random House, Inc., New York.

DEL REY is a registered trademark and the Del Rey colophon is a trademark of Random House, Inc.

ISBN 978-0-345-51376-2

Printed in the United States of America

Book design by Simon M. Sullivan

This book is dedicated to the memories of Punkin and Chessie McCaffrey and Kittibits (Bonnie Dundee) Scarborough, who would be Barque Cats had they been born a bit later, and to Treat Scarborough, whose quirky personality made him the model for Pshaw-Ra.

It is also dedicated to Dr. Tony and Jeanette Rogstad for their dedication to the health and well-being of cats, dogs, and any other animals in need.

CATALYST

"How much for that pretty kittycat you got there, young lady?"

Janina started, jarring Chessie out of her brooding nap. Chessie laid her ears back, stretched, and gazed up into the face of the man who stood smiling down at them. He was a grizzled-looking spacer in the middle of the human life span, she judged, wearing a uniform, the arms of which sported a collection of ships' patches bearing insignias she did not recognize. But then, Hood Station, where they had just docked, was a backwater facility providing the interface between the agro-based planet Sherwood and the rest of the universe. A wide variety of human types roamed the corridors. Though the man didn't seem threatening, he certainly seemed ignorant about cats, as Janina, Chessie's Cat Person, immediately informed him. Had Janina been a cat, Chessie thought, she'd have been bristling.

"Excuse me, sir, but if you are referring to Thomas's Duchess, descendant of Tuxedo Thomas, the original Barque Cat himself, she is not for sale at any price." Janina tightened her arms protectively around Chessie's kitten-heavy body.

"Beggin' your pardon, miss, I had no idea the lady was such a celebrity. She's just such a beauty and I'm looking for a cat for my kid. Looks like she's going to litter soon. How many kittens do you reckon she's got in there?"

"Dr. Vlast says no fewer than five and perhaps as many as eight!"

Janina replied proudly. "Chessie is a good breeder and a good mother."

"Glad to hear it. Glad to hear it. Still, that's a lot of kittens. You'll be looking for homes for them, won't you?"

This fellow just didn't get it, did he? Chessie knew her kittens were far too valuable to be given away as pets! How could a spacer not know the history of Barque Cats? Had she been able to speak to Janina, she'd have asked, "Doesn't he know we save lives, that we patrol the tight areas of our spaceships, keeping rodents from eating the coating on cables, smelling hazardous gases and even escaping oxygen?" Chessie looked into Janina's face, which was flushing a pretty pink, and mewed her confusion.

"Chessie's—the Duchess's—kittens were spoken for three litters ago, sir," Janina informed him politely, then added, reeling off the little speech the crew's communication's officer had prepared for her, "They are highly prized, as her progeny are not only superbly bred but have all grown into the best ships' cats in the universe. The sire of this particular litter is Space Jockey, a cat as renowned as the Duchess herself for his breeding and spirit."

Hah! The truth was that although Jock was a handsome tom, he was a terrible brawler. That trait accounted for the rambunctiousness of these unborn babies of his. Chessie had never carried a more active litter, and that was saying something! She had borne twelve litters in fewer years, barely having time to train one kindle of kittens in the space ways before the next lot was born and the whole process began again. She couldn't actually remember many times when she had not been pregnant. It made patrolling the ventilation ducts and interior passages of her ship, the *Molly Daise*, a bit difficult at times, but there were always half-grown kittens to go into those few places where she could not fit her belly.

"Is that the truth? Well, I'll be. Could I pet her? Would she mind? She's such a pretty cat."

"I suppose it would be all right," Janina said, with a glance down at her.

The girl was already a bit more skittish than usual, and Chessie knew it was because she had opposed this latest pregnancy. Chessie couldn't agree more, but she graciously lifted her head to meet the man's fingers and felt Janina relax somewhat. The man had a gentle touch, and his fingers smelled pleasantly male and of a recent hearty meal. She gave the back of his hand a lick as he pulled it away.

"What a darlin' girl," the man said, smiling at her. He had a very nice white smile that made his rugged face look younger. Chessie approved. He could probably snap a rat's neck with a single bite with teeth like those!

Janina beamed. Chessie's young Cat Person took as much pride in Chessie and her babies as Chessie herself did. They had been together ten years, all of Chessie's life and over half of Janina's, who had been a mere human kitten when Chessie was born and the girl became hers. Some ships' cats considered their Cat Person to be a cross between a caretaker and a colleague. Chessie had thought of Janina as an older sister initially. But over the years, through her many litters, she had come to regard the girl almost as one of her own kittens. A grown kitten able to help with birthing the others, but still so young and in need of reassuring nuzzles and purrs.

"I'm sorry, but I really need to keep moving," Janina told the man. "We're on our way to Dr. Vlast's clinic now for her prenatal checkup."

"A prenatal checkup for a cat? She must be really special," the man said, keeping pace alongside them.

Chessie wanted a bath but couldn't start one while clasped in Janina's arms. The kittens were trying to pounce each other while still inside her, judging by the way it felt, and bouncing about the space station wasn't helping. She shifted her weight so her pretty fluffy tail draped over Janina's arm, making more room for her pretty fluffy rear. She mewed up at Kibble, as the rest of the crew called Janina. Apparently, a lot of Cat Persons on other ships had the same name, but Chessie was sure none of the others were as sweet and kind or took such good care of their Barque Cats as her Kibble did.

The man seemed to have appointed himself as their escort, walking easily beside them when the way was clear, breaking up clusters of thoughtlessly chattering people when it wasn't with a cheery, "Gangway! Pregnant lady coming through!"

Janina said, "Thank you. Poor Chessie and her kittens have such a great reputation, and fetch such a big price that she hasn't been given enough time to rest between litters, in my opinion. I want Dr. Vlast to check her over and make sure she's okay. I thought her previous litter should have been her last for a while but I was outvoted."

Chessie wished Janina had won. Motherhood had always been easy for her before, but this litter was disturbing. She dreamed of these kittens all the time—she couldn't remember doing that before. Or having the cravings she'd had with this pregnancy, like those deliciously crunchy shiny beetles she'd discovered in the last shipment of fresh fruit from Jambago Trine. She couldn't seem to get enough of them. Just thinking about them made her hungry.

"Those kittens must be worth quite a bit for the crew to risk stressing out Mrs. Puss here like that."

Janina told him what the babies from Chessie's last litter had fetched—a price that made the man whistle in appreciation.

"As much as that, eh? I knew that some of the Federated ships had cats, but I never knew they were so important, or that some were so much more special than others."

"Oh my, yes. Chessie and her kind have been specially bred for service on shipboard and have saved countless lives! Having the right cat is like having the right engineer, or the right navigator."

"That's amazing," the man said with the proper degree of awe.

Chessie was amazed too. This man must be serving on very low-class ships not to know the importance of Barque Cats, to have missed the story of the founding of her breed and profession. The entire crew loved to tell the story, over the com or when getting together with the crews of other ships. A ship's Barque Cat was a great bragging point for the crew, especially since kittens from the most remarkable cats were highly prized and went to the best homes and earned the crews extra treats. Even Janina, who never preened herself, was apt to carry on at nap-inducing length about Chessie's ancestry, breeding, history, personal qualities, and job performance. Chessie liked it that her friends boasted about her, but there were limits!

Janina had become so nervous about taking her to see Dr. Vlast—as Chessie could tell from her rapid heartbeat—it was as if *she* was the one who would be poked and prodded and have a thermometer shoved up her bum. Since Dr. Vlast had taken over the clinic, Janina seemed much more concerned about her health than ever before. Since the arrival of the good-looking young vet, she and Janina usually visited the clinic several times at each docking, even if she felt perfectly well. This time, the girl seemed to be welcoming the distraction of being able to talk to the curious man about her favorite subject—Barque Cats in general and her in particular. Kibble launched enthusiastically into the familiar story as they made their way through the space station to the clinic.

"Chessie's many times great-great-grandsire, Tuxedo Thomas, originally belonged to a lady named Mrs. Montgomery, the wife of Captain Mason Montgomery," Janina told the man. "She and Thomas lived on PS Station until she was killed in a ventilation accident. Thomas must have blamed himself for not preventing the death of his mistress, because when Captain Montgomery returned to the station, he found Thomas patrolling the ventilation ducts, apparently looking for leaks. Thomas didn't stop the behavior when the captain, out of respect for his wife's love of the cat, took him aboard his cargo ship, the SS *Flamboyant*."

"I can see where the cat might have been a big help on cargo ships with foodstuffs," the man conceded. "Maybe keeping down the vermin, the rodents and bugs, but surely any cat could do that—and traps and sonic deterrents and other devices would serve the same purpose."

Hmph, Chessie thought, revising her opinion of the man downward. He must be a dog person!

"Up until then, animals were only cargo, not crew members," Janina continued. "But Tuxedo Thomas proved himself over and over, finding tiny oxygen leaks and breaches in the hull and drawing the crew's attention to them, as his descendants like Chessie do today. Of course, he caught vermin too, but before long he mostly acted as a self-appointed morale officer. He would visit sick crew members, sit beside others of the crew during long watches, again, all the things Chessie and her colleagues do for us today. Which is why they're so carefully bred and expensive."

"And your regular kind of cats don't do those things?" the man asked. Chessie's ruff bristled. His posture, which had initially seemed protective now felt predatory, and his light teasing tone, indicated that the story was not as new to him as he wanted Janina to believe. There was excitement in his scent too, anticipation, which was odd. It was a good story, but most people didn't react to it *that* much.

Janina, focusing on her story, didn't notice. Chessie knew that in spite of herself, her girl was thinking of Dr. Vlast. She liked him because he was a good doctor, with a way about him that made each of his patients feel as if he was *their* person. During the few times when Chessie had stayed at the clinic, she'd heard other cats and even dogs and horses each talking about how if anything happened to their humans, they knew they'd be okay because Dr. Vlast would take care of them. She liked him, but he affected Kibble a bit like catnip affected Chessie.

It had more to do with the fact that unlike the previous vets, he was young, only a few years older than Janina, and he smelled good in a strong male sort of way. Janina was always sneaking looks at him when she should have been paying attention to her, so Chessie supposed that by human standards he looked good too.

Whatever the reasons, Janina seemed to come in season every time she was around Dr. Jared Vlast, though it was difficult to tell with humans. When Chessie was in season, she was in season. With most humans it only seemed to happen when they were around specific other humans. They were an odd, unpredictable race, even the best of them.

"Oh no!" Janina said to their new acquaintance, and Chessie could tell that the girl's emphatic denial amused the man. "Why, these cats are so valued that every ship carrying a Barque Cat is required to bear a chartreuse sign with the legend 'COB'—Cat on Board. That way, if the ship is wrecked and the humans all perish, other ships coming by will check to see if the cat found a last tiny chamber of oxygen and was somehow saved."

"Huh," the man said. "If the cat is the only one left, seems to me it might not have been doing the job you said it does—you know, finding leaks and such."

Janina shifted Chessie so she couldn't see the man's face anymore. The girl was quivering a little as she came to the defense of Chessie and her kind. "With all of the patches on your uniform, sir, how can you fail to understand that there are many hazards in space that even the most experienced human crewmen—much less a cat, however specialized her breeding and training—could do nothing to stop—meteors, unfriendly fire, all manner of things. Thank you for walking me to the clinic. It is time for our appointment."

Well, that told him! Chessie was sure she heard the man chuckle as he walked away. She would have wondered at his odd reaction to Janina's snub except that Dr. Vlast was opening the clinic door for them, and the kittens had decided to play tag inside her swollen belly.

Chessie purred as Dr. Vlast took her from Janina's arms. Even the kittens quieted down. Despite his regrettable tendency to subject her to medical indignities, Jared Vlast was a great favorite of Chessie's as well as her girl's. The two older vets previously operating this clinic had been very brisk and businesslike, and not at all respectful of Chessie's importance to her ship. Janina, then little more than a child, had whispered to the kitten Chessie, "Never mind them, Duchess. Those kinds of doctors think only livestock animals are important—cattle, sheep, pigs, horses. A lot *they* know!"

For the first time, Chessie noticed that her *doctor's* heart was also beating fast and *his* pulses were thumping as he smiled at Janina, who was trying hard to look calm and professional but couldn't help how big and round her eyes got when she looked up at him.

Hmm. Well well. Good! The attraction appeared to be mutual! Chessie was surprised her human friends couldn't hear each other's chests pounding. Or maybe they could and just wouldn't admit it. Humans were so strange about mating matters.

Janina had of course discussed the doctor with her, for she was not only her best friend but unlikely to spread rumors. Jared Vlast was only six whole years older than Janina, but was already a man of the universe who had actually spent time on other planets, not just their docking stations. He was well-educated, a sort of veterinary prodigy, whereas she had been educated in the Academy, the place where the kittens of spacefaring parents were sent, whether or not their parents were alive. Janina's weren't, and Chessie had heard her say the children of spacefarers who still had their parents were more likely to go on to graduate as officers or ship's technicians. She was an orphan. Not having your parents with you as a kitten was a bad thing for humans, apparently, though it didn't stop them from taking feline kittens from their mothers and sending them—all alone in a crowd of loud tall humans with clumsy feet—onto other ships, stations, and worlds.

Janina evidently considered that her parentless status, despite the fact that she had a perfectly wonderful cat companion, made her somewhat less than the many other females. Silly *mistaken*

Janina had muttered into Chessie's fur that someone with Jared Vlast's potential wouldn't consider a Cat Person as a mate. As if being a Cat Person—especially *her* Cat Person—was not the most important job in the universe! Janina viewed the other females who wanted to mate with Dr. Vlast as prettier, smarter, and *better* than she was. Chessie could only yawn at the folly of such an idea and lick Janina's fingers sympathetically. There *were* no other females, anywhere, better in any way than her.

"She's quite near her time now, isn't she?" Dr. Jared asked as he cradled Chessie in one arm while opening the door for Janina and then shepherding her through the reception room. It was, for a change, empty.

"Yes, but there's something odd happening that I wanted you to check," Janina told him.

"So you didn't get my message?" he asked.

"You sent me one?" Chessie heard her Kibble's heartbeat picking up speed.

"Yes," he said, keying the door lock and ushering her inside his main office. "I'm hoping you can help me. Bill's on home leave, and I need someone in the left-hand seat. There seem to be some unauthorized horses showing up dirtside."

"Seem to be?"

Oh dear, Chessie thought, it's the cat hotel for me! He had borrowed Kibble before to help him when he had to go dirtside, to the planet the space station orbited. Chessie had stayed in the cat hotel then too. It was lovely, but she missed Kibble. And when she'd been here before, the other guests had been horses, who stayed in another part of the clinic, though she could hear and smell them. No other cats.

"George Varley said he spotted some broken-colored stock in one of his fields. He has purebreds and none of them are broken-colored. Varley doesn't want to be accused of stealing them, so we'll chip them if they're not already chipped and check that they're healthy enough to mix with his herd." He showed her into one of the cubicles and gently deposited Chessie on the examination table. "If they've been tagged, I'll be interested to see how and when they came to be here. I haven't seen a piebald or a skewbald since I left Earth."

He chirped encouragingly to Chessie, and she lifted her head for him to give her a proper scritch behind her ears, her favorite place for petting. Purring, she stood up on the table, gave Janina an accusing glance, and stroked Jared's arm with the side of her face. But she knew Kibble would go. It would take more than looks to make her give up alone time with Dr. Jared Vlast. Such a fuss over those silly chips! Couldn't the humans tell which horses were theirs by sight and smell?

As Jared then moved on to a quick, competent feel of her fecund belly, he asked Janina what was concerning her.

"Well, she's been regurgitating a lot, and it's strange looking." Janina showed him the vial that contained the latest of her spit-up. Humans collected the strangest things! Janina turned it in the light. "You see it's got these sparkly bits that I can't account for at all."

Jared peered at the vial, which Janina rocked so he could see the tiny bits that did pick up the light.

He reached for it and examined it more closely, then shook his head. "Well, as usual, you have more foresight than the others."

"The others?"

"Uh-huh," he said in a thoughtful tone. "Four other cats are spitting up the same sort of mucus, whatever it is, but you're the only one who thought of bringing me a sample. I can't do a detailed analysis of it right now because I've got to check out Varley's trespassers."

Chessie yawned and sat and watched them, switching her tail softly.

"Is she eating well?"

Janina sighed. "Like she thinks food is scarce."

The vet grinned, petting Chessie's head again. "Well, she's feeding at least seven kittens. Is that how many you've sold off?"

"No, we've secured buyers for eight this time. Even runts would be welcome with her breeding," Janina replied. "Not that she's ever had any."

"Which is why she's eating so much." Jared scratched Chessie's ear vigorously, and she leaned into his caressing hand. "She's due soon. But not today, I think. I could really use your help tagging, Nina. What do you say? We can either take her back to the ship or leave her here in the peace and quiet. Isn't your ship loading?"

"It is and she should have quiet," Janina replied, stroking Chessie's thick and silky coat with a soothing rhythm. It felt lovely. "Not that anyone would disturb her."

"She can have the whole kennel to herself," Jared promised. "Plus, I have some chicken livers that she might deign to eat."

Chicken livers! Chessie licked her chops at the very idea. She *loved* chicken livers. Maybe some quiet time away from Kibble and *Molly Daise* wouldn't be so bad after all.

"Dr. Vlast! I think you planned this—you know that's her favorite," Janina said. "You sure know how to get around her!" Chessie thought that cats were not the only ones the vet knew how to get around.

He grinned. "Jared, please. I'm glad this works out for all of us. When I got my consumable shipment from downside yesterday, it occurred to me—since the *Molly Daise* was in port—that you might bring her in for a checkup." He ducked his head, and Chessie could see that Janina was surprised to see a bit of a flush on his face. Both heart rates increased tempo and intensity.

Humans could be so adorable—and dense. Why did the girl think he kept dragging her off to romantic rendezvous to tag animals or do mass livestock inoculations if he wasn't smitten? Of course, for the horse thing, which had apparently caused an epidemic on another colony world, he'd rounded up all of the Cat People in port, but he'd chosen to work with *her* most of the time. The girl reported dreamily that he had told her she was efficient and good-natured under extreme conditions. Possibly he was miraculously unaware that any conditions including him would be good conditions as far as Janina was concerned. She'd described in awe-stricken detail the wonders of catching sheep all over the planet, touching down wherever the records listed horses, inoculating them and adding the information on the ID chips all the animals on Sherwood were required to have. They had actually found a couple of *bad* chips, Janina said, though that was up to Jared to deal with, not her.

"I'd better clear my absence with Captain Vesey, Jared," Janina said.

He handed her a phone. "I'll just check the kennel and put down the livers and fresh water for Chessie, then," he said with a grin, and backed out of the cubicle.

Captain Vesey readily okayed the shore mission for Janina and the vacation for Chessie.

Her kennel suite was large enough for a big dog. It had a sleeping platform in one corner, well-lined with soft comfy bedding, a drinking fountain that poured a lovely private waterfall very nice for cooling a paw in and pretending to fish, a tree stump for clawing, and the bowl of rich brown chicken livers that Chessie sniffed as Jared deposited them in the kennel. She practically flung herself out of Janina's arms to get at the treat, and barely heard the click as Jared turned on the security camera and speakers that would allow her humans to check in on her at a distance. She was much too busy purring delightedly over her meal. After all, she was eating for many.

When at last she was replete with chicken livers, Chessie slept on her platform, happy to have nothing expected of her for a change. While aboard the *Molly Daise*, in addition to her usual workload, she had searched the vessel from stem to stern, not for the hazards or vermin she usually stalked, but for a likely birthing nest where the kittens would be safe from prying eyes, where she could do what she had done so many times before. Only once had she been able to actually use her secret nest, and she was sorry afterward because Janina had become quite distraught searching for her. Everyone wanted her birthings to be observed, assisted, and otherwise interfered with.

Well-bred she might be, but by this time her philosophy of raising kittens was to let the little buggers grow and crawl and feed their tiny round tummies. Once they were born, she intended to feed the needs of her exhausted body with blissful sleep. She thought she could sleep through anything at this point. When she recalled the pleasure she had enjoyed raising the first litter, the second, the third, even the fourth, she purred. But now, many litters later, the thrill was gone. Her crew liked to brag about what a good mother she was, but it made her tired just thinking of having more kittens to bear, to wash, to carry until her jaws ached. She would once more train them in their jobs and their basic feline survival skills, then, just as she was getting used to having them around, she'd lose them when they were sold to other ships. Never mind. She would miss them, but they would be someone else's problem. She opened her eyes a slit, sighed, rearranged her paws, and fanned her plumelike tail over them so its tip covered her nose. As soon as the kits were gone, there'd be some new tom thrust at her, giving her the same old song and dance that meant, in time, more kittens.

That was all very well for toms. *They* only had one career, spending their time cruising their ships, hunting space vermin, snuggling with and cadging occasional treats from crew members, and being called upon to breed the poor queens who then had to bear the consequences and the kittens.

She dreamed of pouncing on the next tom like she would

pounce on a rat. She purred in her sleep and had a lovely, lovely rest, rising only to nibble on more delicious food before sleeping again.

It was a most excellent vacation, exactly when she needed it, and she hoped Janina and Dr. Jared would be gone a long time on their errand.

Sometime later she woke with a start to the screams of horses and the smell of smoke. Where was her Kibble, and why wasn't she back yet? She had to warn her about the smoke! And then she saw rough human male hands reaching for the front door to her cage . . .

CHAPTER 2

Jubal Poindexter left the barn door open while he sat on a hay bale sharpening the scythe his dad had promised to sharpen before he left. Jubal had learned a long time ago not to set much store by his dad's promises. The farm would have gone to wrack and ruin if Jubal and his mama depended on the old man to keep his word.

Jubal really had hoped his dad might remember about the kitten, though. His birthday had been two weeks ago and Dad promised him, "Just between us men." Jubal couldn't even tell his mama why he was so disappointed when his dad didn't come home when he said he would. Mama didn't like cats, which was why that particular birthday promise had been secret. That, Jubal suspected, and Dad would have to make up wild stories about how his failure to keep the promise was definitely not his fault for one less person.

How could Mama not like cats? They were so pretty—and useful. This old barn was overrun with vermin of all descriptions—rats, mice, lizards, snakes, all manner of bugs, including the shiny beetles there seemed to be so many of nowadays. A cat would sort them out in no time flat, and also be his friend and someone to play with. He didn't mind a lot of Dad's broken promises—even though he was barely eleven years old he could already do lots of the work Dad should have been doing—but a kitten wouldn't have been hard to come by. Unwanted kittens were given away all the time. Jubal only needed just the one tiny free kitten and he'd have had himself the best birthday yet. But no, his dad was an important man with important space stuff to do. Horsefeathers!

A single shameful tear of self-pity welled up in his eye, and he rubbed at it furiously. Something streaked across the sunlight streaming in through the open barn door. His head snapped up, but by then whatever it was had leaped into the shadows and was scattering straw hither, thither, and yon.

Setting the scythe carefully beside the bale, Jubal stood up and took a cautious step toward the commotion. Might be a fox or a weasel after the chickens, though most of them were outside this time of day, pecking up their feed. Maybe whatever it was had chased one in here!

But it wasn't squawks he heard, just a single terrified squeak, before the straw exploded up and a pair of muckle-colored pointy ears emerged, followed by a pair of round shiny eyes and a big old mouse where a mouth ought to be.

A saggy-bellied tortoiseshell cat tripped toward him with paws as dainty as any great lady's slippers. Her bright eyes looked up into his as she laid the mouse at his feet. Then she stepped back and sat down with her tail curled around her front feet. When he didn't move for fear of scaring her away, she looked up at him, tilting her head, then glanced down at the mouse.

He'd wanted a mouser, hadn't he? Well, she was applying for the job, and here was proof she was fit for it.

Jubal hunkered down to pat her head and tell her what a fine cat she was but she bounced up as a shiny green beetle scuttled past. Snapping it up in her jaws, she crunched once, then came back and sat down in front of him again, a little farther away this time. Her fur was long, shiny and soft looking, though bits of straw and leaves clung to it. Her tail, though sprigged with straw, was long and plumed and luxuriously furry. This was a really fine kind of cat. An ordinary everyday cat, maybe, but a beauty, and furthermore, a practical mouse-catching kind of cat. Even Mom would have to see how worthwhile a cat like this would be.

But best of all, that round belly with all those heavy pink nipples swinging underneath told him that she was about to be a mama and soon he'd have not only this fine cat but a whole litter of kittens besides.

He leaned over to pat her but she backed off and gave him a purely annoyed look that hurt him at first, then tickled his funny bone. "Okay, kittycat. I got it. You're a working cat and we got ourselves a business arrangement. I can see you have your own ways and you don't know to trust me yet. I just hope your babies are a little more cuddly because I sure would like one for a pet, and I promise I would treat it and you really well."

The cat stropped herself against his legs once, quickly, as if in agreement, and bounded heavily back into the straw again. He was a little disappointed she wasn't a friendlier, cuddlier cat, but then, he couldn't blame her much. Cats on Sherwood were common as dirt and not always treated nearly as well.

But she was a cat of *her* word. The next morning there was a line of rats, mice, lizards, and bugs at the barn door when he opened it. Minus her commission, signified by the tail at the end of the line and by the satisfied way she sat cleaning her paws.

⌐ ⌐ ⌐

"It shouldn't take us long to get to the Varleys'," Jared said as they left the kennel area. "I've extra gear for you and you already know how to manage a tagger." He gave her a grin and then stepped past her to open a cabinet and haul out a warm flight jacket, a helmet, and two bags of tagger equipment. He hoisted one to her shoulder and the other to his. Janina carried the bag proudly. Jared was a very important part of the station and the agricultural world it serviced. The colony worlds needed to move animals from one to the other to acquire new breeding stock, but it was imperative the animals reach their destinations disease free, so as not to contaminate existing stock. By Galactic governmental regulations, animals arriving at the station were examined and chipped to indicate origin and arrival date. Animals who became ill en route to other worlds were also cared for at the clinic before being released to continue their journeys.

Of course, once they arrived on the surface, the animals still needed periodic vaccinations, and their microchip tags required updating, and Jared did that too, as well as providing care for pets. It was a huge job.

"I've got a good tracker, new model. We'll be done and back in no time."

"Famous last words," she said, waggling a finger at him. Now that she was actually with him instead of just thinking about being with him, she no longer felt nervous or flustered. He was so comfortable to be with that she fell into the teasing she often did with her fellow crew members on the *Molly Daise*.

"I know, I know, " he replied, grinning again, remembering one of their earlier trips to Sherwood, which he had promised would be quick but lasted two weeks. He'd only just got her back to the space station in time to reach her ship before its scheduled departure.

The tracker was docked in the small bay adjacent to the vet clinic. They seated themselves in the vehicle, checked with Traffic and were assigned a time, cleared their orbit, and recorded their destination.

Jared was a good pilot, and Janina sat back to enjoy the flight. As soon as the docking bay doors retracted, she could see the green and blue bulk of the planet Sherwood. As they descended, the long valley between two minor mountain ranges that constituted the Varley ranch zoomed in beneath them. It was a rich holding, and Varley was known as a successful but responsible settler who took good care of his stock, so she understood why he would want to make sure all his animals were being imported legally. It wasn't as if the breeder couldn't afford to pay the costs of legitimate additions to his stock.

That didn't mean that someone else couldn't have brought the horses to Sherwood. There were always ways to elude notice. Pirates and smugglers could likely make an unseen landing when the station eclipsed the planet. Even Traffic couldn't monitor everything. But why would anyone go to the trouble of smuggling stock to boost someone else's herd? It didn't make sense.

Jared had a brief, earnest conversation with Traffic, after which he seemed lost in thought most of the time. He glanced at her once or twice to smile encouragingly, and she knew he was happy to have her help, and, she hoped, her company.

But as excited as she was to be off on another mission with him, and reassured as she was by the precautions he took to ensure Chessie's safety and their own, Janina felt a twinge of worry and guilt about leaving her charge. She compulsively checked the security camera monitor every few seconds, sure that Chessie would go into labor the minute she wasn't looking. Chessie was still sleeping soundly, though the chicken livers were now gone. Janina knew it was silly of her to worry, but she wouldn't have been a Cat Person if she had not.

 ✶ ✶ ✶

The broken-colored horses were rather surprising. They didn't act wild or even worried when they saw the humans.

The first lot of them, six in number, were grazing when Janina and Jared arrived, and after several coy sidelong glances, one of them, with a black saddle and rump and one rather rakish black eye, trotted cautiously over. Jared had armed himself and Janina appropriately. She proffered an apple as a bribe and the mare sidled in more closely, finally accepting the apple from her palm. Meanwhile, Jared clipped a halter across the horse's neck. The mare whuffled but did not interrupt her treat long enough to seriously protest. He clicked the scanner and shook his head. No chip.

When he tagged her ear, she started, neighed, and reared in protest, dropping the remains of her apple. The DNA smear from her saliva would establish whether she was related to any of the local herds.

"Shhh, shhh, it's okay," Janina said soothingly. "That's all there is to it. Don't be such a big baby. My cat barely noticed when we did hers, although hers is here." She touched a spot on the back of her neck. "It's how we know who you are and can find you to help you if you get into trouble. Everyone has one. You don't want to buck the tide of fashion, do you? Now stand still and I'll undo the halter."

The mare whickered, and Janina retrieved the slobbery apple and offered it in apology. The horse took it with more of a snap than her first polite bite, but allowed Janina to release her, after which she hopped sideways, kicked up her heels a bit, and trotted over to the other horses. Jared and Janina watched, fully expecting the little herd to flee. The weather had turned damp and the grass was a luminous green under the ruffled gray sky. They stood in a valley between the low hills bounding Varley's property and the steep rocky ridges of the Hood Range beyond. A slight breeze carried the rich scent of fertile ground, growing things, and horse sweat. It chilled her where it touched her skin, evaporating the sweat she had generated while reasoning with the horse.

The other horses crowded close to the tagged mare, touching noses, shaking heads, and for all the world looking as if they were conferring.

Another mare with a white face blazed with black stepped forward as if looking for her own treat. Janina obliged her while Jared tagged her. This time there was no fuss. The mare flicked the ear afterward as if testing it, then returned to the herd, having finished her apple. The work went quickly after that, as the horses had evidently decided that the tags were a small price to pay for the treats, and each could hardly wait for a turn.

Jared chuckled, patting the last brown and white neck with a strong hand, its back laced with little white scars that were no doubt souvenirs from former, less cooperative patients. "Have you ever seen such unhorsey cooperation from wild creatures?" he asked.

"You say Varley claims he doesn't know where they came from, but wherever it was, they seem to have been gentled already," she said.

He nodded, looking as puzzled as she felt, and they gathered their gear and began striding back toward the tracker, which they'd left at some distance to avoid spooking their patients. "There are six more over the next ridge, according to Varley's last siting. I think we've earned a spot of lunch before we move along to them, don't you?" Jared asked, and Janina realized she was indeed quite hungry. "There's no hurry and there's quite a nice café in Locksley. We can eat there if you like or they'll pack us a picnic to take along."

"A picnic sounds lovely," she said, then, fearing he would realize she was angling for time alone with him, she added, "I mean, that would be most efficient and we could have it in a field where the pintos could become accustomed to us while we ate." Furthermore, the horses would be unlikely to spread gossip if they caught her gaze lingering too long on the handsome Dr. Vlast. Nor would they mention to anyone if in some small way he— She should put that right out of her head. But she couldn't help feeling as if the gravity had suddenly lightened when he grinned warmly down at her.

"That's what I'd prefer as well," he said.

The breeze freshened as they strode along, and Janina found it at first cooling and then chilling in spite of their brisk pace. The scent of smoke mixed with the other woodsy smells of Sherwood, and in spite of the cozy, homey, warm things that smoke indicated on a place like Sherwood, the smell made Janina uneasy. One seldom smelled smoke on shipboard, and if one did, it was not a good thing.

When they reached the tracker, the monitor showed Chessie had shifted position slightly, and though her tail tip twitched now and then, she was otherwise sleeping soundly. Chessie was fine, Janina thought. *She* was the one with the problem.

Locksley was a typical frontier settlement—a single circular main street with businesses around the outer diameter and along the spokes branching out into the residential district beyond, where the roads became fewer, leading off into the countryside where horse farms such as Varley's occupied square miles of fields. The businesses along each spoke were separated into malls according to the sort of wares they sold. There was a food mall; a hardware and repair mall; a clothing, shoes, and fripperies mall; a children's mall; a housewares mall; and a livestock mall containing feed, horse tack, and home veterinary supplies. She'd heard new settlers express wonderment at the strange arrangement of their town, but the prefab wedges that formed around towns had been the shape carried most easily in the early round-hulled ships. Some of the houses had been delivered that way too, but other, humbler and more primitive dwellings were made of native organic plant life and stone. She liked the look of them, as each was different from anything she had seen before.

While Jared went into a café in the food mall to order their picnic, she ducked into the adjacent clothing spoke to shop for the gifts Captain Vesey had requested she purchase for his family. It was nice that he made an effort to show them he was thinking of them no matter where he was.

Bypassing the sections containing uncomfortable-looking shoes and colorful clothing, she headed for the jewelry and accessories. Captain Vesey's oldest daughter was horse-crazy, so Janina selected a bracelet beaded with running horses for her. For Mrs. Vesey, she found a hood and collar of soft loden green mohair, locally grown. The hood and collar were a nod to the hero of Terra's original Sherwood Forest. The colony's marketing team had decided on that theme for their souvenir industry, but this was a new product, something Janina hadn't seen before. That was why Captain Vesey liked the dirtside malls. The space station's shopping center held a far more cosmopolitan array of goods and services, but each planet had certain lines of items that could be found only on the surface. They made fine collectibles, and the captain said Mrs. Vesey was an original who liked unusual things. Janina had seen pictures of the captain's family and thought the hood would suit Mrs. Vesey's green-gold eyes and rather dramatic bone structure very nicely. For the youngest girl, she found a little lavender drawstring bag decorated with a bow and arrow motif outlined in shiny purple crystals.

Her shopping complete, she returned to the tracker. Chessie had switched positions so that her face was now to the wall. Janina held her breath for a moment, thinking Chessie seemed too still, then a delicate ear tuft quivered and the long tips of her upturned whiskers twitched. Janina relaxed. Poor Chessie had needed this rest badly.

CHAPTER 3

Carlton Pontius—Ponty to his shipmates, Carl Poindexter more familiarly to his local Sherwood associates—had not forgotten his son Jubal's birthday cat at all. Or rather, he had momentarily forgotten his promise but remembered it immediately when he saw the *Molly Daise*'s Cat Person and her prize queen.

Ponty was a man whose capacity for inspiration had often come to the assistance of his aspirations. Like the cat in the little lady's arms, he usually landed on his feet and got the cream while he was at it.

He had been a soldier until he saw the light and started working as an arms dealer and a sales rep for pharmaceuticals of both legal and illegal status. He had served in every conceivable rank and capacity aboard ships, chiefly those that smuggled prohibited technology from world to world for a price. His sales experience had made him a valuable asset to such crews. His was a competent medic and a mostly self-taught geneticist, having reared several clones from test tube to maturity en route to their most lucrative destinations. Among his other less legitimate talents, he was a consummate con man.

But even he had never in his wildest dreams imagined that he would someday include cat rustling in his résumé.

Oddly enough, it was his child's innocent wish for a pet that alerted him to the opportunities awaiting the imaginative man in the feline relocation industry.

Raising the groceries for his family's sustenance had put his knowledge of the shadier branches of selective breeding to good use. Since horses were big money business on Sherwood, when he first arrived he'd experimented with equine embryos and tended them faithfully. Then he'd been called away before he could return to care for the resulting foals. The best he could do was to borrow a couple of maternal mares from a neighboring herd to look after the little shavers near the line shack where he'd stashed them. Due to the financial demands of his household and the shaky state of his marriage, he'd only been back for brief intervals in the meantime and had no idea what became of the foals. If they survived, they should be full grown by now, with a couple of generations of descendants unless they were sterile, and he had no reason to think they would be.

Cats were smaller, easier to smuggle, and according to the cat girl, some of them were even more valuable than horses. Every ship he served on had a ship's cat, of course, though none were of the hoity-toity lineage of the furball the girl had been toting. If one of those ships had gone down, the cat would have perished with the crew. The last thing his ships' masters wanted was to draw attention to their vessels with a big fancy sign, whether or not they were derelict. Cargo could always be retrieved later, but not if some interfering busybody boarded a dead ship to save a cat.

He had known about the Barque Cats and seen them occasionally when he did business with ships whose missions were less shady than his own. They were pretty enough beasts and good hunters and all that, but in spite of what the cat girl said, he didn't see any difference between them and the standard Maine coon moggie that patrolled the barns, yards, and houses of his feline-inclined neighbors. No matted fur on the pampered highborn beauties, of course. No fleas, ticks, ear mites, or parasites either.

When Ponty saw the girl toting the pregnant cat, it hadn't taken much mental arithmetic to figure she was on her way to Vlast so he could tend the furball. He had promised his boy a kitten, and that was, he told himself, the reason he had approached the girl. A man could ask about a kitten for his kid, couldn't he?

It had been a revelation to him that ships would actually pay so much to have a kitten with the right pedigree on board. Crews apparently gave more for a fancy-bred Barque Cat than he had ever been paid for a year on any of his voyages. Well, they might be too good for him, but nothing was too good for his boy. Jubal wanted a kitten, and his son was going to get the best kitten his old man could get for him. If he happened to make enough money off the sale of the cat and all of the other kittens to support his family and future enterprises for some time to come, it was no more than his reward for being such a great father. He could have always settled for one of those poor little Sherwood kittens that were lucky to find a berth as a barn cat, luckier still to be a pampered pet, but if that cat girl said her cat was better, and worth more money, he figured she ought to know.

Personally, he didn't see—unless these cats had their kittens through their noses or in some other special way—how anyone would ever be able to tell the difference between a kitten born to Thomas's Duchess and sired by Space Jockey from a kitten born to Haystack Puss and sired by Back Fence Tom. There was ID hardware, of course, with the DNA code on it, but that could be counterfeited easily enough.

So, in his natural fatherly solicitude for his boy, he formulated a lapse into not-so-latent larceny. Using the Duchess as his seed cat, so to speak, he could use her DNA samples to maybe elevate some otherwise undervalued kittens to her lofty and lucrative status, sort of like placebo cats, or a control group. As expensive as the real thing, of course, but all misrepresented in a spirit of scientific inquiry. If they didn't know the difference, would his clients adopt the barn kittens and believe them to be as good as Chessie's real kittens? It was a far far better thing he planned to do, a redemocratization of that most independent feline species. He would be undermining a silly human value system that falsely overinflated some animals while leaving others homeless and forsaken—when they could be going to good homes for a healthy profit to him. He was nothing, he liked to think, if not softhearted.

His own kid would get a bona fide Barque kitten, of course. His kid deserved nothing but the best.

⸙ ⸙ ⸙

Jared returned to the tracker swinging a large woven basket, and he and Janina took off over the ridge to the field Varley had indicated, where six more broken-colored horses watched curiously as the humans unpacked their lunch. Included in the picnic provisions was a healthy supply of apples and carrots.

A café lunch might have been more private, as it turned out. These horses were no more frightened than the others had been, and were also so nosy as to be intrusive. Janina and Jared sat together on a blanket, close enough to pass food and close enough that she could feel his body's warmth radiating through the chill of the afternoon breeze.

"Janina, you've been a tremendous help," he said, handing her a plate with some cheese and apple on it. "Did your Cat Person training include being a vet tech?"

"Not really," she said. "Just certain things. Like birthings, treating wounds, emergency cat medicine, recognition of the usual cat maladies."

"Not all of the cat handlers I've met seem nearly as well-versed in all of those areas as you are," he said.

"What they gave us at the academy was a bit sketchy. I was lucky to be assigned such a wonderful cat to work with as soon as I'd finished the Cat Person elective in my schooling. And not all of the cabin boys and girls who care for a ship's cat have even had the academy training I did. Some ships acquire a cat without having a properly trained Cat Person in the crew, just a youngster to feed the cat and change the commode. They don't all know how to monitor the cat's hunt and search activities properly, to do the most good for the ship. When I meet some of the untrained ones, I try to answer questions and make suggestions. Most of them at least do love their cat."

"You've done remarkably well with the knowledge you have," he told her.

She felt her skin growing warm from more than the sun's heat. He had the most beautiful eyes, and they were totally focused on her.

"I study everything I can from the courses in the data banks, and take classes at our ports of call when we dock for more than a couple of days."

"Excellent. Have you thought about later?"

"Later?"

"When Chessie—retires. She's not a young cat, and all of these litters are taking a toll on her."

Janina studied the grass intently for a moment or two while her eyes stopped swimming. She knew he didn't mean actually retire. Chessie wouldn't leave the *Molly Daise* until she died. Then, if the ship hadn't retained one of her kittens for an understudy, they'd have to buy a kitten and assign a new Cat Person, someone young and small enough to follow the kitten into places where an adult couldn't go. "I—I'd probably train my replacement," she said. But the thought of trying to do that after Chessie passed—she didn't know how she'd face it. She couldn't bear the thought of being without Chessie. They'd been together since she was eight years old and Chessie fit into the palm of her hand.

"Will you return to your family on your home world?" he asked, pretending he hadn't noticed her discomfort.

"I don't have a family, not that I know of. My mother was killed in an accident when I was small. My father was away—no one ever told me exactly where—and has never returned. I haven't been able to learn anything about him. I'm not really sure what I'll do when Chessie—"

He cleared his throat, and this time he seemed a little nervous. "I actually had something I wanted to ask you about that," he said.

She didn't catch the rest of it. A brown and white muzzle intruded between them and lipped the apple off the plate, leaving a smear of sparkly slobber on the cheese.

Both of them bent over the plate. "Look," she said, pointing, "that looks like what Chessie's been coughing up."

Jared was already fishing a specimen bag out of his inside pocket. Lifting the cheese slice with the edge of the disposable fork, he deposited it in the bag. He frowned. "This is very irregular, since a ship's cat and a wild horse are hardly on the same diet and don't even breathe the same air. I can't think what they'd have in common that would produce this"—he waggled the bag at her before tucking it into his pocket—"in both species."

Janina felt suddenly sick with apprehension. "You don't suppose it's some sort of alien plague, do you? Like those diseases that used to kill so many Terran animals before they developed vaccines?"

"I hope not. But we'll need to tag this lot before we process this," he said. "We'll want to be able to identify them again, in case it's necessary to isolate them."

But when they rose to return to work, they found the attentive horses had all vanished. Returning to the tracker, Janina and Jared followed the beasts into the hills, down into another valley, and then into a thick birch wood, where they lost them. The tracker's scanners showed that the horses were still there, but when they tried to follow on foot, no fruity inducements were enough to persuade the horses to show themselves.

Finally Jared shook his head and said, "We're wasting our time here. We'll need to have a talk with Varley. He's going to have to round this lot up for us to tag. Not a word about the specimen, though, all right? He's not likely to be cooperative if he thinks we may be looking for something that could endanger his herd."

Janina nodded gravely, her former high spirits thoroughly dampened.

* * *

Jared set the tracker down in the wide drive outside of Varley's extensive ranch home, which was bigger than the bridge and the crew quarters of the *Molly Daise* put together. The house was surrounded by a vast garden with an array of flowers in a rainbow of colors. The gardener, Hamish Hale, stood up as they exited the tracker.

"Hi, Doc Vlast," he said. Hamish owned a black lab named Rollie who had a hip problem. As they drew nearer, Rollie looked up at them from his place beside Hamish's feet and wagged his tail. Jared greeted them both, patting Rollie's head, and asked if Mr. Varley was around.

"In the stables, Doc," Hamish said, waving his trowel in the direction of the building that was the size of one of the Locksley malls.

Two large red dogs came bounding up to meet them. One of them leaped to put its front paws on Jared's shoulders, and he held them and danced the dog around as if they were at a ball. The other settled for pats from Janina, when it was clear his doctor was tied up with another patient.

"Roscoe, Roary, down," a man's voice commanded. Varley himself strode out to meet them and shook their hands briskly.

"Get the mustangs tagged already, did you, Doc?" he asked in a jovial tone.

"One lot, but the second spooked and hid in the woods. They wouldn't come out for love nor bribes, so you'll have to have your hands corral them and call me back."

"The ones you did check—they look okay to you?" Varley asked. "Healthy, no mutations or anything?"

"Other than their coloring and undocumented origins, no," Jared said.

"Because I'm thinking I should probably sell them offworld—I'm not one to look a gift horse in the mouth, but on the other hand, I don't want to get fined for owning a herd of them when I can't say who the giver is."

Jared nodded. "They look healthy enough to me, and I would say most are young and sturdy as well. But as long as we're here, I thought we might take the annual specimens from your other stock. Save us all time later."

Varley screwed his mouth up considering, then shrugged. "It's up to you. They're not due for six weeks, though."

"I know, but I figured you'd like to get it over with."

He shrugged again. "Your call. You know where to find them." He signaled toward the stable area. "When you're done, you and your helper come on up to the house for refreshments, why don't you?"

"Thanks," Jared said, waving as he strode toward the corral, Janina trailing behind him. Roary and Roscoe, wagging and bouncing as if they'd never before seen such a wonderful man, followed their master to the house.

It took another two hours to gather the necessary specimens. Only three of the stabled horses exhibited the sparkly saliva, which obviously puzzled Jared as much as finding it had displeased him. But neither he nor Janina said anything about it as they sat sipping iced tea and nibbling fresh baked biscuits from Mrs. Varley's dessert plates. The biscuits were dusted with cinnamon and melted in Janina's mouth. She thought she'd never tasted anything so delicious. She was biting into her second when one of the hands, dressed in blue work pants and a matching shirt with the tails hanging out, strode into the room.

"The station's on the com, sir," he told Varley. "They said they've been trying to raise Dr. Vlast on the tracker com but can't."

"Is it an emergency?" Jared asked, setting down his glass and plate as he rose.

"I think it may be, sir. They were wondering if you can explain why there are horses, dogs, and sheep running through the station."

Janina felt her stomach clench with anxiety.

Even before entering the tracker, they heard the com unit squawking at them through the closed hatch. Janina's dread swelled to near-panic as she made out the first words of the message. The security monitor that had last showed Chessie peacefully napping was now black.

"Fire," the com unit was saying. *"Fire in the animal clinic!"*

CHAPTER 4

*T*raffic diverted the tracker from its customary bay near the clinic, and security contacted them as soon as they docked. *"Dr. Vlast, station ops requests that you and your assistant round up the animals who escaped from the clinic and examine them for possible injuries and smoke inhalation while we are securing the area."*

They didn't need to be convinced. Jared's patients were his top priority, and Janina was frantic to find Chessie. She triggered the cat's locator beacon, hoping against all odds that it would lead her to a Chessie calmly setting her whiskers in order with a dampened paw. But there was no answering signal from any part of the ship.

By the time she and Jared had rounded up the horses, dogs, exotic birds, and the boa constrictor wreaking havoc throughout the station, Janina was sick with worry for Chessie.

But when at last the animals were secured, examined, and lodged in whatever space available until their owners could collect them, and Jared and Janina returned to the clinic deck, they were still denied access.

"Toxic fumes," a guard, barely distinguishable as a female in her hazmat suit, told them. "The fire seems to have started in the hay in the horse stalls, but it ignited a lot of other substances that give off poisonous gases when they burn. Good thing the animals got loose before that happened or they'd have all died from inhalation. As it is, some of the fire crew are in sick bay now."

Frustrated, they turned away, and Jared went to the station master's office to fill out paperwork.

Janina roamed the station with Chessie's locator, calling and listening, but saw no sign of her, though two other cats stopped hunting long enough to regard her curiously from a safe distance.

Finally, after hours of fruitless searching, Jared called her on the com to tell her the area had cooled and the air supply had been cleansed enough that they would be allowed in as long as they wore masks.

Steeling her nerve, Janina followed him into what was left of the clinic. It was hard to believe that this rubble was the same neat, hygienic place where she had left Chessie. She picked her way through the clinic, the pools of melted stuff, the collapsed ceiling, the twisted metal exam tables. She had felt sure that Chessie was alive, since all of the other animals appeared to be accounted for and unharmed, but since she could not find her charge alive, she began to dread finding evidence that she was dead—charred fur, bits of bone, her locator chip . . . Jared set off in another direction to examine other areas of the clinic. Perhaps he too couldn't bear to see proof that the kennel where Chessie should have been safe had become a death trap. If Chessie had died, Janina only hoped it was from smoke inhalation, quickly, while the cat still slept, dreaming of her new litter.

"Careful there, miss," the guard called. "Some of the floors have buckled and pulled from their moorings. You could fall through in some places."

"Thank you," she replied without looking at the woman. Her eyes were on the twisted wire door lying halfway across some beams two doors away. She picked through the rubble toward it over upended file cabinets, their bent-open drawers filled with the blackened remains of the hardcopy records, the shattered blind screen of a computer, and charred and melted plastic chairs from the waiting room. Chessie's kennel had faced a large viewport, to give her sunbeams to bask in, since sunlight was said to be health-

ful particularly for ships' cats much deprived of natural feline plea-
sures.

She looked back at the guard and asked, her voice muffled by
her mask and husky from a throat already scratchy with the remains of the smoke: "Did the first responders who rescued the
other animals find a pregnant cat and save her too? She would
have been over there." She pointed to where the husk of the kennel remained standing.

"I think the other animals escaped on their own, miss. No one I
know set them free. I'm sorry, but I've seen no pregnant cat nor has
anyone mentioned such a one."

It was no more than Janina had expected, but her spirits sank a
little more. Still, she slogged through to the room where she had
left Chessie.

Even when creatures were cremated, there were ashes, shards of
bones. She knew if she saw her cat's remains, she would recognize
them.

As she drew nearer the burned-out kennel, she could clearly see
through the blackened wire mesh that the sleeping shelf appeared
untouched, although the cat bed was no longer there.

But better yet, the door hung slightly ajar. Chessie got out!
Someone had let her out!

Janina allowed herself a deep relieved breath, then coughed
over and over, her throat and chest burning.

She stumbled back through the ruins, pressing Chessie's button
again and again. She had to have survived, had to. She could not
have run far, fleet of foot as she was, with her belly full of young.
Whoever had saved the other animals must have saved her too, but
instead of setting her free—perhaps realizing the pregnant cat
would not be fast enough to outrun the fire—had taken her far
away from the once-safe haven that had become a deadly inferno.

Janina collapsed to the deck in the outer corridor.

Jared, his face ashen, turned his back on the ruins and hurried
toward her and then past.

"Jared, what—" she began.

He stopped, took a step back and gave her a look full of sorrow and pity, letting his fingers brush her hair, then strode on without speaking. But not before she saw the tracks of tears through the soot that covered the exposed part of his face. He was as stricken by this tragedy as she, but he had not lost the creature dearest to him in the whole universe. She had—but the loss was not hers alone. She rose and straightened her uniform. It was time to face her crewmates.

✶ ✶ ✶

Her feet felt so leaden she thought she'd dent the deck as she boarded the *Molly Daise* and marched to the bridge.

The ship's officers were waiting for her. That was unusual. A Cat Person was normally not important enough for such an august assemblage. She didn't flatter herself that it was her welfare that concerned them now. Not only were most members of the crew fond of Chessie, but they had plans for the money they'd receive from the sale of her new litter.

The officers' faces were not accusatory or unkind, however, and somehow that made her feel worse. She had thought she was doing the right thing by Chessie, leaving her at the clinic. How had it gone so horribly wrong?

To put off having to say anything, she hauled the gifts she'd bought for the captain's family from her pack and silently handed them to him. He took them with a distracted frown, not inspecting them. "Are you all right, Janina?" he asked her.

"I am well enough, sir, but—" Her throat closed with aching and she couldn't finish the sentence.

"Did you—find her?" asked second mate Indu Soini, her voice holding a strange restrained mix of hopefulness and dread.

"I did not, ma'am. She was not among the rescued beasts from the clinic—"

"Oh no!" said Engineer's mate Charlotte Holley, who of all of her section was the one fondest of cats in general and Chessie in particular. "Janina, why did you leave her there? You could have brought her to me. I'd have watched her."

"She had my permission," Captain Vesey said. "It seemed best at the time. The cat needed a checkup and a rest. The vet needed Janina's help with tagging some horses on Sherwood."

"But she's the Cat Person, sir!" Charlotte protested. "Her duty was—"

"Her duty was where I permitted it to be, Techmate Holley. Hear the girl out."

Janina looked from one of them to the other. Charlotte was right. What was she going to say to them? What could she say? Instead of staying with Chessie, as she should have, she'd gone off gallivanting with Jared, and she would not fool herself into thinking it was for duty or helpfulness. She was eager to go off and leave Chessie so she could enjoy the pleasure the vet's company gave her. Picnics! And poor Chessie, how she must have cried for her Kibble when she sensed the fire.

Charlotte, communications officer Bennie Garcia, Purser Mick Yawman, and Indu all seemed at a loss. Captain Vesey had returned his attention to the instruments without signaling that his officers do the same.

Years seemed to pass.

"Thank goodness you're all right, anyway," Indu said at last, stepping forward to give Janina a light hug. When Indu stepped back, her contact with Janina left black sooty spots on her immaculate uniform. The hug made Janina feel worse, much as she appreciated it. She knew she didn't deserve it.

"We were all loaded and onboard when the port officials hailed us and informed us of the fire," Indu told her. "We feared you and Dr. Vlast might have been injured, but it looks as if you're fine."

"Yes, of course, we're glad you and Dr. Vlast are okay," Bennie Garcia said, "but the question remains: if she wasn't with the other animals, where *is* the Duchess?"

Captain Vesey had brought up a scan of the ruins on the com screen.

Mick Yawman, the purser, was staring at the screen, his jaw tight and his pale blue eyes starting to water as badly as Janina's. Chessie had seen Mick through a bout of flu turned to pneumonia that nearly killed him a year before, and she often took her naps under his chair as he did the ship's accounts.

Charlotte followed Mick's gaze. "She wasn't—did you look?" she asked.

Janina nodded in mute misery.

Mick dropped his head and his hands fell to his sides. She realized the other crew members looked as grim and shocked as he did, and realized they had misinterpreted her nod.

"Oh—she wasn't in there," Janina admitted. "Her kennel was empty and the door was ajar! She got out! I just know she got out. But though I've combed the station, I've not found her."

"Did you try her locator signal?" Charlotte asked.

"Of course I tried it, over and over again, but I didn't get any response."

"But if she survived, you'd get a signal," Bennie said.

Janina shook her head so hard soot rained off her face. "Not necessarily. I don't think she's dead. I really don't."

"What are you saying?" Bennie asked. "That the chip was damaged by the fire but Chessie wasn't? Does that mean she's lying up somewhere injured?"

"I looked all over," Janina said, "and I'll keep looking. But I think someone took her. Someone let the animals out, and I think they saw that she couldn't move fast enough on her own and they carried her away."

"And they just *kept* her?" Charlotte asked indignantly.

"We can only hope," Mick said, bringing her up sharply.

She knew she had let them all down. She was guilty of dereliction of duty, even though Captain Vesey was defending her. She still had to face the other crew members, who'd been counting on the sale of the kittens for all manner of improvements in their lives. They might not openly accuse her of betraying them and neglecting her mission, but they'd resent her all the same. It didn't matter. Whatever they said, nothing was worse than missing the touch of Chessie's silky fur, the delight of looking into her large gold-green eyes. It left a throbbing pain in her heart.

"We'll offer a reward, of course," Mick said finally.

"Can't," Indu said. "We're due to take off and we're on a tight schedule. There'd be no one here to identify the Duchess or to authorize payment."

"There's Dr. Vlast," Bennie said.

"Look at that mess," Indu replied, gesturing to the ruins of the clinic on the com screen. "Dr. Vlast just lost everything. He may have to relocate until they can rebuild his clinic. If they can. There've been all those budget cuts."

"I'll stay," Janina said. "And if she's—if it's possible, I'll find her. Captain Vesey, sir, have I permission?"

"Yes, that seems appropriate," he agreed, and left the bridge abruptly—to tend to some other duty, perhaps, or maybe so the others couldn't see that he too was upset. He used to stroke Chessie's tail as she laid across the back of his command chair.

"You'll be on your own, you know," Indu told her. "No berth, no provisions . . ."

"That's right, I'm afraid," Mick said. "We haven't the budget to keep you on your salary now, even if you stayed with the ship. No cat, no job for a Cat Person. Will you be okay here? If you need a loan, I've a bit I could spare."

"Thank you, Mick, but I'm sure I'll manage," she said. "I've put a little aside for emergencies, and it shouldn't take long to find Chessie. When I do, I'll notify you so the reward can be paid and you can pick us up on the next trip." She was trying hard to sound cheerful and unperturbed even though her happy life on the ship seemed to be crumbling around her along with the loss of her dearest companion. All because she'd been a bit too anxious for someone else's company.

"Maybe she's hiding somewhere while she's having her litter," Indu suggested brightly. "Probably we'll no sooner leave the station than you'll be telling us it's time to return for you, Chessie, and the kittens."

"I hope so, Indu," Janina said, and turned away to march back down the corridor.

r r r

Feeling bereft but also a bit relieved when the *Molly Daise* departed without her, Janina returned to the clinic deck, hoping for another word with Jared before she decided how to proceed.

He was more himself again, though somewhat distracted as he poked through the ruins. He asked her what she was doing back when the *Molly Daise*'s departure had just been announced. She told him the story.

"I'm so sorry, Nina, but you mustn't think you're to blame in any way. Chessie should have been perfectly safe. Who would have thought an arsonist would attack my clinic? Everyone on Sherwood uses my services."

"Arsonist?" she gasped, though she realized the thought had been in the back of her mind.

"That's what the fire brigade thinks, and it's the only explanation that makes much sense. The fire started in the hay storage area of the large animal stalls, after the horses had been released. Apparently an accelerant was used, though it wouldn't have taken much. Thank goodness the criminal seems to have been humane enough to spare the horses and the other patients."

"Which means that he probably spared Chessie too!" Janina said, her spirits rising. "I knew it had to be something like that! I just knew it. Maybe it sounds silly, but I think I would feel it if she were dead. The crew is posting a reward. Surely someone saw the person who took her and will report it if there's money to be made."

"We'll hope so. I am so sorry about this, Janina. Look, I'm currently short of a duty station myself. I'm going to set up a makeshift clinic on Sherwood until the supplies can be flown in to repair and rebuild the station facility. Funds will be short but I'll have to do a certain amount of commuting between Locksley and the station, so I'll need extra help. I'm afraid the budget won't stretch much, but I could pay you something to keep you going while you look for Chessie. I'm about to return the other clinic patients to their owners on Sherwood now. Do you want to ride along?"

Janina hesitated momentarily. What if Chessie *was* still here and hurt, her ear damaged so that her locator tag no longer functioned? She could be holed up, too weak to move, waiting to be found. But if Chessie was here, there were lots of other people who knew what had happened who would keep her safe until she could collect her. The reward had been posted and was on the station's computer system, and it was substantial enough to afford someone a nice vacation to a resort world, or to buy new ground transport, a horse, or even one of Chessie's kittens.

If the kittens had survived.

"Janina?"

She took a deep breath and nodded. Chessie would be found if she was in the station. Sherwood was another matter.

Chessie had smelled the newcomer, heard her kennel door release, and felt the large hands reach in to lift her from her sleeping platform shortly after the first whiff of smoke reached her sensitive nostrils.

The hands were fairly gentle, though a bit tighter than she'd have liked around her swollen middle, and she was glad to be released into a carrier. She assumed this was one of the vet's assistants, moving her long enough to clean her kennel, though she certainly hadn't soiled it by any means.

"Come on, old girl, I'm saving your furry tail," the man told her.

She had heard this voice not long ago, when the man stopped Kibble in the hall. What was *he* doing here? And what was that awful smell? Eyes widening with fear, she emitted the growling battle cry intended for prey larger than herself. By then the smoky smell had grown stronger, underlain by the stench of terror as she heard the whinnies, barks, hoofbeats, and paw pads of other animals running past them to escape other parts of the clinic.

When the man carried her from the room, she saw the back of her prison through one of the airholes in her carrier. Flames blossomed and flowed along the floor. Then the man clicked the hatch shut behind them, blocking her view, running down a side corridor at a brisk trot.

Chessie caterwauled and scratched and poked her paws through the airholes, trying to snag her captor in a way to let him know this was no way to treat a lady and an expectant mother. What did he think he was doing? Where was her Kibble? Where was Jared? Who did this man think he was anyway?

He was carrying her and her unborn kits to safety, away from the fire, and that was good, of course. But there was still something very wrong. Why hadn't the sprinklers been set off to douse the flames? Where were the other rescuers?

Hoofbeats clattered down the tiled corridor. Dogs barked behind them. The man paused now and again, then hurried down several flights of stairs, reaching the flight deck. Halfway there the com system began blatting the fire alarm. Her rescuer paused, lowering her carrier so that all she saw were running feet, racing from the direction of the flight deck and past them to emergency duty stations. She meowed, hoping a more familiar person would take charge of the carrier and release her, but her cry was lost even to her in the continuous bleat of the alarm. By the time the alarm stopped and the calm voice began instructing crew members from different areas of the space station to proceed to different areas of the clinic block with their extinguishers, the smell of smoke was filling the staircase. The landing crews were running toward them, away from their duty station. This chaos was quite unlike the disciplined order aboard the *Molly Daise*. Chessie didn't like any of it one bit. She was unaccustomed to being hauled about by strangers. Still, she supposed the man must be taking her back to the ship and to her Kibble.

But he didn't go to her ship's dock. Instead, she saw him run up to a small utility shuttle, the sort colonists used to haul goods from the space station to their businesses or homes on the ground. It was on one of these that she had captured the interesting bug on their last trip here before her crew had introduced her to that cocky Space Jockey responsible for these wretched kittens. She had just weaned her previous litter then, and had spotted the shiny irides-cent insect scuttling away from a USV—a utility service vehicle, as the air-to-ground shuttles with cargo space were called—just be-fore the sterilizer was turned on it. She had pounced with alacrity and devoured it in one bite. Afterward she'd caught several more aboard the *Molly Daise,* probably taken aboard with provisions, the same way the ship acquired most of her prey.

The man hoisted her carrier into the USV's co-pilot's chair and strapped it down. What was he doing? She hissed and clawed at the airholes, sticking as much of her paw and leg as she could through them to try to claw his clothing or skin. But suddenly the shift in the light, the pressure of the air, told her they were in space again, and moving farther and farther from her ship and her people.

The man paid no attention to her protests and had been smart enough to position her carrier where she couldn't reach him. Her struggle quickly exhausted her meager reserves of strength. She needed to rest, to be ready for when the kittens came. The move-ment in her belly told her they would be arriving all too soon.

After a bit more grumbling, she fell asleep. It could have been mere moments later when she awoke as the shuttle set down on the planet's surface, with an aqua sky overhead, in front of a crude build-ing with a three-cornered roof. It was constructed of some sort of rus-tic organic material. Beside it, at a short distance, was a smaller structure with rectangular ports and hatches and a peaked roof.

A collection of machinery littered the bare grounds close to the buildings, beyond which stretched wide green and gold fields. Some of these contained bovines. That much Chessie could see. She heard the cluckings of fowl. It all smelled richly organic, which was not unpleasant of itself, but alarming in that it was defi-nitely not her ship.

The carrier bumped along beside the man, who opened one of the double doors to the larger structure. "I know you're not a barn cat, old girl, but the best place to hide a cat is where people expect to find cats. Barn cats don't have chips in their ears, so nobody will expect you to have one either. You'll be fine out here. Lots of nice hay and milk cows to keep you company. Play your cards right and I can promise you all the fresh milk you can drink. Your kittens too, when they're big enough."

The man talked a lot but he wasn't making any sense. He acted as if she was going to have her kittens *here*!

He set the carrier down in a stall and went away without releasing her. She began yowling for all she was worth.

"Take me *home*!" she demanded repeatedly, over and over, until her throat was sore. She stuck her paws through the airholes again and clawed futilely. "Let me out! Let me out!" she cried. Her right front dewclaw caught in the wire and tore, bleeding into the fur of her leg.

"What are you *on* about, anyway?" The question came to her along with the scent of another cat, a female and pregnant. "And what are you doing in *my* barn? I found it first."

"I don't *know*," Chessie replied dismally. "I don't want to be here. I want to go home to my ship and my Kibble and crew."

"I guess they left this barn sitting catless too long. The rats and other vermin have really taken over. I don't know what the man expects you to do about it from that box, though. It suits me. I'll line up my kill and show him how much he's needed me before he lets you out. Then he'll know who the working cat is here and take you back where you belong. I need this place. I'm going to have my kits any day now. Believe you me, it hasn't been that easy catching rats the size of the ones in *this* barn."

Chessie hissed, which showed how upset she was. "He doesn't want me to catch rats, you stupid creature. He wants to steal my kittens."

"He steals kittens?" The other cat sounded puzzled, then she laughed. "That's a good one! Barn humans don't steal kittens, at least not before they're weaned. Sometimes they give them away— or worse. But they don't have to steal them. There are too many cats who would kill to live in a warm cushy barn like this one. As excited as that boy is about my kittens, he wouldn't steal them."

"What boy? Who *are* you? Where is this awful place? I want my ship!" Chessie cried. "Please make them take me back."

"Do be *quiet*," the other cat growled. "I'm sure when the man finds out the position is filled, he'll get rid of you and your spawn at once. The boy should have told him about me."

"You're wrong," Chessie told her. "That man talked to Kibble in the corridor. He wanted a kitten. She told him they all have homes to go to and now he's taken us *all*. More than likely it's *you* he'll get rid of."

"Not me! I've caught many mice and rats and one frog already. I'll show you."

The other cat turned tail and waddled away. Chessie immediately felt lonely, even before she was out of sight. The other cat was not as unfriendly as she could have been, and Chessie was used to being surrounded by friends and admirers, not to mention her Kibble. She cried out for the other cat to return, and the tortoiseshell padded back toward her. She had a lot of red in her mottles, looked to be the same breed as Chessie and as heavily pregnant, though perhaps a little younger, and she was dragging a huge rat, which she dropped in front of Chessie's carrier. Then, despite Chessie's entreaties that she stay, she waddled away again to return with another rat, then the frog, several small mice, and some other things Chessie had never seen before.

"Good catch," Chessie said, one expert hunter to another.

"And these are just the ones I haven't eaten yet!" the other female said. She was sitting erect, guarding her prey, and at Chessie's comment, her chest puffed out so that it almost protruded more than her kitten-filled middle. Her nipples looked as swollen as Chessie's felt. This was a clever and able cat, Chessie thought, and a possible ally when she escaped to return to her ship.

"I'm formally called Thomas's Duchess," she said. "But my shipmates call me Chessie."

"The boy hasn't called me anything yet, except 'momcat,' " the other replied. "But before him, others said 'Git!' when they saw me, so I guess that must be my name."

"Git—succinct, efficient, no nonsense about it. It suits you."

"Do you think it's short for anything grander, like yours is? I have no idea what Duchess means but I like the sound of it."

"Possibly it's your name and coloring. Your real name might be Grizabella. That is quite a venerable name among Barque Cats so probably it is among dirtside—land cats—as well. It must be an acronym—the first letter of each word. 'Grizabella Is Tortoiseshell' might be your real name."

"Oh, that sounds very grand. Why do you suppose they only use first letters?"

"It's kind of a code. They're fond of using letters for codes. The health op used to say to my Kibble, 'It is time to take Chessie to the V-E-T.' As if I didn't know what that meant!"

"They're really confusing," Git said. "Some cats want to be house pets, but me, I'll be happy for a warm barn to raise my family and plenty of game to hunt. A kind word once in a while is nice but it's not like I'd want to depend on humans."

"My Kibble and crew are very reliable," Chessie said. "They will come looking for me. I'm sure they won't take off without me and my kittens. I doubt the ship will even start unless I'm there."

"If you're so important, why did they send you here?"

"They didn't. I told you, I was abducted. But my people will find me. There's a chip in my neck."

"A chip? Does it hurt?"

"No worse than an insect bite when they put it in. It has my ancestral record in it and my duty station and its signal, but it also transmits my whereabouts. Kibble uses it to track me when I'm patrolling places too small for her to fit."

"Can't say I'd care for that," Git said disdainfully. "You set a lot more store by humans than I do. In my experience they'll more than likely let you down."

"I told you I am worth a great deal to them. That's got to be why the man stole me. He wants these kittens."

"You'll see. It will be as much as either of us can do to keep him from drowning or shooting us all if he reckons there's too many."

"Not *my* kittens. My kittens patrol ships all over the universe. They are much sought after as vermin-control agents."

"What's that?"

"Hunters. Killers. We're very good, you know."

"Better than me?" Git growled, and hunkered down to glower menacingly in through the airholes. "Could you or your kittens catch more prey than this in a single night? I don't think so!"

"Oh, no," Chessie said quickly—and truthfully. Git's proficiency as a huntress surprised her. She'd had no idea that simple land cats, whom she had always heard were inferior to Barque Cats, were so deadly. Perhaps this cat had been stolen from a ship as a kitten by the same man? But no, she had said she'd only just arrived in the barn a short time ago herself and the man didn't know about her yet. She did *look* like a Barque Cat, though, with her long, though slightly matted, fur, tufted ears and paws, plume-like tail that puffed to considerable circumference when she was agitated, and large shining golden eyes.

"I'm hiding when I have my kits and keeping them out of sight until they can fend for themselves. I'd advise you to do the same."

"I don't think he'll let me," Chessie said, and it came out as a wail. "I am stuck in this box with no food and no water and I've already soiled it. It won't be fit for my kittens and they're coming any time now, I feel it!"

Git nosed an airhole and stuck her tongue out, trying to give Chessie a comforting lick.

"What's all the commotion?" the man said, entering with a number of bewildering things in his hands. "Who the frag are you?" he asked Git.

"She's mine, Dad," a younger male voice piped up from behind him. "She's my new barn cat. She knew I wanted a kitten and she brought me a belly full of them." He rushed forward, putting himself between his father and the cage so that his legs blocked Chessie's view. "Lookit there! Lookit what she caught already. She's a good cat and a pretty cat—good as that one you got. Take that one back. We don't need her."

"Okay, calm down, son. You can keep the barn cat out here. But I brought this fine lady cat here so you can have your pick of her litter for your house pet."

"How about the others? What are you going to do? Gruder's dad killed his cat's kittens and Cellie's mom sold some to a lab. You wouldn't do that, would you, Dad?"

"Calm down, son. It's okay. This cat here is a special kind. She's very valuable and her kittens are too. We can make enough from selling them—no, no, not to a lab, to good homes that will pay a lot of money for the privilege of having them—to fix up the house and hire a hand to help with the stock so you can concentrate on your schooling. You're just like your mama. You worry too much."

"Okay," the boy said. "You're not connin' me, are you, Dad?" His voice implied that whatever connin' was, it was something his dad did often.

"Son, trust me. I got this cat so you could pick out your own kitten, like I said. Once we sell all the kittens but yours, we'll be able to make something out of this place."

"And how about the other cat's kittens? Can I keep them too?"

"How about picking up that board over there and helping me build up that stall into a little room for the mama cat to have her babies in where nothing will disturb them? I don't want anything to damage those little gems."

"What's that thing?" the boy asked, pointing to the little machine the man had brought with him to the barn.

"Something else we need to do to protect our investment, son. I'm going to install it right above the barn door, and that will keep anybody from bothering the mother of your future kitten."

✱ ✱ ✱

Jubal suppressed his excitement about the kitties all through supper. Mom had made egg pie, which he had come to love in recent months. Something had improved the flavor tremendously and the shiny bits in it looked very appetizing. He hated to think about it, because it was kind of gross, but he suspected it was because the chickens had been pecking up those shiny beetles that infested the barnyard. Like the beetles, the eggshells were shiny, sparkling like they'd been coated in sugar sprinkles. He'd actually been saving the shells because they were so pretty.

But much as he loved everything made with eggs, Jubal was too anxious to get back to the kittens to eat much that night. When he muttered, "'Scuse me," and started to leave the table, his mom asked him where he thought he was going in a tone that said no matter what he answered, she probably wasn't going to like it.

"To do my chores, Mom," Jubal said with wide-eyed earnestness. "I want to get them all done before I start my homework."

"Right, and I'm Maid bloody Marian. You doing your chores before you even check to see if there's dessert, that doesn't fly, my lad. What's the use of having the biggest liar on Sherwood for a daddy if you can't fib any better than that?"

Pop looked up from a forkful of his second helping of the pie. "Leave him be, Dorice. He's just going to check on the livestock."

They hadn't told mom about the cats yet. They'd have to sooner or later but hoped to stall as long as possible. She probably wouldn't raise too much fuss over the barn cat because even a cat-disliker had to admit that barn cats served a good and useful purpose. But Pop had said he didn't want her to know about the fancy new cat yet.

Jubal was pretty sure it was because there was something fishy about the way Pop had come by Chessie.

If Mom knew what they were up to, she wasn't saying anything. Jubal thought she might have a good idea about at least some of what was going on. He'd caught her staring at some cat hairs on his overalls, wrinkling her nose when he hadn't washed off the smell of cat pee good enough. Dad's industriousness, if nothing else, was enough to rouse her suspicions. Suddenly he was doing all the men's jobs in the barn, the ones Jubal couldn't do that she usually had to do since the old man, for a retired guy, spent a lot of time in space.

She rolled her eyes and pointed to the door as she bit down on a biscuit. Even if she had guessed the whole thing, Jubal wasn't too worried.

Mom had stayed married to Pop in spite of everything he did that made her mad. She usually managed to be looking the other way when Pop pulled a lot of his shenanigans. If she didn't see it, she wasn't responsible for it. She was a very practical lady. She had scruples but they were flexible.

Pop said they just needed to keep her in the dark until the kittens were born and he could sell a couple, because she was apt to be more reasonable once she saw they were the start of a lucrative enterprise.

Jubal kept himself to a walk until he reached the kitchen door, then lit out for the barn as fast as he dared.

The cats were settled down snug and cozy in the little rag beds he had made for them in the hay. They seemed to be getting along fine. The momcat had moved right in with Chessie to the stall room Pop and he had built to protect her—and to protect Pop, Jubal was pretty sure.

The momcat meowed and yowled about the closed door, though, so Pop took the truck to town and brought home one of those cat doors that could be keyed to open only for a cat wearing a special collar. It took both Jubal and Pop to put the collar on the barn cat, which she obviously considered was taking undue liberties. She had not liked that collar even a little, but being a sensible cat, when her gyrations and scratchings didn't get it off, she seemed to forget about it and went about her business.

Chessie didn't get a collar but didn't seem to mind the door. Pop said she was used to being indoors and in confined places a lot so he figured she probably liked it that way.

Jubal opened the door a crack. If he'd been a little taller, he could have looked through the crescent moon carved through the front of it. The door had been on the privy that used to stand in back of the house, before they got hooked up to the Locksley sewer system. They'd had to saw off the top and add a board to the bottom to make it fit, but it worked okay. It still stank a little, but cats didn't seem to mind that kind of thing.

He meant to just peek at them before bringing the cows in for the night, feeding the chickens, and milking, but when he saw both cats licking a sticky-looking kitten while part of another kitten was coming out of its mom's back end, he couldn't leave. Even though he'd seen that other newborn animals were a sticky mess just out of the mama, he somehow thought the kittens would be all fluffy and cute and bright-eyed.

But the first kitten out of the chute had its eyes stuck shut, and what little fur it had was glued to its teeny-weeny body with sparkly slimy stuff from its mother's insides. Its tail was no longer than Jubal's pinky, and the rest of the entire kitten would have fit inside a teacup. When he reached out with one fingertip to pet the kitten's head, which was now fairly clean, its mother gave him a dirty look.

"Don't worry, girl. I wouldn't hurt your baby. You know me, right? We're friends, aren't we? I was just going to pet it."

Chessie turned her head to give him a long look too, calmer than the momcat's but a warning. It came to him all of a sudden that the kitten was probably too little and too new to be petted right then. "I didn't know, okay?" he said. "Gimme a break here. I haven't seen baby cats get born before."

The little kitten might be blind, but it found one of its mom's teats quick enough and set about nursing while she popped the rest of the next kitten out. The two cats were doing an assembly line kind of thing: the tortoiseshell momcat popping them out, Chessie washing one end while the new mother washed the other, and then if Momcat was busy with birthing the next kitten, Chessie would nudge the clean kitten over to get its dinner.

He was still watching when he heard Pop call, "Jubal! How come the cows are still out in the pasture? It'll be getting dark soon."

"Pop, come and see this!" he cried without getting up. In a minute the latch was raised and Pop came in behind him.

"Well, looks like your barn cat is showing her ladyship how it's done. I don't reckon they need supervision, son."

"But, Pop!"

"You go do your chores before your mama wants to know why you didn't. I'll make sure the cats are okay."

And that was that. Jubal hung around the barn as long as he could, going out in the yard to feed the chickens, putting down fresh food and hay for the cows, getting the milking gear ready for when he brought them in. Pop slipped out in the middle of the milking and came back with a piece of equipment that he took into the cat room with him. Jubal wondered what it was. Pop wouldn't hurt the cats or the kittens, he was pretty sure, but it was hard to say for certain what he *would* do. He wasn't exactly a predictable kind of guy.

When Jubal put the cows into their stalls and was measuring out their food, he heard a cat squall. He hastily set down his bucket and ran to the cat room, flinging open the door. Pop had one of the kittens in one hand and a syringelike thing in the other hand, the tip against the kitten's neck. Momcat was snarling at him.

"I'm not going to hurt your offspring, madame," Pop told her. "I am elevating him—or her, as the case may be—to a higher station in life. You'll thank me for this later."

Jubal didn't think Momcat was buying it.

CHAPTER 5

CHESTER'S STORY: A BARN ON SHERWOOD

Having finally attained the maturity and skills to render a full account of the events surrounding my entrance into the universe, I can now tell the story of my birth, the births of my siblings, and our fate at the hands of our captors.

Because of the humans' interference, my mother wisely chose to deliver her litter in the middle of the night. I was born first, the most beautiful of the lot, my mother assured me, though I heard her say the same thing to each of my subsequent siblings. I had to take her word for it since my eyes were still closed.

Inconvenient bit of biology, that. Fortunately, my blindness made my other senses preternaturally acute and I quickly assessed my surroundings. My nose led me to a source of nourishment.

"Hey, you, new kid, that's *our* milk you're stealing!"

"Yeah, get away from our mother and go back to your own!"

These were the unkind and uncouth cries that greeted me from the other youthful feline denizens of our lair, the offspring of my mother's companion and my sometimes nanny, a tortoiseshell queen named Git. Though lacking our careful breeding, Git nonetheless proved herself to be a noble creature of the highest order. Fortunately for me, Git's kittens had been born only the day before and were also blind and of precarious balance, so their feeble swats at my poor unsuspecting newborn self did no harm except to them as they fell back on their own tails with the effort of swinging their paws.

"Now where *did* I put that kitten?" I heard my mother's melodious voice inquire. "I hope I didn't sit on him while I was birthing this one. Git, have you seen—"

"He's right here, Chessie. Causing trouble." Larger paws and a nudge from an adult muzzle herded me back toward my own mother, who nudged me toward an appropriate dispenser of sustenance.

"Ah, not my fault, Git. He gets that from his father's line. Space Jockey is a notorious brawler."

"Aren't they all?"

My sister was already at an adjoining milk outlet and we applied ourselves to nursing with great zeal while two more siblings were born, washed, and deposited beside us. Then things began to go badly.

I noticed this because I was sleeping on top of Mother when she began heaving and panting to a degree that I have since felt only during take-offs, landings, and meteor showers. My brother did not survive. Neither my other siblings nor I found this terribly distressing as it meant more available food for us, but Mother was vexed, rather ashamed, she complained to Git, since she had never before lost a kitten, and, by the time she finally succeeded in pushing it out, she was hurt and bleeding to an apparently irregular extent.

"Where is that boy now that he might come in handy?" Git asked, dumping her own brood unceremoniously, as I divined from their indignant minuscule mewings, and trying to help my mother clean her injuries.

"Kibble! I want my Kibble!" Mother cried. "She would know how to help me. We've done this together many times and I never lost a kitten. Oh, Kibble, where are you?"

Her cries, strong at first, quickly grew softer as she lost more blood. The tang of it was strong and it made the straw sticky beneath our paws.

Git's louder complaints were joined by the sound of her claws rending some resistant substance followed by the thud of her body against the same. "The dirty rats locked my entrance!" she cried. "How are we supposed to provide for these young'uns if we can't hunt? Let me owwt!"

I did not understand the full implications of the situation, nor did any of the other kittens, poor blind stumbling little things that we were. But we could hear that Git was distressed and sense that Mother was in mortal pain, so we added our feeble squeaking voices to those of the older cats.

In between my verbal complaints, I licked my mother as she had licked me to clean and dry me. Although I had not the words to articulate it, I knew that she was on the verge of leaving us, that help must be sought, if only to remove the barrier Git found so irksome. Mother trembled beneath me, and her heartbeat—our steady and strong companion as we awaited birth—had become too quick to give proper emphasis to each thud. Were we all to end before we had made a proper beginning?

"Boy!" Git called over and over again, and suddenly I saw as clearly as if my eyes had opened a strange-looking biped with blue hind legs and chest, dirty white hind paws, furless arms, and spidery looking forepaws with wormlike things on the ends of its pads. A large round head bore the only fur on the boy's entire body, and he seemed to have no ears. His eyes were also closed when I first saw him, but when I gave an inner exclamation of surprise, they opened. They were the first eyes I saw, although mine remained closed. They were large, a lighter shade of the same color as his legs and chest. Their initial expression was one I would come to recognize as startled. It quickly shifted so that his whiskerless face with its flattened, split muzzle reflected the fear I felt rising from my mother and through me. I smelled his fear but I also smelled his wonderful boy smell, tangy and warm mixed with wood and dirt and a bit of what I later identified as onion.

I had at the time no idea how I conjured this apparition, but was as gratified as I felt after nursing when a short time later there were rustling steps outside, a rattle, a snick, and a rush of clean air, along with a beam of light I saw even through the membranes covering my eyes. "Chessie! You're having your babies. What's the matter, girl?"

The boy's large warm presence loomed over us and one of the wormlike things descended to stroke my mother between the ears and then me, from my ears to my tail. The sensation was not un-pleasant. The boy stroked each of my siblings in turn, then Git's kittens. Git had taken advantage of the opening to leave the en-closure, but I heard her return and the sound of her fur brushing the boy's hind leg and paw, which were cramped awkwardly be-neath him.

Then the boy said, "What's that? Looks like you lost one of your babies and—shite oh dear, kitty, you're bleedin' like a stuck pig."

He rose so quickly that Git fell sideways and, without closing the opening, he thudded away, yelling, "Dad! Hey, Dad!"

My memory gives me no account of what happened next. Al-though I now possess the maturity and faculties I mentioned pre-viously, at the time I was newborn, with closed eyes, had been through a great deal during my first few moments of life, and I needed my rest.

I can say only that my mother and I survived, as did the three siblings that were born after me. That made it even. Four of us and four of the others, Git's get. The boy announced that he would call me Chester. Mother said I was the spitting image of her illustrious forebear Tuxedo Thomas. I am largely black, with a white chest and paws. My younger sisters were Silvesta, a silver tabby whose stripes twined into butterfly shapes on her sides, and Buttercup, gold and white with deeper orangish stripes along her legs and decorating her tail. My brother Sol, when he was little, was pale peach and cream-striped and insufferable. No matter which outlet on which mother I chose, Sol was right there to argue with me about it.

The kittens born to Git were our seniors by a day, according to her. They were all males. The boy called them Virgil, Wyatt, Bat, and Doc, after dead humans whose exploits he had read in stories. Apparently Bat was the one whose name came first, since he batted at the boy's finger when the boy tried to pet him. The other names came by association.

We got to know Git's get quite well, as they were essentially also our littermates and shared our meals. While Mother recovered, Git often gathered us to her to nurse and give Mother rest.

Then came the time when their eyes began to open while we were still in the dark. It seemed wrong somehow that we, who Mother and Git agreed were quite special and of celestial lineage, should be blundering around blindly while Git's kits pounced us, rolled us over, and generally behaved in an exceptionally aggressive and aggravating manner, punctuating their attacks with squeaky growls.

"You had better stop that," I told Wyatt, who had landed on me while I was suckling. "The boy and the man are coming, and they don't want to see any of us damaged. We are valuable."

"You are whupped, that's what. I don't hear the boy's steps or the man's so don't try to get out of it that way. No one can save you now from the paws of doom!"

Then he heard the footsteps too.

"How'd you hear them before me?"

"I saw them," I told him. "I see the boy."

"Hah! You can't. Your eyes are closed."

"I have my ways," I told him mysteriously. It was not hard to be mysterious since I didn't understand it myself. However, ever since my cries for help had summoned the boy to my mother's side, I had retained the ability to see him through my closed eyes and to compel him to do my will. This would have given me a great sense of power except that most of the time I had no idea what my will was concerning the boy. My urgent needs, as I understood them, were met by Mother and Git. If my littermates had similar powers and visions, they didn't mention it. Perhaps it did not occur to them that such abilities were not a normal part of a cat's equipment, but I tend to think that theirs took longer to develop than my own, as I was the only one to know in advance when the boy was coming. When the man came to tag us, I tried to hide under Mother, but to no avail. I was scooped up and my neck stung for a reason I did not understand. I cried lustily at the cruelty and injustice of it all. Afterward, Mother gave my poor neck a weak lick, but I forgot about my injury almost before her tongue was back in her mouth.

That particular day stands out in my memory, however, because, as the boy scooped me up and put me on his shoulder, where I huddled under the fringe of hair curling down his neck— the part of him that seemed most like Mother—I slowly realized that I could see not only him but the man as well, and that I was looking down at my beautiful mother, at Git, and my littermates. The light was not good and colors were not strong but my new eyes were very sharp and I could see everyone and everything around me. I began mewing excitedly, and the boy plucked me from his neck and turned me to face him so that his huge blue eyes looked into my new ones.

"Pop, look, Chester opened his eyes!"

"Excellent! That means the rest of the litter will soon. Not too much longer and we will be wealthy, son."

"But not Chester, right, Pop? We don't have to sell them all. You said I could keep one and I want to keep him. That's okay, right?"

The man sighed as Mother sometimes does when we are exploring her too actively. "I'm sorry, son. I meant it when I said that you could keep one when I brought the Duchess home, but with her only having the four kits instead of seven or eight, like we thought, our profits were cut in half. So how about picking out one of Git's babies instead? You can have any one you want."

"No, Pop. Chester is the one who likes me."

"Cats like whoever feeds them, Jubal. And he's likely to get a better life than you do once we get him a good berth. Now you look after them while I'm gone and don't let on to your mama, you hear? I have a little job to do on the station for the next few days."

"You know I'll take care of them, Pop."

To the best of his ability, he did too, and the tragic events that followed were not really his fault. He was simply doing what we wanted.

* * *

During the time the man was gone, we kittens began to grow hungry for something besides milk. This became apparent the day Virgil, while nursing, bit Git and got himself slapped tail over nose into the hay pile.

Then she shook all of the others off and stretched her forepaws out in front of her and her hind end toward the ceiling and whipped her tail back and forth a few times before announcing, "Time for you young'uns to learn to hunt."

I'd like to say that this happened at once and we all became the superb predators we were always destined to be, but first we had to learn to eat solid food. The boy helped. He brought us table scraps of cooked meat. The others growled and fought over it, but I realized immediately that the meat lacked something in juiciness and savor—that indefinable quality that I was hungry for without even realizing what I was missing. I looked up at him and mewed. He picked me up and asked, "What's the matter, Chester? Don't you like rabbit?"

Git rose and went to the door—that was what the opening was—and scratched.

"Okay, girl," the boy told her. He pulled something out of a pouch in a fold of his blue hind leg, reached down, and buckled the long tail-shaped strip around Git's neck. "You can go hunting now if you want."

Git streaked through the door. "Freedom!" I heard her cry as she disappeared.

The man returned and entered our room. "Hmm," he said. He took something from *his* coat, very small, and aimed it at us. Several times light blossomed around his hands and the colors of our coats, the hay, the boy's clothes and skin, all became bright and distinct.

Mother blinked placidly.

"What's that?" I asked her.

"I think it's a camera, my boy. So the man can show our images to others. Come here. You've a tuft of fur sticking up on the back of your head. Let me fix it for you."

The weeks passed quickly, though back then I had no idea what a week was.

I slept. I nursed. As my legs grew stronger, I practiced pouncing and running. So did the others. Our play was the work of kittens, which is a far more serious thing than it looks.

I don't know what the others dreamed of, but in my dreams I often did what the boy did. We fed chickens, rode horses, washed dishes, ate things that for reasons unfathomable to me seemed to appeal to him and his mother. We also read books, and this was extremely exciting, the stories we shared leaving lasting impressions on my thirsty young mind.

Yes, our strange connection let me participate in many of the boy's activities and learn his feelings and thoughts on more matters than actually interested me.

Of more interest were Git's expeditions, after which she would bring in strange edible creatures for us to tear apart with our ferocious claws and needle-sharp teeth. We were fierce, voracious, and merciless.

But of course the early prey was dead.

When we got live food and started to attack it, Git growled us away, smacked it dumb and bit the back of its neck, severing the spine in her strong jaws. "This critter was a living thing," she said. "It had a mama, like you, and maybe young'uns like you too. Its death helps you kids to keep on being living things your own selves. Treat it decent. Put it out of its misery. It's an ill-brought-up cat that tortures its food to death. Quick and clean, just the way you'd want to go if it was your time to be something else's supper."

I was to remember that admonition ruefully the day Git took us hunting outside for the first time. She had taken her own kits the day before, one at a time, and Sol, Silvesta, Buttercup, and I lurked at the edges of her portal, waiting for her to bring them back, desperate to see what had happened. Wyatt and his brothers were cocky enough already, lording over us their day's lead in life. What would they have to brag of now?

When Git herded each through the door carrying parts of prey proudly in their jaws, I was overcome with jealousy. I tried to snatch Bat's rat rump from him but the others abandoned theirs to jump on me and thump me soundly. When they turned back, they saw that Silvesta and Buttercup had cornered two of their mangled prizes and were daintily gobbling the bits. When the boys squalled, my sisters gave them withering looks from their bright round eyes and continued dining.

"The female of the species is more deadly than the male," I said. It was something the boy had read in one of his books, and my brethren looked startled to hear me say it but they didn't disagree. My sisters might smell better than we did but they were the same size and didn't mess about when it came to hunting. Mother and Git both favored them, actually, reminding them that someday they would have kittens to feed and teach too.

Wyatt and his brothers abandoned the pilfered prizes and began fighting over the remaining piece and thumping on Bat, trying to get his away from him.

But the next day was our turn. Git hauled me up by my scruff and I hung there, twitchy with anticipation while she took me into an outer world I had seen only through the boy's eyes before then.

Everything smelled stronger, moved faster, and looked much bigger when I saw it with my own eyes.

Git set me down just inside the barn door. Outside it was bright and vast—there was more world out there than I could have imagined on my own. I oriented myself quickly, though, since I had been here before in the boy's mind. The chickens wandered the yard. The house was over to the left. I couldn't see the fields where the horses roamed but the waving of the grass in the wind fascinated me.

I took a couple of steps forward when Git returned with Sol.

"Stay put, both of you," she said, "while I fetch your sisters."

She taught us how to hunt through the barn that day, but only Buttercup caught anything.

"Mrrrr," Git said. "Seems I've done too good a job. It was hard finding enough for the boys yesterday. Fine, then. You're not likely to have a nice barn to hunt in all your days. Before I found this place, I hunted the meadows and fields on the way. There's lots to be had but there's farther for the critters to run. I'll show you the way today but don't be fussed if you don't catch anything. It takes practice to run a meal down. We're fixing to go farther than you've gone before. I have to carry you in and out of the cat door for my collar to work for you too, but you need to run on your own paws now. Understood?"

At first we kept up fairly well, running, leaping, tumbling after her. The blades of grass looked as tall from my own height as trees did to the boy. The wildflowers, purple-belled ones and frothy white, bobbed seductively enough that Sol temporarily forgot he was actually a voracious carnivore and attacked the plant. A bee flew out and would have stung him if he hadn't jumped back in a hurry.

Deeper and deeper into the meadow we went, until Silvesta said, "I can't see the barn anymore."

Git, whose fine fluffy tail had been our beacon through the bush, turned back on us. "Good. Now then, I'm going to flush something your way. Before you go back to your mama, I want you all to catch enough to eat that you won't be troublin' her for milk. It's high time you wean."

She disappeared into the grass, but in a moment there was a thrashing and a small sparkly thing hopped toward us. These bugs were my favorite treat, and as eldest and the first one of us with open eyes, I figured the first kill out here at least belonged to me. Following Git's instructions, I vanquished it far more easily than I would have believed possible and proceeded to eat it with pride while Sol skittered after a lizard that slid through the grass toward us.

Buttercup, full of her barn catch, had lagged behind us. It was Silvesta, waiting with waggling hindquarters for her turn, who heard Buttercup squeak.

Git heard it too. Although we had not seen her for some time, suddenly she bounded over us, snarling.

There was an answering snarl and then nothing.

A bite of my prey was still in my teeth. I looked up, surrounded by the waving grass and the blue sky up above. But with my inner eyes I saw the boy come out of the barn with the feed bucket in his hands. As if he saw me too, he dropped the bucket and began running.

Somewhere he picked up a stick. "Leave them be, you mangy mongrel!" he yelled, waving the stick.

But I knew even before the canine sprinted past us, our protectress dangling from his jaws as prey had so often dangled from hers, that the boy had come too late. Where our second mother's strength, energy, and alert attention had crackled through the air, there was only stillness. The emptiness filled up with the boy's panting breath and the smell of the dog trailing behind it. Then came the first yowl of Silvesta's life as she stood over our sister's mangled body.

Git's sacrifice had not been swift enough to save Buttercup.

The boy picked both of my sisters up. Buttercup was so small, he slipped her body into his chest pocket, and blood seeped through the fabric. Silvesta continued to cry, and the boy searched through the grass until he saw the cowering Sol and lifted him too. I, who was closest to him, was the last to be lifted up, but I knew even in the midst of terror and bewilderment that it was because the boy knew exactly where I was, and that I knew he was near.

Mother washed us all when the boy took us back but she couldn't wash the life back into Buttercup, though the boy showed her the body, now oddly so much tinier than ours. Finally, Mother gave up and began washing Silvesta, and the boy took the body away again.

Wyatt and his brothers could not grasp it at first that their mother was gone. They searched the straw, they sniffed at us, who still bore her scent on our skin, and they prodded our mother looking for theirs. Wyatt understood first and stood by his mother's cat door and mewed a pitiful, lonely keen, more mournful for being so squeaky and small.

Sol and I just stared at him and the others. They had always been bigger than we were, had bullied us, but now they were lost. I sidled up to Wyatt, bumping my weight against him, trying to purr consolingly. He hissed at me.

He and the others hid separately, forlornly, until Mother rose shakily and one by one rounded them up and brought them to nurse, then called us to join in.

We all fell asleep before we finished eating, but when we awakened and had fed again, Mother shook us off, rising onto her haunches, her forepaws planted like columns beneath her feathery chest.

"My children—and you are all my children now—the time has come to teach you one of our most time-honored and useful rituals—bathing. A clean cat is a healthy cat, a respectable cat, and furthermore, a serene, deliberate, and decisive cat. Cleansing one's fur refreshes the mind as well as the body."

Washing hardly seemed as important as hunting, especially at a time like this, when we were all stricken by the sudden loss of Git and Buttercup. But Mom's voice continued, demanding our attention. Perhaps she was trying to distract us from recalling the deaths.

"This skill is necessary for every cat ever born on the ground or among the stars," she began. "But for we of the long fur, the plumed tails and full manes, the tufted ears and fur fringed pads, it is absolutely essential. Without proper grooming, our fur quickly mats into great clumps that hang from us like disgusting growths, that pinch and pull and catch on things when we are stalking, skulking, or attempting to slink. If you are fortunate enough, as I have been, to have a Kibble to care for you, she can assist you with the more difficult bits, but daily, hourly, and momentary maintenance are your responsibility, your duty, and your pride.

"Everybody, lick one of your forepaws."

"Why, missus?" Doc asked. "It'll just get dirty again."

"Just do it," Mother said firmly.

Doc looked down at his paw as if he had never seen it before and gave it a quick lick, as if expecting it to grab his tongue and strangle him.

I did the same, giving mine as long a swipe as my little pink tongue could manage. Silvesta and Sol followed suit.

"Now, this paw will be your tool to clean those parts of you that you are unable to reach by direct licking. Pass it over your face, thusly," she said, and demonstrated. She swiped it down over her ears and nose, licked it again and passed it over her long elegant whiskers, both the uppers and the lowers on the same side as her paw. Then she switched paws. I hoped my whiskers would be so magnificent when I was big.

Virgil got his paw stuck behind his ear when he tried. Bat would only dab at the areas in question. If I do say so myself, I did a splendid job on my first try.

Silvesta took a trial lick then began crying again. She missed Buttercup even more bitterly than the rest of us did. It was painful to listen to, and it interrupted the lesson. Mother cuffed her ears, swiping a paw across their tips to get her attention, then licking one tufted tip to take the sting out of the reprimand.

"Pay attention, my darling. You will have kits of your own to teach one day."

Silvesta trembled with grief, for this was the sort of thing Git used to tell her and Buttercup with every lesson, but she moistened her paw and washed her face.

When Mother had demonstrated the procedure for washing each bit of ourselves—and some bits were far more awkward than others—she said, "There is a language to the bath understood by other creatures as well as cats. Even humans are somewhat attuned to the meanings of the various postures. Washing is a built-in diversion, a time-out, you might say. In the annals of feline-based literature my Kibble used to read aloud to me, a wise cat named Jennie instructs a newcomer: 'When in doubt, wash.' Sage advice I pass along to you with these elaborations on the language of public bathing. When conveying confusion or when you are in need of clarification, wash your face. To express nonchalance or self-assurance, wash your shoulder. To indicate that you are considering a situation, lightly groom one of your front paws. And a fine time to groom that critical area under your tail is when you wish to demonstrate your indifference to the insignificant events around you, or to demonstate contempt for an idea or individual. Grooming one's abdomen indicates trust and should only be done in the presence of those you actually do trust. A full bath, with or without the assistance of a fellow feline, ideally should be undertaken only in privacy or in the company of one's Kibble."

"Or the boy," I said. "The boy's all right, isn't he, Mother?" My siblings and now foster siblings murmured agreement. The boy had just saved us.

She gave a short, noncommittal purr but I thought I saw a cloud cross her great gold-green eyes.

*   *   *

Mother had vowed that she would continue Git's work in teaching us to hunt, but alas, she never had the chance.

Inside that little dark room, we could only hunt each other, but even my reckless foster sibs realized that killing was out of the question.

We had only a few more days to nurse, to feed on the kibble and soft food the boy brought us, and to practice washing and pouncing before the man returned.

The boy sadly informed him of the deaths of Git and Buttercup. He frowned, shook his head, and patted the boy's shoulders.

But all he could say was, "They've grown, I'm going to have to take a whole new set of pics."

He took one of all of us nursing, then had the boy hold up each of us while he pointed the little flashy thing at us.

The boy held me close to his chest and I felt his heart thudding through it. "Don't worry, Chester. You and me are a team. Pop said I could have a kitten and I choose you, whether he likes it or not."

I pressed my ear to his heart and purred as loudly as I could. Of course the boy would stay with me. Why would I know everything he did and most of what he thought if he wasn't mine? He was my Kibble in the way that Mother's Kibble was hers, except Mother didn't know where hers was and some tiny part of me always knew where the boy was.

Nobody could fathom the mind of the man, though. He was trickier than the canine that had killed Buttercup and Git.

CHAPTER 7

When she wasn't helping Jared in the makeshift clinic in the Locksley Mall, Janina was out plastering every available notice board with flyers featuring Chessie's ID pic and the reward for her return. She talked to everyone she could stop and told them about the fire and how Chessie was missing and asked them to look for her.

One day she stopped a woman laden with parcels, boarding a battered farm tracker.

Janina showed the woman the picture.

"Just a minute, honey," the woman said, setting her parcels in the passenger seat and turning back to Janina. She shoved back her long dark brown hair, the plait of which had loosened during her shopping, wiped her hands on the thighs of her blue denim pants, and took the picture from Janina, glanced at it, grunted, and returned it. "Sorry," she said. "Don't recall seeing one like this."

"You'd notice her," Janina insisted. "Not only is she beautiful but she was about to have kittens when she disappeared."

The woman shrugged and started to walk away. "Hmm, well, I'm not much for cats. But kittens, you say? When was it she disappeared again?"

The woman's expression was both annoyed and speculative. Maybe she had a lead!

"Nearly two months ago, after the fire in the vet clinic at Hood Station."

"Huh. Well, what a shame. That crew must set great store by her to be offering such a hefty reward."

"Oh, yes, ma'am, and her kittens too. She's a very valuable cat, but more than that, we love her and we need her on our ship. She's an important part of the crew."

The woman glanced at the flyer again, her eyes lingering on the line about the reward. "Well, I hope you find her, honey." Then she turned back to put her parcels in her flitter.

Janina said, "Ma'am, if you see her or hear from anyone who might have seen her, please would you call me at Dr. Vlast's clinic in Locksley? I'm working with him until the new clinic is ready on Hood Station."

"Umm-hmm," the woman said. "I sure will."

𝄐 𝄐 𝄐

Since Janina began posting the flyers, people had shown up at the clinic with cats of all coloring, ages, and both sexes, some with kittens, some without, trying to claim the reward. A few had short hair or showed the Siamese strain. Did they think the large long-haired tortoiseshell Chessie had somehow managed to don a disguise and go incognito?

Jared said it was the triumph of hope over common sense, something he'd seen a great deal.

Some of the cats were so matted they looked to be made from balls of dirty felt instead of fur, some were battered and scarred, many looked starved, and all looked frightened. Jared did what he could for the pretenders to Chessie's throne, but ultimately they had to be returned to the arms of their disappointed bearers, though some were abandoned at the clinic. Janina made it her job to look after these and tried to find homes for them, though it was clear that most cats were not highly valued on Sherwood. Often they were considered to be as troublesome as the vermin they hunted.

She kept hoping as she continued her rounds of cleaning and filling feeding dishes, mucking out stalls, hosing down kennels, and changing litter boxes. It was useful work and she didn't mind it, but the familiar routine of caring for the cats tore at her heart, even though she was glad to be able to help them. They wound around her ankles and purred up at her and she patted them and spoke kindly, but they were just not Chessie. She and Chessie had been a team for ten years—more than half her life, and all of the best part. She missed her desperately and also missed the camaraderie with the crew.

Under other circumstances, the prolonged opportunity to work with Jared would have cheered her, but he was run off his feet now that the people (and their animals) of Sherwood had him all to themselves. They called him night and day to attend difficult births or accidental injuries, and he was often so exhausted he barely seemed to recognize her. When there was a lull, he spent it in his makeshift lab, preoccupied and focusing on his work.

She often found him frowning at slides and tubes of the mysterious glittery substance, which they were finding in more and more animals, but when she asked him about it, he shrugged and said only, "I'm checking it out."

* * *

Two weeks later, she was grooming the last poor matted moggy brought in by a hopeful. He was a gray and black male who had been spitting mad when he arrived. His temper hadn't improved much since. Jared had long red scratches running down his hands from this fellow, but the cat seemed to like females—or at least Janina—somewhat better. She was clipping one of his mats when the office door jingled.

"Nina, there are people to see you," Jared called from his exam room in the front of the clinic. She wished people would make appointments instead of popping in any old time with the poor imposter cats for her inspection. Every time they did, her hopes rose, and every single time they'd been dashed. Bracing herself for another letdown, she plopped the recalcitrant tom back into his cage, washed and dried her hands, and walked deliberately into the waiting room.

She saw two people at the desk, a woman and a boy, each carrying something. She was trying to remember where she had seen the woman before when she heard the plaintive mew.

The mew.

"Chessie?" she asked, thinking surely her ears were deceiving her. But she heard the mew again and knew she was not mistaken. "Chessie!"

"So you do recognize her?" a slightly familiar female voice asked. "You'll not deny that she's the very cat you told me about. The one you're looking for?"

Hurrying toward them, Janina recognized the woman she'd spoken to in the mall. The woman peeled a blanket farther away from the beloved furry face with its long magnificent whiskers. Chessie appeared uninjured. Her tufted ears had twitched forward at the sound of Janina's voice.

Janina reached for her. "Oh, Chessie!" The bundle the woman relinquished was much lighter than the beautiful cat had been when Janina placed her in the kennel at Jared's station clinic. "You've had your kittens, haven't you?" she asked, lifting an edge of the blanket to see the rest of Chessie more clearly.

"She did but they was all lost save this one here my boy's got," the woman said, indicating a bright-eyed fluffball peeking out from the shelter of the boy's arms. "And she's been poorly he says."

"Poorly?" Janina's heart dropped. Was she to regain her friend only to lose her again? She hurried to the examining room door and popped her head in. "It's her! Someone found Chessie but she's sick. Jared, she's light as a feather. I can feel her bones."

"Take her in exam room two. I'll be right there," he said, and he sounded happier and more excited than he had since the disaster.

"Even if she doesn't make it, I still get the reward, right?" the woman asked anxiously, following Janina into the exam room, the boy trailing reluctantly behind them.

"If you had her and you knew she was sick, why didn't you say when I met you before?"

"She didn't know about it till my dad and me had it out when he tried to take Chester with him," the boy blurted out. "Dad found your cat and kept her in the barn. He said not to tell Mom because she doesn't like cats and wouldn't let me keep her."

"But I tried and tried her locator signal and got no response."

"I reckon it must not work out our way, honey," the woman said. "Jubal didn't know she was yours. Don't take it out on him. He saved her last kitten. I didn't know a thing about it till I heard them carrying on and saw your cat. I recognized her right away."

While the woman explained, Janina laid her bundle down on the exam table, a rather rickety metal folding table of the sort set up in meeting halls and at fairs. Chessie was indeed much thinner than she had been. Her nipples were still distended.

"She had a really hard time when she birthed the last kitten," the boy said. "It died, but Pop wouldn't let me call Dr. Vlast. He said she'd make it or not, and she did."

"She only had the one other kitten?"

Tears welled up in the boy's eyes. "No, ma'am. There were more but they got caught out when they were learning to hunt . . ." he said, his voice quivering. Janina wanted to cry herself. Poor Chessie! Poor baby kittens.

Jared entered the room and examined Chessie thoroughly. "She'll need some repair," he told Janina. "I can't be sure but I'm rather afraid her breeding days may be over. However, she should be able to return to her other duties before long, as long as she has her able assistant." He nodded toward the kitten, who was batting a string the boy dangled for it. "I'll tend to her now."

He carried Chessie from the exam room back toward the operating theater, and Janina, who couldn't bear to be separated from her—having finally found her—started to follow.

But the voice of the boy's mother stopped her in her tracks. "So, how do we collect the reward?"

CHAPTER 8

CHESTER

I clung to Jubal as if he were Mother, since she was otherwise occupied and in the hands of others. I did not like the woman, Jubal's
mom, and I knew she did not like me or Mother either. But she
liked Jubal and vice versa, so I seemed to be stuck with her. By my
mother's joyous mew, I knew that the girl who first greeted us at
the clinic was Kibble, her friend from the ship. She seemed harmless enough, and Mother was so happy to see her I'd have been
jealous except that Jubal was there. Everything was fine as long as
Jubal and I were together.

On the man's last trip home, when he tried to carry me away
with him, Jubal fought with him, yelling and clinging to his legs to
prevent him from carrying me to the shuttle in the little bag that
smelled like my brothers and sisters. Jubal had been afraid he
might try something like that, and smuggled me into the house
with him.

But the man had crept into Jubal's room at night and plucked
me from the pillow.

It took Jubal a few moments to respond to my entreaties for his
assistance in fighting off his father who was stuffing me into a bag.
When I finally clawed through the boy's dreams to wake him, he
thudded through the house after us, his bare feet on the floor-

boards. When the man left the house and carried me toward the shuttle, Jubal chased him, banging the screen door after him as he tackled his father.

"You can't take Chester!" Jubal yelled at his father as he tried to snatch my carrier out of his hands. "He's mine! You took all the others but you can't have him."

"Whoa, boy," the man said, lifting me aloft so high I feared he meant to dash me to the ground, dodging his son as he leapt to take the bag back. "You're going to kill him if you keep that up. Now stop it and let's talk about this."

"You didn't want to talk when you stole him from my bed," Jubal said.

"I'm taking him to a new home, son. I told you I was going to have to."

"Yeah, and you told me I could have a kitten too. I want Chester and I want him back *now*."

"That was before the queen lost so many of her litter. Even filling in with Git's kittens, we're still down a couple. All I'm doing with these little kitties is finding them good homes. Best thing that could happen to them. With their bloodlines—and, well, for Git's babies, the fake ID tags I've given them with the queen's DNA codes—they'll be treasured ships' cats, just like their mama. Nothing will be too good for them. Don't you want Chester to have that kind of a life? He was born for it, you know. If he'd been on the ship, he'd be going off to a new home now where he'd be top cat, with his own personal servant and bodyguard to look after him."

"He's got that now. He's got *me*. Pop, come on, just this once keep your damn promise. I love Chester and he loves me back and doesn't want to go on any spaceship. You don't care about what kind of a life he'll have, just how much money you'll get for him."

"That money is for you and your mama, son. I can get you anything you want, maybe a scooter even, and fix up the place for your mama."

"I don't want a scooter. I want Chester! He's mine. Give him back."

"Son, now, I've explained why you can't have him—" the man began.

Jubal was unimpressed. "Mom's right about you," he shouted at his father. "You are just a rotten good-for-nothing liar and you welsh on your promises when it suits you."

"Look, soon as I get back I'll take you to the feed store and you can pick out another kitten from their cat's new litter."

"You don't get it, do you, Dad? If somebody took me away, would you take Mom to an orphanage and tell her to pick out a new kid?"

"You're being overdramatic, Jubal. I admit you get it from me, but on you it isn't becoming. Now, I am taking this kitten and selling him for enough money to keep food on the table for this family. I am your old man and that's what I'm supposed to do, so you keep a civil tongue in your head and keep your voice down before you wake up your mama."

The man turned his back on Jubal and started for the shuttle. Then I had the strange experience of feeling the man fall while I also felt Jubal tackling his father's legs and bringing him down. My bag went flying and I yowled in protest.

"Chester!" Jubal cried. I called back that I was fine, just shaken up, but my answer was lost in the explosion and the man's bellow.

"Carlton Poindexter, you mangy lying sack of manure, you leave that boy alone or so help me I will blow a hole in you a horse could jump through!" a woman hollered from the house.

"I wasn't hurting him, honey. He attacked me over nothing. I was just going off to work and the boy went wild as a ricocheting rocket."

The boy looked back at the woman, who held a smoking metal object in front of her. "I know him and I know you, Carlton, so I know who's at fault here. You think I'm an idiot? I knew you were up to something in that barn, since you were so all-fired anxious to relieve me of any chores out there. I knew it was cats 'cause I smelled them on Jubal. When I saw that poster about that missing space cat, I thought you were probably the culprit since you never have seen much difference between what's yours and what's someone else's. But I thought you were doing it for me and for the boy. I know he wanted a cat and you two were in cahoots about something I wasn't supposed to know about. Jubal's been so happy, I looked the other way. But now you're going to cheat him too? What kind of daddy are you anyway? No, don't bother to answer that. You just get out of here and don't let me see your sorry butt around this place ever again."

"But, baby," the man began, then said, slyly, "Okay, I just need to go get some stuff from the barn."

"You don't need squat, Carlton. Now git before I have to traumatize our son with the sight of his mama killin' his daddy."

While his mother held the man's attention, Jubal left his father to snag my bag and hug it to him. I tried to claw my way out of the bag and he released me. I climbed his head, sat on top of his hair, made myself big, and hissed at the man.

The man headed for the shuttle, "Okay, Dorice, but you're making a big mistake. Those cats are worth big money and I've got it."

"Shut up and get out. And you're not taking the shuttle either. Hit the road running, Carlton, if you value your lying hide."

"But, sweetie, I thought we were so happy!"

Another blast from the object in the woman's hands and the man ran very swiftly for a human.

As soon as he was gone, the woman lowered her weapon and walked over to Jubal, but stood well back, no doubt frightened of my fierce and bristling stance. "Oh, honey," she said in a weary voice, shaking her head.

"Mom, I know you don't like cats but I'm keeping Chester, no matter what."

"Yeah, I get that," she said. "But since I ran your daddy off, I think you and I had best have a look at what's in the barn. If it's what I think it is, there's a nice reward for her and it'll keep us going until I figure out what to do next."

Shortly afterward, Mother, Mom, Jubal, and I were in the shuttle and then at the door of the clinic, where Mother was reunited with the girl, Kibble.

Jubal's mom made him promise not to tell the girl about his father selling my littermates and milk brothers, in exchange for which she would allow him to keep me.

"If they knew we'd been part of it," Jubal's mom said, "we might not get the reward, and now that your father's gone, we're going to need that money."

I heard the man's influence in Jubal's thoughts as he told himself that all he wanted was for us to be together, his mom did need the money, and his father had said the other kittens all went to homes where they would be valued crew members. He reckoned as long as they were okay, his mom got the reward money for Mother, and he had me, we'd be fine.

While the doctor was taking care of Mother, the girl Kibble helping, Mom and Jubal and I sat in the office. Mom fidgeted, impatient and suspicious. Jubal fell quiet as he mulled over the events of the day and consequences he hadn't previously considered. I slept.

✶ ✶ ✶

"Can you put her right, Jared?" Janina asked anxiously as the vet made the first incision. She was monitoring Chessie's vital signs under the effects of the anesthesia. Her fragile feline charge had been X-rayed and partly shaved, the shaved area cleaned with antiseptic.

"I can help her stand on her own four paws again and get back to work as ship's cat, but I'm very much afraid . . ." He zapped a tiny bleeder with cautery and blotted the area with sterile gauze to see the inside of the wound he'd made. " . . . that her days as a breeder are done. Her uterus and birth canal were damaged by that last delivery and—ah, here's the cause of her drainage." He pulled something out and plopped it into a basin. Janina looked at it curiously then looked away again. It was bloody, whatever it was. "We'll have to spay her," he said.

Once Chessie was out of danger, sleeping off the anesthetic, Janina relayed a message to the *Molly Daise* via the station.

In a few minutes the clinic's com screen filled with the faces of Captain Vesey, Indu, Bennie, and Mick.

"You've found her!" Indu said. "I knew you would, Kibble. No doubt whatever."

"How many kittens?" Captain Vesey asked.

"I'm afraid only one survived, sir, a male, but—"

"The crew will be disappointed but she can always have more, after a suitable rest, that is."

"I'm afraid not, sir," she said. "There were complications. Dr. Vlast had to spay her."

"Well, we'll have the little male, then. His bloodline is as illustrious as hers and the crew will have the stud fees to split instead of the price of kittens."

The office door opened behind them and the woman and boy stood there, the boy holding the sleeping kitten. "We can't wait all day, you know," the woman said. "We've animals to tend to at home. Give us the reward and we'll be on our way."

Catching site of the newcomers in the com screen, Bennie's eyes lit up. "Is that him? Is that the kitten?"

"Yes, it is," Janina began.

"His name is Chester," the boy said.

The kitten woke, stretched his tiny paws up the boy's arm, and yawned before climbing onto the boy's shoulder and blinking at the room, the other people, and even the com screen. Chessie had never paid much attention to com screens unless there was some interesting movement for her to observe. The kitten regarded the remote crew members with the same curiosity he showed toward Jared and Janina.

"Chester because of his little white chest?" Indu asked. "It suits him! What a handsome little fellow he is! He'll be the heartbreak of every Barque female in the universe."

"Not a chance!" the boy said adamantly. "You got the mother cat back but Chester is mine."

Janina looked toward Captain Vesey, but he was shaking his head. "I'm sorry, son, but he's not. Chessie and her progeny belong to the *Molly Daise.*"

"That wasn't the deal," the boy's mother said. "You only mentioned one cat, and it's one cat we're returning. There was nothing on the flyer about the kittens. Kitten. My boy has fed and cared for both cats, not knowing the female was yours, and we're out the money for the food and his time . . ."

"I'm sorry," Janina said. "I made up the flyers and I left out anything about the kittens, it's true."

The woman said in a hard businesslike tone, "Kittens would be extra, then, even you would have to agree."

The crew members nodded at one another. "I'm sure we can come up with a bonus on the reward for the return of the little fellow as well. Another 750 credits perhaps?" Captain Vesey said.

"No!" the boy said. "He's mine. You can't have him!"

The woman sighed and put one arm around her son's shoulders, including the one with the kitten, who sniffed at her uncertainly, bobbing his fuzzy tail behind him as he investigated. "Well, there you have it. My son is very attached to his kitty. I'm afraid it's not worth it to me for 750 credits to disappoint him."

Mick cleared his throat and said, "These cats belong to the crew, ma'am, and we aren't wealthy people. We offered the reward as an inducement to returning them, not in place of a purchase price. As I understand it, when Chessie left, she was pregnant with at least five kittens, of whom you still have only one. Furthermore, you've brought her back in such a condition that she can't bear us any more kittens. We're pleased to have her back as acting ship's cat, but we'll need the kitten for her to train as her successor, and to continue her line. The truth is, as things stand, he's the more valuable of the two to us. So . . ." He looked around to the others, who depended on their purser for negotiating the ship's business. ". . . I'm afraid that if the kitten isn't returned with his mother, the reward will have to be considerably diminished—to about a tenth of our original offer."

"You can't do that!" the woman said. "I'll take you to court! I—"

Captain Vesey cleared his throat. "The cat disappeared under mysterious circumstances—arson and considerable damage to station property and to Dr. Vlast's personal records and effects. I'm sure the court will want the Locksley Guard to investigate fully how our cat—who is very talented and clever but who, as you know, has no wings—left the station, made it down to Sherwood and into your possession. The *Molly Daise*'s parent company has a pretty good fleet of lawyers and investigators."

"But we need that money!" the woman said. "All of it."

"Then we'll be needing both cat and kit, madame," Captain Vesey said. "Once Ms. Mauer, Chessie, and her kitten have reached the space station, the money discussed in the reward, plus the bonus I mentioned, will be deposited in your bank account. Not before."

The woman bit her lower lip as she looked down at her son. "Hand Chester to the lady, Jubal."

"No! Mom, no." The kitten slid down the boy's shirt front and under the bib of his overalls. "See? He doesn't want to go!" The boy turned to the com screen. "He can't be a ship's cat like his mom. He can't! He's—He's afraid of heights. He closed his eyes all the way here."

"Give it up, son," Bennie advised.

"Janina will take good care of him," Indu said.

"Let them have him, Jubal," the woman said in a no-nonsense

voice. "We need that money to keep a roof over our own heads now. It's time for you to grow up and realize we don't always get what we want in this life."

Janina's heart, so full now that Chessie was back with her, went out to the heartbroken child, but the cool expressions of her crewmates and Jared made her feel that perhaps she was being naive. Although she didn't see how such a young boy could have had anything to do with the clinic fire, she sensed that the others were suspicious of him and his mother. She knelt in front of him and looked directly into his eyes. "Jubal, I have been with Chessie since she was no bigger than Chester. I have helped her birth many many litters of kittens, and loved every single one and had to part with them, so I know how you feel, I really do."

"No you don't!" he said in a tight, stubborn voice, his fingers clutching the bulge snuggled inside his overall bib.

"Maybe not because I'm not you. But I loved them and they loved me, and I know how that feels. Chester will be well-loved and will have great adventures. But do you know what? I don't think he'll ever forget you."

The boy's chin quivered, much against his will, and he looked down at her and quickly back up again to hide the tears welling in his eyes, threatening to flood down over his freckles.

"Jubal Alan!" his mother said sharply, startling Chester, who poked his little black head out of the top of the overall bib. Jubal's mom reached down and pinched the scruff of the kitten's neck between her thumb and fingers and lifted. The kitten's needle claws clung to the boy's shirt and it squealed a high-pitched indignant protest. But Jubal, outnumbered and beaten, reached down and unfastened each set of claws.

"Go on, Chester," he said as his mother deposited the wriggling kitten in Janina's outstretched hands. "Go be a space cat. You'd probably just get it like the others if you stayed with me anyway."

CHAPTER 9

For the next two weeks, while the *Molly Daise* was en route to Hood Station to collect Chester, Chessie, and the girl, Jubal dreamed of Chester every single night. In his dreams he repeated everything he had done that day, except in the dreams Chester was with him. The first night this happened, when he woke up alone in the morning, he choked up remembering what had really happened, but as he shared his world with Chester every night after that, it made him feel better to think that as soon as he fell asleep, he and Chester would be a team again.

His mother thought he had forgotten all about it, though he couldn't hide how mad he still was at her for making him give the kitten up. But he did his chores and he didn't have to be told to go to bed.

But on the twelfth night, the pattern of the dream changed, and instead of Chester helping him with his chores, Jubal was carried with Chester through the space station, awesomely huge and clanking and whizzing with all kinds of mechanical and electronic contraptions, and taken aboard a ship. On the ship's bridge, they saw the captain and a bunch of other people, among them the ones Jubal had seen on the com screen at the vet clinic.

Janina Mauer lifted the cats from the carrier and the people all petted Chessie and made a fuss over her. Then the cat girl passed Chester from crew member to crew member to be admired, and everybody oohed and ahhed over how cute he was. When the captain said it was time for the crew to get back to work and prepare for departure, Janina took the cats to their quarters and slipped a harness onto Chessie, who accepted it, purring and rubbing her face against Janina's hand as the girl snapped its straps secure. She picked Chester up, and her fingers tickled his chin and belly gently as she fastened a similar harness on him. Jubal knew Chester didn't want to like this, but his mother told him proudly that all of her kitten apprentices from previous litters had been harnessed to her until they learned the tricks of the trade.

When Chester and his mother were securely attached, she took him through the ship, trying to teach him her trade. He thought it was play and refused to take it seriously, though he enjoyed poking through the nooks and crannies, as he had in the barn. Despite his mother's encouragement, however, he didn't try to hunt and he didn't want her to, except for catching an occasional beetle. Every time his mother started waggling her hindquarters, Chester remembered Git and Buttercup and tackled her. Hunting was dangerous. He didn't want to lose his mother too.

There was another visit to the clinic, but Chester slept through a lot of it, and it was overshadowed by what happened afterward.

They returned to the ship, boarded, and Janina harnessed the cats together again. Suddenly there was a loud noise and the ship began to move. Moments later Chester and his mother floated around the cabin in what Jubal knew must be zero g. Chessie thought it was fun and tried to show Chester how to cling to things with claws and push off again. Chester clung to Chessie, quaking.

And suddenly Jubal was wide-awake. It was still the middle of the night. He tried to go back to sleep, but when he did, he didn't dream at all and he woke again a few moments later with the bleak knowledge that when Chester's ship whizzed off into space, the kitten's dream connection to him had snapped. That was it. He would never see Chester again. He was just too far away.

He lay there crying into his pillow to muffle his sobs, mourning the loss of his friend all over again. His window was open to the warm night and the scattered stars with Chester's ship among them. The yard was quiet except for the usual noises, the lowing of a cow, night birds calling, the rustle and sigh of the breeze through the leaves of the taller trees.

Then he heard light footsteps and the creak of the barn door as it opened. He slid out of bed and crept to the window. He wasn't at all surprised to see his old man's back as he snuck into the barn.

He'd come back for Chessie, apparently, not knowing that Mom had turned her in. He intended to take Chessie—and probably Chester too—and escape in the shuttle.

As Jubal's mom often said, the old man was so predictable it was a wonder his past deeds hadn't caught up with him a long time ago.

Maybe he'd be coming to the house to get Chester, like he'd tried to before, then take off into space for good? Jubal had other ideas.

Still barefoot in his pajamas, he grabbed his pants and shoes, crept down the stairs, opened the door quietly, and streaked toward the shuttle, which was thrumming and ready to go.

He opened the hatch and slid behind the front seats. The blanket his mother had carried Chessie in had been tossed back there, and he threw it over himself. It occurred to Jubal that if the old man did go to his room and found both his son and the kitten gone, he might think to check the shuttle before he took off. The barn door creaked open, and the footsteps crunched on the bare dirt and shushed through the grass, then snicked on the paving stones leading through Mom's kitchen garden to the back door. Jubal rose from the floor to peer out the port. The old man was standing there, inside the screen door, scribbling away on something he then placed on the doorsill. It looked like an envelope. Then he turned and strode back toward the shuttle, way less careful of the noise he made than he had been before. Jubal barely had time to scrunch down and cover up again before the hatch opened and the old man was in the driver's seat.

He hoped he was right about where his father was going. Since

Mom had run him off and the cats were gone, there would be nothing for his father to do but go back to work before the people on Chessie's ship or the vet figured out who he was and maybe had him arrested, or at least try to sue him for the damage to Chessie. Pop would be heading for the station to find a berth on an outbound ship.

This time the old man was going to take him along, like it or not. Everything was his father's fault, and even if he wouldn't help get Chester back, his father would at least get Jubal closer to his cat. Jubal knew he sure couldn't do anything while he was stuck on the ground and Chester was in space. He'd gotten the impression that the *Molly Daise* docked at Hood Station at pretty regular intervals. He reckoned the ship probably docked at other stations fairly often too, and met up with other ships. He just had to get himself to the right place at the right time.

r r r

It was a long uncomfortable ride wedged behind the seats. He didn't dare go to sleep for fear he'd snore and Pop would discover him and take him back home. Mom was going to be mad, he thought, and then she was going to worry and send people looking for him, but he wasn't going home, no matter what. Let her worry. All she cared about was getting the damned reward money. She didn't like cats, and whatever she said, she didn't really want him to have Chester or she'd have let him get a kitten a long time ago. She was brought up on Sherwood, among farmers who thought animals were just for eating, or riding, or catching mice. She thought loving them was dumb and something he'd grow out of. Well, he wouldn't. Besides, she was wrong. Those people on the ship were all adults, seasoned spacers, and though they talked about how valuable Chessie was and how much they needed her, he could tell they cared about her. And the girl was crazy about her. His mom was just cold, hard-hearted, money grubbing, and *weird* sometimes, that was all.

The ride to the station seemed like hours, but when the shuttle began its docking routine and he checked the watch Pop had brought him for his last birthday (although he hadn't actually given it to him until six months later, when he returned home from his latest—and better not discussed, according to Mom—venture), Jubal saw that it had only been about forty-five minutes. Shuttles were poky on the ground but had that second mode for extreme outer atmo travel that made them practical and even essential for the colonists on Sherwood.

When the transport settled down, Pop unstrapped himself, opened the hatch and said, "You'd better come out now too, Jubal. If you were planning on waiting for a ship associated with the circus you're planning to run away to, you may have to wait a long time. Meanwhile you'd best stick with me."

Jubal poked his head out from under the blanket, feeling foolish and a little like a turtle. "How'd you know I was here?"

"Never try to kid a kidder, sport," the old man said. "I got eyes in the back of my head."

"Yeah sure. And thanks for the ride, but I don't want to stick with you. I want to find Chester."

"Where is he anyway?"

"Mom turned him and his mother in for the reward," Jubal told him. "The people on the ship wouldn't give her all the reward money unless she gave them Chester too, so she did." He had intended to be as calculating in what he said as the old man always was, but remembering what happened at the clinic got him all stirred up again and he told his dad just how much trouble he had caused, how the vet and the people on the ship had treated them, blaming them, though they didn't exactly say so, for the loss of the clinic and the cat and kittens to begin with. "If you hadn't made her run you off by being such a—"

"Careful, kid."

"By making her mad," Jubal said, altering his course slightly in the interests of avoiding getting thumped. "She wouldn't have been so worried about money and let them take him."

"So it's my fault no matter who took your kittycat, is that how you've got it figured?"

"That's about right," Jubal agreed, narrowing his eyes resentfully at the old man, who clamped his lips together and made a popping sound with them, which always meant he was thinking about something that did not please him even a little bit.

Then he ran his hand through his thinning hair and shook his head. "Damn, I wish she wouldn't go off half-cocked like that. You neither. You both should have known I was working on a plan. Now I wish I hadn't left her the money from the sale of the other kittens. She'll have enough from selling the Duchess and Chester to last for a bit."

"You left her that money? When?"

"Just awhile ago, when I went up to the house. I didn't know you were in the shuttle then or I'd have hung onto our assets."

"Yeah, maybe we could have bought Chester back," Jubal said.

"You are a single-minded little sonofagun, aren't you?" Pop asked. "I think we can get your cat back but it's going to take some doing."

"How?" Jubal asked. "We can't just steal him. That girl and the vet know who Mom and I are and where we live."

"I can grow us another one," Pop said, shrugging. "I've got DNA from all the cats, including the mother. You may not know it, but cats have been cloned longer than any other species except sheep."

"I don't want a clone or any other cat," Jubal said stubbornly. When his father looked angry, he added, "Pop, it wouldn't be the same. Chester and I—well, don't laugh, but I think we can read each other's minds."

"No kidding?" his father asked mildly. "Well, well, well, that's special."

"Yes, it is," Jubal said. He wasn't sure what the old man was making of it. He didn't sound exactly like he didn't believe him, but he didn't sound like he took him seriously either. He sounded like he had a use for the information. "If you're thinking we'll get him back so we can do some kind of hokey psychic act like at the Universal Chatauqua show last spring, forget it."

"Me? Put my own boy in a hokey act? No siree, nothing like that. I admit I couldn't see what the big deal was until you told me about you and your kitty—"

"Chester," Jubal said. "His name's Chester."

"Yeah, that's the one. But I think with a slight change of plan and quite a bit more trouble and risk on my part, we can still make the cloning thing work for us. In fact, it opens up a number of other interesting possibilities."

"Whatever," Jubal said. This was sounding all too familiar, like some of the old man's other crazy schemes.

"Meanwhile, though, we're going to need a grubstake and—ah, I see just the ship!"

"I was going to wait here for Chester's ship, the *Molly Daise*, to come back," Jubal said, still not willing to trust his father again, though he was feeling a little better about him. If it hadn't been for Pop, after all, he wouldn't have ever had Chester to begin with. "I thought maybe the vet could use some help around the clinic."

The old man dismissed that plan with a wave of his hand. "He's not going to hire you if he thinks you had something to do with the fire."

"I guess not," Jubal admitted.

"So, what do you say? Are we a team or what?"

"Might as well, I guess."

"You want to call your mother before we leave the station?"

"Nah. If she got your kitten money, she'll figure I'm with you, and if I call, she can track us."

They continued down the ramp of the docking bay, in search of a ship with two open berths.

CHAPTER 10

Chessie took up her duties again as if she had never left, and at first it looked as though she and Chester were going to make a good team. The kitten trotted along beside his mother, alert, attentive, curious, and very fast. Janina realized how much Chessie's perpetual pregnancies had slowed her down. In spite of her recent surgery, she was much quicker now that she was free of her litter. Amazing how rapidly cats recovered from even the most drastic surgeries, once they'd been set to rights. Of course, Jared was an excellent surgeon, and that helped.

Chessie caught several rodents and one of the shiny bug things in the first week she was back aboard the ship. Chester clung to her side and didn't give her enough maneuvering room in the tight passages where she did much of her stalking.

Chessie was patient, licking and comforting him. Some members of the crew observed the cats hunting and were critical of Chester's behavior. "Sure you got the right kitten, Kibble?" Siegi Shively, a ship's steward, asked. "This one doesn't seem to have Chessie's spunk, or Jockey's."

"We paid a good bonus for him," Zane Beres from maintenance said. "But if he's not going to hunt, might be we should sell him to a ship that can afford to keep a cat just to breed."

"Don't be daft," Thielk Sulin, the galley chief, told him. "They're not going to want their queens bred with a tom that won't hunt. Better we sell him while he's still a trainable kit and buy our Chessie a new assistant. Her kittens have all been good workers in the past, but there's always one in every family."

Janina was thoroughly chagrined by their words and knew they'd spread the criticism of poor little Chester to other crew members. How awful if they ended up selling the kitten after all the fuss that took him away from the boy who obviously loved him! Chessie might be upset too, although she had relinquished all former kittens with equanimity. Would it be different with this little one, her only remaining baby—and the last she would have? Did she realize that? It was hard to tell about cats, even when the one in question was a close companion for ten years.

Janina explained the situation to both cats in reasoning tones, petting them in turn, though Chessie kept getting between her hand and the kitten.

Later that night when Chessie began her rounds, she suddenly hunkered down, her tail's feathery plumage dusting the floor as she switched it back and forth, winding herself up for a pounce.

Chester watched his mother anxiously, and just as she sprang, ran between her legs. She backed off with a hiss and swatted him so soundly the kitten rolled ears over tail back against the bulkhead. "Stop hindering me and pay attention!" his mother said sharply when he looked up at her and mewed."This is what I do, and it's what you were born to do."

For the next week, Chester behaved himself in the manner expected of a ship's cat, and made several kills of his own. Talk of selling him to another ship died down. They were still docked at the station while they waited for another ship to bring them one more consignment of cargo before they resumed their previous mission.

Janina was glad of the reprieve, as it gave her a few more opportunities to see Jared and observe the progress in the new clinic. The clinic was being improved upon as it was rebuilt, with more exam rooms, a larger operating theater, much nicer kennels, and a far more efficient fire detection and prevention system. The floor coverings and upholstery were all made of substances that would not produce toxic fumes if they did burn, would not mildew or mold, and were delightful to cats wishing to sharpen their claws. Janina begged an extra piece for new coverings for Chessie's scratching posts.

Jared hardly had time to see her, though when he did give her his attention, he seemed glad of her presence and her company. She took Chester and Chessie back for one last checkup when five of the broken-colored horses from Varley's "bonus herd" arrived at the clinic for outprocessing before being shipped off to buyers on another colony world.

Jared immediately became distracted, almost agitated, again. Janina was about to accept—as she always had before—that he had other business to attend to and tell herself that she'd taken up enough of his valuable time. But he looked so tired, as if he weren't sleeping well, that instead she gathered her courage and asked, "Jared, are you all right? I don't want to intrude but you seem—well, troubled."

He sighed and leaned against the exam table, arms crossed over his chest. "You're not intruding, Janina. In fact, I've considered asking if you had any thoughts on this matter already. I may be taking an entirely wrong, even disastrous, path here, and I've been wracking my brain trying to decide what to do. I should follow protocol and report my findings to the center for disease control. But it isn't really a disease, you see, not as far as I can determine. Nevertheless, precedent in times past has been for the center to step in, put down every beast in the affected area, ruin the lives of the owners, and damage the reputation of an area for years to come. So I've been trying, discreetly, to learn just what is causing the sparkle in the spittle and some other bodily fluids of the animals from Sherwood, and some from this station, like your Chessie."

"You think they'd order you to *destroy* Chessie?" Horrified, Janina hugged the cats close to her. "And the horses and—and—"

"And every beast they might have come in contact with, yes. The thing is, this seems to be a recent phenomenon, and I've yet to see that there's any harm in it, but analysis doesn't reveal what is causing the sparkle in the secretions or what its effects might be. On the one hand, it doesn't look as if Chessie, for instance, has suffered any harm from it. However, it might have been responsible for her losing some of her litter . . ."

"Or more likely, it was the fire and being carried off when she was so far along in her pregnancy," Janina said, clutching harder. "She's been doing very well since her operation, and Chester seems perfectly healthy too." She thought it best not to mention the kitten's apparent aversion to hunting. He had improved in the last few days, after all. His problem wasn't physical, as far as she could tell. He seemed more frightened than anything.

But she saw now that Jared was even more worried about the consequences of his actions, whichever course he chose. If he said nothing to report the aberration or to quarantine the affected animals, including Chessie, and the substance did prove at some later date to be symptomatic of a disease process, the entire settled portion of the universe could become infected in an incredibly short time. If he did report it and the center decided to be as proactive as in times past, thousands of innocent animals would be slaughtered, settlers who depended on them would be ruined and stranded on colony worlds with no way to make a living, and others—like the crew of the *Molly Daise*—would be heartbroken with the loss of a valued crew member and possibly forbidden to do business until they were certified free of contamination.

While she was considering this, Chester suddenly wriggled out of her grasp, leaped to the floor and chased something across it. He leaped right over it swiftly, corrected his trajectory and landed on it with an impressive *snick, crunch*. Then, like a modest conquering hero, he picked it up in his jaws and took it to Jared, laying his kill at the vet's feet.

It was a small iridescent insect. Janina had seen the cats catch these creatures before but had never examined one closely.

Jared squatted down, gave Chester a scritch under the chin, grabbed a glove from his equipment counter, picked the creature up, and popped it inside another glove. Chester paraded back and forth, thoroughly pleased with himself, emitting wild raucous cries, which clearly meant, "What a mighty hunter am I!"

Janina laughed. "And the crew were worried he wouldn't hunt! I think he also fancies himself a detective—"

"Or an entomological epidemiologist," Jared joked. "You notice that just as I was discussing the sparkling matter in the animals' saliva, he made a point of catching this." He peered inside the glove at the crunched creature. "Come to think of it, I don't actually recall seeing these things until lately. Could be that they're some new species, possibly accidentally imported from another world, and have made their way into the food chain, with the results that we've seen."

"I don't see how they can be harmful," Janina said hopefully. "The cats have been catching them since they've been back aboard the ship, and I'd vow I saw Chessie catch one before. Apparently they're right tasty because neither cat has ever gifted one to *me*. Chester must really like you."

Jared cocked an eyebrow at the kitten, who sat looking up at them, waiting for something. Probably more praise. "Either that or he understands Standard and was making a suggestion."

✂ ✂ ✂

Janina half expected a reluctant Jared to prevent the *Molly Daise* from disembarking, but that did not happen. Five days after the ship returned for her and the cats, it departed the space station, two cats and one Cat Person richer.

By the time they were a day out, Chester's behavior changed again. From a 'fraidy cat and a happy hunter, he morphed once more, this time into a listless, indifferent little lump with a vacant and vaguely resentful stare. He did not want to eat, he would not hunt, and he followed his mother and Janina around only, she suspected, because he did not wish to be left alone.

Janina began to fear she had reassured Jared as to the cats' health too soon. What if he made a disastrous decision based on her support? She lay awake when she should have been catnapping with her charges, imagining a terrible plague—the first symptom of which was the shiny spit and mucosa—wiping out the animals that ate the shiny bug, infecting each other with whatever vile disease it might carry, and finally contaminating the entire universe. The animals would die. The disease might even spread to people. And again the blame would be hers; Jared, who had only tried to do the right thing, would be destroyed professionally when the origins of the disease became known.

She whimpered and tossed in her berth until she finally did sleep, exhausted by her dreams and then comforted by purring cats, Chessie having crawled on top of her chest, while the kitten—more animated than he had been since they left the station—curled up between her head and shoulder and sang into her ear.

All of which made his lackluster performance when they next patrolled more puzzling than ever.

* * *

Ponty found the ship he was looking for. The captain and crew of the *Reuben Ranzo* were respectable enough that he didn't mind taking the boy there, but not so respectable that they could afford to be too inquisitive about Ponty's own schemes. The captain was a divorced man whose ex-wife—a memorable woman Ponty recalled with painful clarity—made him look like a saint. He had a little girl about Jubal's age. Ponty's other criteria for a ship was that it not be one to which he had delivered a contraband kitten.

Not that Jubal was going to secure a berth simply to be a play-mate for the captain's daughter. Fortunately, the boy was a hard worker and handy at a number of practical pursuits of the kind that had never interested Ponty. His mother's influence. He was good at building things and taking them apart, good with machinery, and even seemed comfortable fixing plumbing.

And Jubal liked it that the *Ranzo* had a ship's cat; not a fancy Barque Cat, just a jumped-up mangy old alley cat. In spite of what the kid had said about not wanting another cat, he immediately befriended it, though the captain said his daughter, the self-appointed Cat Person, considered Hadley to be her own. Hadley was black and fluffy, like Chester without the tuxedo and spats. He seemed to be a laid-back animal and graciously spread himself around enough to include Jubal, a possible new source of food and pets.

Once the kid was installed and helping load and stow the equip-ment and cargo, Ponty went about his business. He needed to ac-quire a few things to furnish the homegrown lab he intended to establish shipboard, an enterprise he was sure would interest Cap-tain Loloma—nonviolent, low risk, and potentially quite prof-itable. He already had the DNA of Chessie and her litter. Cloning her and her kittens was only illegal if he got caught, and there was little chance of that. To most people, one cat looked a lot like an-other.

The equipment and supplies he couldn't filch or acquire by calling in favors, he had to buy at the station commissary, a huge megamall encompassing one entire deck of the station. He was looking for a particular reagent when he felt an ominous poke in his back.

"If it isn't my old friend Ponty," a familiar but entirely unwel-come voice growled in his ear. "You weren't planning on leaving without coming to see Mavis, were you? You know how she gets when she feels snubbed by them she's shown kindness to."

Translated, this meant Mavis had noticed he hadn't repaid the advance she'd given him on one of his earlier projects that had not turned out as well as he'd anticipated. The kitten money would have covered his debt had he not left it with Dorice.

"I know I'm a little late, but I've been working on something new. Tell her I'll be able to repay her 'kindness' soon."

"She'd rather hear it from you, that and another little item, with all the details. At length, while you start working it off aboard the *Grania*."

The *Grania* was Mavis's ship, the *Grania O'Malley*, named for the famous Irish woman pirate. Mavis claimed descent from her, which seemed doubtful, considering she appeared to be of Asian descent, despite the long red dreadlocks she habitually wore. Nobody knew how old she was, but he had once heard that her real name was Mai Ling.

Mavis was not a pirate, of course. Piracy was against the law, and in order to survive, ships had to be able to dock at all of the usual stations and at least appear to abide by all of the usual regulations. Mavis was an entrepeneur and a financier, and he'd have said she was a gambler except that she wanted every gamble to be a sure thing and was a very sore loser.

"She thought about sending the law after you," Mavis's henchman told him.

"She wouldn't want to do that. You know how snoopy they get." If they found out about the cats, it would not just be his neck— they'd more than likely go after Dorice and Jubal as well.

"Yeah, that's what she said you'd say. So why don't you just come along with me now and join us on a little voyage."

He thought about trying to escape and get back to the *Ranzo*, but that would lead Mavis's thugs back to Jubal. They could decide to use the kid as leverage. They could find out about the cats and send someone to take the money from Dorice, which was unlikely to go well for anybody. Especially him, the next time he met either his wife or his creditors. No, best leave Jubal where he was and keep him out of it. Maybe he could convince Mavis to release him if he told her about his current project. It would be easier to do his experiments on the *Grania* than the *Ranzo* anyway. Captain Loloma was a little too inquisitive, and more law-abiding than made for comfortable working conditions.

The kid would be fine in the meantime. Ponty hoped he'd get over being mad at Dorice and send her a message to let her know he was okay. He had planned to suggest it to Jubal later on, when they were well out of range. In his current situation, however, it didn't seem like a good idea to draw attention to his wife while under Mavis's iron thumb. Not that Dorice in the right mood wouldn't be a match for Mavis and her entire crew, but he didn't want to be in the middle. You never knew about women. They might decide to join forces, and that would be extremely bad for his health.

CHAPTER 11

Imagine the vet making such a fuss about the shiny stuff in our poop! I was surprised the doctor hadn't deduced that the glittery bits only showed up in our leavings when we ate the keka bugs. They didn't make us sick. They were delicious, and I for one always felt better after eating one. It was fun to hunt them too. They made a tiny sound when they scuttled, their crunchy shells clicking, that sounded like *keka keka keka*, the sound we cats make when watching prey. I could say that's how I knew to call them keka bugs but the truth is that it just came to me, the same way the boy's thoughts and activities came to me in dreams and sometimes even while I was awake, if the need was great.

Sometimes they didn't want to be eaten, that was true, and that led to a lot of hacking up, but nothing serious or prolonged. The shiny bits that didn't digest were certainly nothing to panic over.

I was very anxious to please the girl and the vet that day, because I hoped another visit meant the boy would be there. He had been in my dreams every time I closed my eyes, and I knew he was thinking of me. I thought we'd be together again soon. The girl was kind enough, but her friends talked of selling me—they didn't think I could understand them, but I could, of course. I may not share dreams with everyone, and require a lot of cat antics to make myself understood to people who are not my boy, but having been connected with him from my birth, I understood his language perfectly well. Naturally, my vocabulary was limited to words he knew, and I had only a sketchy notion of many human concepts, but I considered those to be the humans' concern and of no interest to me or my species. However, I understood perfectly well what the vet meant when he said all animals might be "destroyed." That was not good, and I was glad to be able to straighten him out about the connection between our "symptoms" and our prey.

I was somewhat deflated when Mother asked, "Why did you catch a keka bug for the doctor, dear? Humans don't eat those, you know." I had to explain my act of selfless heroism to her—after all, keka bugs are delicious and I gave that one away without knowing if I'd ever catch another one.

Although I was disappointed that the boy had not appeared in person at the clinic by the time we left, as I'd hoped, I continued to feel his presence with me, as I had since we were parted.

I danced back to the ship, running circles around Mother, pleased with my accomplishment and certain that there never was a young cat cleverer than I. I was sure I had been chosen to spend my life doing Great Things.

But shortly after we returned to the ship, it departed the space station. We floated in what Mother called "free-fall," and although I was frightened at first, I soon started to enjoy it. Then someone turned on the gravity again, gradually, so that we were lowered to the deck.

The separation happened then, and it wasn't gradual. It was as if someone had snipped the harness that bound the boy and I together, the way the harness on the ship bound Mother and I together.

Without warning, the boy's warm bright presence vanished, leaving only a cold hollow void. I could not hear his thoughts or see what he was doing. I curled up for a nap, thinking to find him while I slept, but he was not in my dreams, which were instead of wild canines breaking into the barn, hunting tender kittens, then stalking the space station while they somehow brandished laser rifles while standing on their hind legs. They clamored at the ship's hatches and my mother cried. My boy had been with me almost since birth and now he wasn't! It was as if I was suddenly blinded, or had lost my paws.

"Get up, you lazy kitten," Mother chided me, unaware of my loss. "You've missed one patrol. Kibble let you slide since you did that showy bit of killing at the doctor's office, but it's time you earned your keep again."

"Let me sleep," I whimpered in return. "I'm trying to find the boy."

"You can't find him, you silly child, because he's back at home. I tried to warn you not to get too attached but you never listened to me. The boy and his father were our abductors. They are not our people."

"The boy is *my* person," I cried. "And I want him back."

"That is foolishness. We are back where we belong, with Kibble and the crew, doing the job we were born and bred to do. And it's about time you got off your tail and did it. I thought you were over this nonsense."

"Mother, without the boy, the canines will get us," I told her, remembering my dream. "Like they got Git and Buttercup."

"Don't be daft. There are no canines here, and if there were, the entire crew would protect us. We're quite valuable, you know. At least, I am, and you will be if you start performing your duties."

I didn't care. The boy was not to be found during dreams or waking, so what did it matter? I wanted him, and until someone produced him, they could expect whatever they wanted from me but I wasn't interested in cooperating.

Mother was quite stubborn, and soon used her feline wiles to convince Kibble to load me into the kitten harness and attach us to each other. I lay down and wouldn't move, but Mother dragged me along.

We paused outside the service opening in the bulkhead, while Mother sniffed and scratched, searching for the source of the tell-tale scrabbling from within.

"This close to the station, there is always more hunting to do," she instructed me. "As we get farther from port, there are fewer and then no creatures left for me to hunt. By then it is time to visit with the crew. There are so many of them, and they all want me to spend time with them. Sometimes it is quite draining, but I do my best not to disappoint my public."

Kibble opened the service door for us and unhitched my harness, scratching my ears. "Be a good boy, Chester, and follow Chessie's lead," she told me, shoving me inside and closing the door behind me. The passage was only one cat wide, with no extra room even for a kitten as small as I was.

But I confess it smelled intriguingly of rodent and keka bugs. The floor lacked claw holds, and one could feel the ship's movement far more clearly than from within the corridors. With no one but Mother there to notice if I failed to live up to her standards as a hunter, there was little point in further demonstration of my lack of worth as a ship's cat. I suppose I thought they would send me back to the boy if I was not what they expected, but I underestimated how much they hoped to profit from acquiring me.

So that day I hunted and made my mother proud. With each kill, she would pick up our adversary in her mouth and carry it back to the service door and scratch for Kibble to open it. When one passage had been cleaned, we were let into the next.

I cooperated. I did what they wanted me to do. But I was not happy about it, and I let Mother take credit for the hunt.

When Kibble tried to pet me and tell me what a fine cat I was— as if I didn't already know that—I took a swing at her with my lethal right paw and drew blood. She looked as if she were going to cry, not because I had hurt her hand to any great degree, but because she expected me to be as affectionate with her as Mother was. Well, it wasn't going to happen. The boy was my person, and I had no room for others, especially not those responsible for separating us.

Mother cuffed me again, but though I yowled as if she'd gutted me, I didn't care. Mother was as much to blame as anyone. Most of my life she had been ill or idle. Git had taught me more than she had. It seemed as if all she did was cuff me or scold me or wake me up from my naps. She wouldn't let me nurse anymore. In fact, since the doctor had fixed her, she didn't smell exactly like she should have. I was thoroughly dissatisfied with everyone and intended to let them know about it.

I was still yowling while Kibble washed her scratch and scooped me up, wrapping me in a towel except for one leg. She tucked me under her elbow, and try as I might, I couldn't wriggle free. I was little more than three months old and no match for a seasoned Cat Person. She pulled out something metal, sharp, and shiny.

"Mother! Help!" I cried. "She is seeking revenge for that little scratch, she is going to chop off my leg! Save me! Save me!"

"Do be still," Mother said, opening one eye. "I need my beauty sleep."

"No! No! Mother, help me! Oh no, she's starting with my toes—she's going to torment me to death, Mother, just as Git said no well-brought-up cat does to its prey. It was only a little scratch! She took liberties with my fur! I was only defending myself. No—no!"

"Janina, will you shut that brat up?" a gruff male voice demanded.

I looked up, afraid another attacker would join Kibble in my torture. I felt a brief tug, heard a snip, and when I looked back, the sharp pointed useful bit of my middle claw was gone! Amputated! I can scarcely relate the indescribable horror of that moment. And then she pressed another toe and another claw poked out, entirely against my will. I cried, I howled, but to no avail. She was without mercy. I twisted and squirmed and freed my back paws and tail, but her shipsuit lent her impressionable flesh armor as impervious to my claws as a turtle's shell would have been.

My hind legs churned and I tried to back out of her suffocating embrace, but once more there was the tug and snip and another claw fell away from my poor mutilated paw. Then three more times in quick succession, and suddenly my paw and leg were free! Free! She had weakened at last. Now she would feel my wrath and be forced to release me.

But alas, it was not to be. Her fingers somehow entangled my disfigured paw in the towel and pounced upon the other foreleg.

I wriggled and cried for mercy, humiliated to be bested by a human who was not even mine. But the worst was to come when she flipped me over just as Mother had earlier smacked rodents into submission, imprisoned one of my free hind paws in the folds of the restraint, and grabbed my right rear leg in a grip so tight I knew she would snap it if I continued trying to pull away from her. Although she was not the boy, I had thought, up until then, that she was adequate as far as humans went. Mother was fond of her, but all I could think was that Kibble had concealed her brutish nature until my attack brought it forth. When I felt her grip loosen this time, I kicked hard and connected with her hand again, but she just laughed, grabbed the paw, and tucked it back into the towel before starting on my other leg. I got in one kick, but all that did was cause her aim to miss, and this time there was horrible pain shooting up my leg, causing me to release the contents of my bladder.

"Kitten, you are a trial and a tribulation," Kibble said to me, and gripped me tighter, her elbow continuing to clutch me to her side while my urine soaked into the towel and my fur. She wiped her hands—one on my towel, one on her trouser leg—and clipped my remaining claws while I continued crying unheeded for mercy.

Then she set me down and went once more to the basin, where she washed her hands. I ran to Mother for comfort, thinking that when she saw what the girl she loved so foolishly had done to me, she would surely relent and groom me lovingly as she had when I was younger. But instead she flattened her ears and hissed at me, and I jumped back.

Cruel hands caught me around the middle and lifted me to the basin. The wicked young woman took a cloth and rubbed it over my soiled fur, then reached for something else—a gun, not as long as the one Jubal's mother had wielded, but the same general shape. She pointed it at the wet fur and I twisted to see what she was doing. Her finger moved, something clicked, and the gun went off, not barking but growling and blowing warm wind into my fur. I knew it was some sort of death ray, the kind the boy had read about in his comic books. But it didn't kill me, and in fact I am ashamed to admit it actually felt rather nice.

When she at last set me down and allowed me to rest from her evil ministrations, I found I was exhausted from the abuse and fell straight to sleep. But the horrors of waking were nothing compared to the pain of a restless, searching sleep where no boy joined with me no matter how hard I tried to find him. When I awoke, desolately lonely, I vowed that my attack of that day would be nothing compared to the campaign of terror I intended to wreak on the heartless hapless humans who held me captive. They thwarted my will at their own peril.

✷ ✷ ✷

I awoke at a different hour than Mother and Kibble, who were attuned to each other's sleep patterns. First I took my revenge on the girl, turning one of her boots over and crawling inside it to relieve my bowels. It is an acknowledged fact that cats could teach entire invaded civilizations a thing or two about guerrilla warfare. Which does not mean that we usually have anything against apes, simply that we are masters at effectively deploying the weapons that our bodies provide against the sensitivities of our adversaries.

Once I had taken care of Kibble's boots, I refueled at the water dish, then used Mother's cat flap to exit our quarters. The captain's boots were next. He was the one who insisted I be snatched from the bosom of my boy and forced aboard his ship. He would pay dearly for that.

CHAPTER 12

Jubal didn't think much about it when his father didn't return. He'd probably poked around so long he had to go straight back to work when he got back to the ship instead of coming to find his only son. Jubal was busy in the crew quarters, making up cots, returning safety harnesses to their proper positions, cleaning lockers and mopping floors, all part of his own new duties. It was the kind of stuff he hated doing at home, but somehow it was more interesting doing it aboard ship.

He was, in addition to his other duties, designated assistant Cat Person, meaning he helped the captain's daughter and cleaned the litter pan, because she didn't want to. The girl's name was Sosi, a quick, black-haired, dark-eyed little thing who seemed to be in a big hurry when he met her. She called herself the ship's Cat Person but she wasn't a professional one like Janina Mauer. She was just the captain's kid who had a big fluffy black garden variety cat, and she'd given herself a jumped-up title to make herself sound important.

The *Ranzo*'s ship's cat, Hadley, was what the old man might have called "easygoin'." He was not an old cat but seemed very lazy. Every time Jubal saw him, the cat was sprawled in a furry puddle, fast asleep. Jubal scrunched the soft dense fur of the cat's exposed side and received a placid purr in return, and a languid opening of beautiful green eyes. His black fluffiness reminded

Jubal of Chester, but unlike Chester, Hadley seemed totally disinterested in most of the people and events around him. His hunting mostly consisted of walking to his food dish and grazing.

The second mate, Felicia Daily, gave Jubal a fast tour and introduced him as "Ponty's boy" to as many of the crew as they encountered. He learned that his pop used a different name when he shipped out—he was Carlton Pontius. Most of the people Jubal met seemed friendly, if busy, but a few acted suspicious and he really couldn't say he blamed them. He wondered what they knew about his old man from previous journeys and supposed they might be worried about what other trouble he'd cause.

It wasn't until he heard the station intercom saying, "*Mr. Pontius, Mr. Carlton Pontius, please report to your duty station aboard the* Reuben Ranzo *immediately,*" that he realized the old man was *still* gone. A few minutes later the ship's intercom advised the crew to prepare for disembarkation, and Dad totally failed to stride down the corridor at the last minute. He wasn't coming.

Another kid, hearing the same messages, might run to the captain, ask where the old man was and if he wasn't aboard, try to leave the ship to go find him. But Jubal simply sighed and strapped himself in the way Felicia had showed him. Although his original plan had been to stay on the station and wait for the *Molly Daise* to return with Chester, he realized now that the scheme was flawed. Mom had probably sent the Guard after him, thinking he'd been kidnapped. It would be just like her to have had Pop arrested.

Nope, Jubal decided, he was better off staying put. And if the old man wasn't around pulling what Mom called his shenanigans and making everybody mad at him—and his son by association—he knew he stood a chance to show his new shipmates what he could do being his own man. He had another plan for finding Chester, one that would be easier without worrying about what his dad would do next.

The person he most needed to make friends with was the communications officer, he'd decided. He'd find out what she liked to eat, maybe, and filch extra tidbits from the galley, as he might for the cats. Give her something, tell her she looked nice, carry messages, anything to make her like him. Then he'd tell her his story and see if she could help him keep track of the *Molly Daise*'s location, and somehow or other set up a circumstance where they could rendezvous. He wasn't like his dad. He wasn't trying to trick anybody or take anything away from them. He just wanted some help getting Chester back.

*   *   *

Jared's last patient surprised him, since she lacked fur, feathers or fins and only had two legs.

Although she was by herself and dressed in expensive-looking new clothes, he recognized her as the woman who had come with her son to the Locksley clinic to return Chessie and the kitten. She was the wife of the arsonist who had torched his clinic and kidnapped Chessie in the first place, he was pretty sure.

"More cats, missus?" he asked the woman.

"No, but that's why I came," she said. "I wanted to ask you to get in touch with that cat girl and her crew. I need to buy that kitten back."

"I thought that was settled. The ship's five days out from port now," he said. "Janina, Chessie, and the kitten are on it."

The woman tightened her lips. She looked no less anxious than she had on the previous occasion. "Five days, you say? Not four?"

Jared found he knew to the hour when the *Molly Daise* and Janina had left the station. "Five days, seven hours, and thirty minutes actually."

She looked puzzled. "No, he's only been gone four."

"The kitten?"

"Jubal, my son. I think he got his good-for-nothing father to bring him back here so he could go after that cat. I thought he'd got over it but then I got up the next day and he was gone, as was my transport."

"He couldn't have just taken it himself? Because if he did, station security would have detained him. It's against regulations for an unregistered, underage youngster to enter the station without an adult."

"I'm pretty sure Carlton brought him," she said, her eyes shifting to the side, indicating she was hiding something.

"Why?"

"There was—a note," she said. "And Carlton—Jubal's father—is an old spacehand. This is where he *would* come. It took me awhile to catch a ride with one of the neighbors who was coming here. I need them to search the station and find my boy. If he didn't get on board the ship with the cat, he could still be here."

"You should be talking to station security, missus, not to me," Jared said.

"I intend to. I came here first because I figured if that girl and the cats were here, I could take the other deal—less money for the mother but keep the kitten for Jubal. I don't know why, but the kid was really attached to that little cat. He didn't speak to me till the next morning, but then he seemed to be all right for a couple of weeks, didn't mention the cat again. He's a good boy and a big help to me with his old—his dad gone, but he's stubborn. Gets that from me, I guess. I should have known he had something up his sleeve when he was so quiet and cooperative. He was just biding his time, I guess. Carlton's more slippery than stubborn, but once that boy sets his mind on something . . . well, the thing is, Doctor, if I get my boy back and not the cat, he's not going to stay and I know that now for a fact."

"Still, I think you'd be better off finding your son first, ma'am. The kitten is on board the *Molly Daise*, and he'll be safe with Janina until you can work something out. But I don't know about your son. He's probably here at the station, if what you say is true, waiting for the *Molly Daise* to return, but if not, ships come and go all the time and he could have boarded one of them."

"I'll do that, but meantime you contact that girl, okay? Tell her I can pay what they wanted for that kitten and to be sure to bring him back with them."

"I'll relay your message," he promised as she turned on one shiny new boot heel and stomp-clicked her way from the clinic. He wondered why—when she and her son brought Chessie back—the reward money seemed to matter to her so desperately, and now she was willing to return a large portion of it in exchange for the kitten. He didn't think she was willing to relinquish the funds solely because of her son's disappearance.

Then his assistant Bill called from the waiting room that they had an emergency. The passenger liner *Tesoro* had brought in their cat, Tess—short for Galactic Treasure—a purebred like Chessie, injured in an accident.

By the time he finished operating on Tess, Jared had forgotten all about the woman.

* * *

When Chessie jumped as gracefully as ever onto Janina's chest to alert her that it was time for their next watch, Janina smelled the cat feces right away. She thought she might have forgotten to clean the box so she rose and sleepily pulled on her shipsuit and then her boots, which had fallen over sometime while she slept. The kitten, probably. Chessie was always as neat about Janina's things as she was about her own fur.

Her toe was only partway in when she discovered the source of the stink. She pulled her foot out quickly. "Chester? Did you do this, you naughty kitten?"

But to her surprise he wasn't there. She looked down at Chessie, who was standing with her tail to the boot and industriously scraping her paws back toward it, trying to bury it. Janina retrieved her boots, slipped on clean socks, and said, "Madame Chessie, I'd like a word with your son," and set off down the hall, stopping to throw her soiled socks down the laundry chute outside the female crew's loo. There, she scraped the contents of her boot into the commode, scrubbed it clean, and spritzed the inside with odor neutralizer. She took off her sock and washed her foot for good measure, then put the sock back on, dried the inside of her fortuitously waterproof boot, checked the other one carefully, and slipped them on.

Janina was wondering where to start looking for Chester when the intercom exploded with a long string of oaths followed by a shout of, "Kibble!" that could easily be heard from the forward corridor without the benefit of the intercom.

As she ran up the corridor, Chessie trotted behind her and the intercom ordered, *"CP Janina Mauer report to Captain Vesey's quarters on the double."*

She opened the door to the captain's cabin, and Chester's furry form flashed out the door past her, heading toward the bridge. Chessie took off after him.

"I found this when I came back from my watch," the captain told her, pointing to his bunk, where a damp spot on the pillow reeked of cat urine. "It looks to me as if this falls into the scope of your duties. The little devil went for the one part of my bed that isn't waterproof."

"He was missing when Chessie woke me for our watch. I wonder how he got in here?"

"Probably snuck in when I went on watch myself," the captain replied. "I must have shut him in." The normally mild-mannered Vesey was cooling off, calming down. "You checked him for UTIs?"

"No, sir, but I will as soon as I find him," Janina promised.

"You go do that, then, and I'll have someone else clean this up."

She clicked Chessie's locator. She was on the bridge, two doors down from the captain's quarters.

For the second time in as many minutes someone bellowed, "Kibble!" and she ran for the bridge, where chaos reigned.

Crew members leaped and lunged, those who were trying to cajole the kitten rampaging across the control panels shouted down by those demanding that he stop. Chester hopped from one console to the next, landing squarely on control buttons while Chessie chased him across the same panels trying to corral her offspring.

Janina calmly planted herself in Chester's path, preparing to grab him before he could climb up one side of her and down the other. The scratches on the faces and hands of others in the crew testified that their attempts at similar maneuvers had been futile. She was very glad she had trimmed his claws earlier or someone could have been injured far worse.

Chester pounced again on another bank of keys, and Janina thrust her hands forward to catch him. She knew she was going to miss when suddenly Chester and his mother levitated toward the ceiling while crew members began floating, then swimming in free-fall.

Chester gave a startled mew. His legs and tail flailed in every direction until his mother caught him with a precision free-fall pounce and grabbed his ruff in her teeth. Someone keyed the buttons the kitten had activated, slowly reintroducing gravity so that cat, kitten, and crew gently sank to the deck.

Captain Vesey walked onto the bridge, carrying a stack of bedding he shifted under one arm before he bent and picked up a printout from the floor, saying, "That kitten is a menace." His voice was mild, even amused, as he looked down at Chessie, who was growling through a mouthful of fur. "Keep him on a leash, Janina, until he learns some manners. If he doesn't learn to use his box properly, we may have to give up on him as a breeder and have him fixed. He'll not fetch such a good price that way but we can't allow cats like this to taint Chessie's line."

"Yes, sir," Janina said, and bent to retrieve Chester from his mother. The kitten laid his ears back and hissed, but Janina kept hold of his ruff while he grrred ferociously and lashed his tiny fuzzy black tail.

Captain Vesey pulled a pillowcase from his stack of bedding and tossed it so it landed on her shoulder. "Put him in that until he calms down," he told her. Janina was shamed. She was the Cat Person. No one else, not even the captain, should have to tell her how to manage her charges.

She expertly swaddled Chester in the folds of the pillowcase and carried him off the bridge. Behind her the crew began returning things to normal, but there was a lot of muttering.

"Is that really Chessie's kid? She's always been such a sweetie."

"I told you we should have looked for a better sire than the Jockey," Charlotte's voice answered.

"Dr. Vlast checked him for rabies and distemper, didn't he?"

"I think he's got mad cat disease."

"What's that? Is it serious?"

"Sounds like they'd have to euthanize the animal for that," was the last comment Janina heard.

"Are you mad, little cat?" Kibble asked as she carried me into the quarters she shared with us. "Did you hear that? They're talking about destroying you, and these are people who admire and respect your mother and your species."

Once inside, I expected her to release me. Instead she opened the door, grabbed a carrier from under her bunk, and popped me inside without removing my shroud.

I had been planning to let her know I was sorry about her boot. Now I wished I'd done the other one too. If my eyes had been death rays they'd have incinerated her where she stood. As it was, a squinty glare and an indignant hiss had to suffice.

I thought she and Mother would then go on patrol, but instead Kibble set me upon the little table where she wrote out her reports of Mother's patrols. "Kitten," she said sternly, "I know you're just a baby and you probably do not understand what I am saying to you, but I think you are an intelligent little cat so I will try to explain this nonetheless. You must never again do what you did just now. Captain Vesey is as kind and caring a skipper as any in the universe. Wetting on his pillow was a naughty, wicked thing to do. But your rampage through the bridge was much worse because it was very dangerous. You could have caused us to lose life support, destabilize our navigation system, any number of things that could cost us all our lives."

All that for pushing a few buttons? Surely Kibble was exaggerating.

Mother was washing her flank with quick little licks. I thought she would agree that the girl was overreacting but when I mewed inquiringly at her she raised her head, laid her ears flat against it and spat at me, saying, "Ignorant offspring, what has gotten into you? The older you get, the more you resemble that tom who sired you. You've disgraced me in front of my crew. Even Kibble is cross and she is never cross."

And now that she had finished her tirade, Kibble's eyes filled with tears and she sniffled a little, then wiped her face impatiently with the heels of her hands. She took another box from the locker beside the head of her bunk and withdrew some interesting looking articles. With her fingers, she quickly wove a little web like the one the boy had called a cat's cradle. He, of course, had invited me to destroy it. It had been one of our games. But she attached shiny things to it and a very long snake. She emitted little wet hiccups as she did so.

"You made her cry!" Mother scolded, and rubbed Kibble's ankles, then hopped onto the bunk beside her, not even trying to leap onto the web thing.

"You love her more than you love me, your own son!" I accused.

"Well, of course I do. Kittens are fine when they're very small but they are very selfish and do nothing but take all of your milk and time and attention and then go to some other home. I wish you had done that too, instead of spoiling my work and angering my crew. Kibble is good to me and takes care of me and loves me. All you do is cause trouble."

"The boy was good to me and took care of me and loved me, and your girl took me away from him and brought me here," I said. "And if that's the way you feel, I won't even let you know when I leave. I'll just be gone and then you'll be sorry."

Kibble let loose of her work long enough to reach over and stroke my mother's beautiful soft fur. My mother didn't love me anymore! But she didn't understand how much I needed to find my boy. I could have done without my tail more easily because he had been half of what was me. Now he was gone and I was left with nothing but a lot of heavy boots waiting to step on me, faces I had to crane my neck to see, and small dark places made of metal. No trees, no chickens, no cows, no brothers or sisters, no reading under his blankets at night, just a mother who hated me.

I didn't mean to do it. I meant to be haughty and disdainful, to show these people how little their opinions and missions counted to me, that they did not, as they thought, own me. But I was suddenly so sad that a mew escaped my mouth like a mouse might slip through my paws.

Kibble opened the carrier and took me out. I hadn't the strength to fight her, nor, as she cuddled me and petted me and made soothing sounds, the will.

"There there," she murmured. "Look, I've made you a pretty new harness, suitable for the enormous cat you are becoming. This will keep you tethered to Chessie or me and out of trouble." And she slipped the web she'd woven over my head and across my back, holding me with one hand and fastening it with the other.

Mother was not fooled by Kibble's sugarcoated explanation of the new harness. "Now Kibble will walk you like a dog," she said, her eyes still slitted. "You will hate it but you've brought it on yourself."

So naturally I decided I wouldn't give them the satisfaction of thinking they'd bested me. I pretended to admire the hateful thing and batted—charmingly, if I do say so myself—at the lengthy bit that attached my harness to Kibble's hand.

Kibble petted my back but told Mother, "I fear he will not like this once we begin our patrol."

Hah! I'd show both of them. Besides, my other plan hadn't worked and I needed to think of something else, some other way to escape my captivity and return to my boy. Although I did not understand exactly what the captain meant when he threatened to have me "fixed," I assumed it involved breaking me in some way first, and that it would not help me return to Sherwood.

So I trotted meekly beside Kibble and behind Mother. Sometimes I made it a point to grab for the tall fluffy plume of Mother's magnificent tail, making her trot more quickly ahead so that I ran to catch up and leaped toward the target just before she whisked it out of the way. When was my tail going to be that pretty? I wondered. How fast did tails change? When I turned to see if it was growing properly yet, I couldn't quite see it. It kept getting away from me when I tried to grab it to examine it more closely. For some reason, Kibble and the crew found this amusing and laughed at my efforts. Finally I sat down to wash it and saw that although it was a little longer and perhaps a bit fluffier than the last time I'd looked, it was only a third as long as Mother's. Maybe they got longer every time you washed them? I began an extensive licking campaign, but was interrupted when Mother and Kibble insisted on continuing the patrol and Kibble unhitched my tether from Mother and picked me up to carry me to the next station.

I very cleverly did not struggle or yowl, scratch or bite, but purred into her ear.

A few days of this and crew members were remarking on what a changed kitten I was. I began hearing words like "adorable," "cunning," and "cute." I was being cunning, all right, but not in the way they thought. Soon they would forget my transgressions and that I had a very definite mind and will of my own. Then, when I made good my escape, they would be unprepared. Only my mother remained suspicious, though she had forgiven me and started grooming me again and allowing me to sleep with her. My kind are stealthy stalkers and patience is part of our equipment. It had just taken me a few false starts to learn that the quickest way to catch the prey may be apparent immobility. The boy read me a book in which some ancient Asian general said the same thing. He no doubt learned it from his cat.

ɾ ɾ ɾ

Jubal made a game out of doing everything quicker and better than he was asked. Some days he won the game, and some days he lost, but the crew was mostly patient with him. It was a lot more interesting keeping busy anyway. He missed the horses and cows, and the cats of course, and he would sometimes pet Hadley and talk to him. But compared to Chester, he was just an ordinary furball, not especially smart or especially dumb, pretty and soft but not much of a conversationalist.

So it helped that a lot of the crew members took to him and after a while were willing to show him stuff about running the ship.

As he'd intended, he won over the com officer first. Her name was Beulah Bradley and she was originally from Sherwood. She had been brought up on a horse farm and liked gardening, so when Jubal was off watch, he dug up a patch for her in the hydroponics garden in one corner of a cargo bay. It wasn't as hard to till as regular earth had been, compacted by rain and snow, baked by the sun, and scoured by wind. He could turn it over with a rake and hoe. When she was off watch, she planted her rows. Weeds weren't really a problem, though some of the other more aggressive plants in the garden tried to invade their patch and had to be set straight.

He watered for her a couple of times when she had meetings or was too tired, and once found her some seed packets that had been dropped when a shipment was unloaded.

And she answered a couple of his innocent questions by showing him the com system, which was more complicated than any he'd encountered before, telling him about its range, which varied depending on the nearest relays and proximity to major stations, moon bases, or dirtside docks.

She accessed the roster of registration codes for him and looked up from the screen, the instruments reflecting in her intelligent blue eyes, their pale red brows almost disappearing into her spacer-pale skin. "Come closer and I'll show you how to read this. I know what you're after, Jubal."

"You do?" he asked. He hadn't told anybody here about Chester. He didn't think they'd care anyway, but maybe Beulah had heard something. Maybe Mom was looking for him, or the Guard.

"You're trying to find your father, aren't you? I called back to Hood Station but no one had seen him since your arrival and he wasn't on the roster of any of the other ships. He must have returned to Sherwood."

"I don't think so, ma'am. He might run into my mom, and they weren't exactly on friendly terms when we left."

"It was that way, was it? Hard to understand. Your father is such a—pleasant man."

Which told him right there that Beulah might be a smart lady but was no great judge of character.

"I was wondering maybe if my cousin had heard from him. She's aboard the *Molly Daise*," Jubal said, adopting the cat girl temporarily.

"What's her name?"

"I don't rightly know her whole name, ma'am. Pop had a lot of brothers and sisters. But if you'd let me know if we're going to meet up with the *Molly Daise* at any of the stations anytime soon, I'd be obliged."

"No problem. Let me see if I can get her position and course from Traffic Control."

She pulled her headset up from where it was coiled around the back of her neck and adjusted the mouth- and earpieces. Her station was within a sound-insulated booth that kept the noise to and from the bridge at a minimum. Her com voice was lower, crisper, and more musical sounding than the way she usually talked. It was a voice that wouldn't be hard to listen to all day, maybe that was the key.

She spoke briefly with Control, nodded, then paused. With one side of her mouth and an eyebrow raised, she asked, "Oh?" and resumed the normal protocol before pulling the headset down again and adjusting her screen. A starmap appeared. She tapped a key, and the picture zoomed. Jubal had seen it when he visited Beulah before, and it usually indicated the *Ranzo's* position with a large red light, but now there was a green light as well and a yellow one.

"Looks like our courses may intersect again at Galport, in Galipolis. The *Molly* deviated from course for a few minutes but seems to have adjusted."

"How can you tell?"

"Signals from other ships and nearby relay stations, mathematical projections from those signals when a ship is out of range. And the *Molly* reported her momentary deviation. But don't worry. She corrected it almost at once."

"What caused the deviation, do you think?" he asked.

She shrugged.

But he had the oddest feeling that it had something to do with Chester.

* * *

Mavis wagged a finger at Ponty. "You been evil again, sweetie. How many times I tell you to leave evil to Mavis? You're not as smart as you think you are."

"If you could have waited a little longer to see me, gorgeous, I'd have paid your loan back to you with big interest."

She waved her hand impatiently. "Sure you would, Ponty. I not worried about that. You got plenty good collateral. But why'd you pass off a counterfeit cat for the real thing? Cost me plenty of money!" She snapped her fingers. "Bring it."

Ponty didn't have to think twice about the kitten deals he'd made. He would never have approached Mavis with any of the little furballs, who were, if not of "counterfeit" lineage, hot. Mavis would know about Chessie's theft and pay him only a fence's price, so he'd approached less knowledgeable clients. Less dangerous ones.

A rough-looking customer of a crewman arrived carrying the kitten on his shoulder next to his ear. Sure enough, it was one of Git's gray and black tabby jobs. The one with the slash of white under its nose, like a mustache. *Doc?*

"I never saw that cat in my life," he said automatically, opening negotiation, as it were. It was sort of true. The little twerp had grown bigger, the tail longer, the fur fuzzier. He'd been a totally different kitten when they left the barn together in search of a wealthy ship in need of a cat.

Doc ratted on him—or maybe it was catted on him—by leaping from the crewman's shoulder to his, nuzzling into his hair and kneading his claws into Ponty's sensitive skin. "Affectionate little critter, isn't he?" Ponty asked with what he thought was a cool suavity, reaching up with a couple of fingers to tickle the kitten's belly. It was purring louder than the ship's engine, which— uh-oh—seemed to be propelling them away from the station. It was going to take a really good present to get back in Jubal's good graces. Something mechanical, maybe, that the kid wouldn't get attached to like he had Chester.

Mavis said, "Wipe the grin off your face, Ponty. I'd smack it off but I don't want to scare the kitten. He's a sweet little fellow, even if he is a phony."

The kneading and purring stopped, the claws retracted, and weight lifted from Ponty's shoulder as Doc launched himself onto Mavis's scrawny bosom. She boosted the kitten to her own shoulder, took a swing, and knocked Ponty to the deck.

He thought he might be safer if he just stayed there, but then they'd probably kick him.

Rubbing his jaw, Ponty sat up and said, "Looks like a real cat to me."

Then Mavis did kick him. "Don't be a wise guy. You know it's the ID chip I'm talking about. His credentials. The DNA code on it matches the high-class queen's and tom's but not the kitten's. The only part of Thomas's Duchess in this little fellow is on that chip in his ear. The rest of him is as bastardized as you."

"Now that's just plain mean, Mavis," Ponty said. "I can see right now that little kitty is getting real attached to you. If he could understand what you said, you'd break his little heart."

"I wouldn't want to do that. So I'm gonna break your neck instead."

"Why? What did you want from one little cat? He looks like a ship's cat to me, meows like a ship's cat, has a chip that says he's a ship's cat, and he has a job on your ship, making him a ship's cat. And that's what you bought, so what's the difference?"

"Several thousand credits is the difference. You're going to have to scoop a lot of cat poop to make it up to me."

"I got something better," he said. "I got the DNA and the codes for Thomas's Duchess and her last litter. The thing is, this little guy is a foster kitten of the Duchess's, suckled along with her own babies when his mama tragically died. The Duchess adopted him and his brothers all by herself. So you see, he isn't a phony after all. He was good enough for her, and he ought to do for you until I can clone you a cat with the right code."

"Is that what you were planning to do with that stuff you were buying back at Hood Station?"

He nodded.

"Sounds to me like you've given this considerable thought already, Carlton. Maybe I misjudged you. Maybe you've been wracking your brains all this time thinking, 'How can I ever repay Mavis for all she's done for me? I know! I'll make her a purebred kittycat just like she's always wanted. And then I'll make a lot more for her to sell and pay back my debt.' That's what you had in mind, wasn't it, Ponty?"

He allowed himself to draw a breath, smiled and shook his head—not in denial but in apparent admiration. "Mavis, I always knew you and I had a special understanding—like you could read my mind."

"Cut the crap, Ponty. You gonna make the cats for me?"

"Just give me a little space to set up my lab and we'll have kittens."

This was good. Very good. It was what he had planned to do anyway, just in a different place. Later, when she was in a better mood and he'd produced several cats for her to sell, he'd produce the Chester clone he'd promised Jubal. The kid would just have to wait a bit longer. It was for his own good.

CHESTER: THE FIRST DREAM OF THE DERELICT

I fell asleep and for a time dreamed the regular sort of dream. Of the barn and fields, of chasing tasty beetles through the hidden spaces of the ship. It was a good enough dream, as regular ones went, but I longed for the dreams the boy and I had shared, after I was taken from him. Then all I had to do was nap and he was with me. The dreams I had dreamed since were lonely and boring by comparison, and although I liked sleeping, hardly made it worthwhile.

But sometime in the course of this dream, I realized I was no longer alone. Another presence, not the boy, was with me, watching, listening, feeling what I was feeling. And then suddenly it all turned around and in the way of dreams I was feeling what he was feeling.

Merging with him, *I knew that I was the last survivor. I huddled alone in the tiny space, as I had so often huddled before, sleeping, dreaming of stepped pyramids whose broad sunny slopes were fine to climb and drowse upon, of walls covered with picture writing in which my own shape was a symbol, of open sun-drenched structures devoted to my pleasure. Of cozy passages filled with funny looking cats and strangely dressed humans involved in a wide variety of tasks. Of a ferocious-looking gigantic cat with a beautiful queen on his head.*

And then, suddenly, I was in exile—banished to drift in space in this small craft, with food stores dwindling, as my will to survive dwindled while I feared rescue might never come. Of being alone and abandoned.

Of my ears being licked . . .

I opened an eye and filled my nostrils. Plenty of food and company after all, not like the dream. That was a relief! I stretched and yawned and stretched again.

"Get up, lazy kit. Time to patrol," Mother said.

I was already up and grooming, pleased to see my tail was growing in length and furriness every day. I could wave it as gracefully as Mother did now.

The watch was somewhat eventful. Mother and I found a pinprick gas leak and we both pointed it out to Kibble with sneezes. She informed the appropriate crew member and it was repaired swiftly.

All during the watch, however, I kept recalling my dream and wondering about the cat whose consciousness I'd shared. He was alone in a ship somewhere, that much I knew, and his own dreams remained vivid in my mind. But where was he now and what did he want? Rescue was the obvious answer, but somehow I felt that lurking behind his implied plea for help was another motive, one I could not understand until the time, if ever, I met him.

CHAPTER 14

As it happened, Beulah was also, if not exactly Jubal's and Sosi's teacher, their supervisor when they did their lessons on the ship's computer. In addition to the basics, they took a very broad course called Galactic Studies that gave them an overview of the history, population distributions, and geographies of the known settled worlds and moons.

Sosi was bored with the whole thing, but not Jubal. Now that it looked like he was going to have a chance to see some of these places, at least from a distance, he scanned the charts with new interest.

He recalled the lessons he'd already had on the subject when he was back home on Sherwood. The galaxy had been settled in waves by the governments and companies from old Earth. The six main reasons the Founders began their Intergalactic Expansion program were:

1. Exploration, the "Bear Went Over the Mountain" syndrome, as it was called, although bears had gone extinct long before the first successful colony was settled, back in fairly ancient times.
2. Overpopulation, especially in certain regions where there were no restrictions on the number of children people could have.

3. Depletion of resources on old Earth, including oxygen, as pollution and global warming destroyed much of the essential atmosphere existing populations needed to survive.

4. Economic expansion. As more and more governments found it necessary to develop their own colonies on other worlds, the megacompanies of Earth were the only ones for whom it was profitable or even possible to supply the transport, life support systems, terraforming, and the necessities and amenities the settlers required to live. Not all of these colonies were successful. It took the companies' big global boo-boos on some of the planets and cost quite a few lives before they got a system down. Once everybody was settled, the profits fell off, so the companies ventured off to new worlds and did what they did *better*, making the new worlds lusher, more comfortable, self-replenishing, and generally desirable, supplying them with well-equipped and -staffed space stations to monitor their needs and see that they were met, and generally oversee their welfare (this was the official version, anyway). Then they sold people on moving from those original, more primitive colonies to the new ones. Most of the old colonized worlds, settled by the same people who had ruined their original homeworld, were pretty well trashed by the time the new ones were ready. Deemed unworthy of refurbishment, the early colony worlds were abandoned by their creators.

5. Resettling refugees from the unceasing wars among people of different persuasions on old Earth. For a time, the entire planet was threatened by governments carrying their quarrels into the space around the Earth. Eventually, wars were avoided or stopped by sending compatible refugees to the less luxuriously appointed worlds, where they were deprived of the resources and equipment necessary to continue their animosities with refugees on neighboring worlds.

6. The nuclear holocaust that finally happened in spite of all of the above measures, finally making Earth totally uninhabitable for human beings. The survivors were also resettled on other worlds, or their moons, inherited by those with whom they had no previous quarrels.

The Galactic Government, or GG, controlled all of the planets, moons, and space stations in the galaxy. Galipolis, the most galipolitan world of them all, was the hub of company and governmental affairs. Everyone said you could find fantastic stuff in Galipolis not seen anywhere else. Traffic from all over kept the space around Galipolis way busier than Hood Station at festival time.

Jubal couldn't wait to see it.

⚹ ⚹ ⚹

Jared had looked Varley's gift horses in the mouth. Since ascertaining that the glittery residue in the secretions and excretions of the horses—as well as the other animals exhibiting the same phenomenon—were simply the result of ingesting the shiny beetles, and not the symptom of a disease, Jared gave the horses a clean bill of health. Varley sold them.

If he'd sold them to another rancher on Sherwood, things would have been fine for a while longer, but he sold them offworld to a man who was unlucky in his neighbors and in his veterinarian.

The first Jared heard of it was a call from Varley.

"You said those wild pintos were healthy," the rancher said accusingly.

"They were," Jared replied evenly, though he had been up half the night operating on a dog who got into a fight with a forklift. "Is there a problem?"

"You'll find out about it soon enough. I sold them to the son of my old friend Trudeau, who just died. His son inherited his place. I only got enough to cover the shipping costs. Trudeau didn't leave a lot of money so I sent the boy the pintos at cost to start a new herd, help get him on his feet. Unfortunately, the Trudeau property abuts a spread owned by the nephew of the secretary of agriculture for the area.

"One of the pintos jumped the fence and on the orders of the secretary's nephew was shot for trespassing. Young Trudeau, the damn fool, made a fuss, and the local vet—who's in the nephew's pocket—did an autopsy and claims to have found something wrong with the horse's corpse."

Jared, remembering the gentle and intelligent pintos mooching food during his picnic with Janina, felt a sick sadness in the pit of his stomach for the horse, as well as apprehension. "Those animals were perfectly healthy when they left the station," he told Varley.

"They've called in the GG's epidemiologists," the rancher said.

"This is the first I've heard of it," Jared said.

"Yeah, well, I imagine they're planning to surprise you. Trudeau warned me that they're on their way here, to investigate my stock and land for this contamination they claim to have found. I expect you to back me up on this, Jared."

Jared said, "Of course." But he had a sinking feeling in his stomach.

If the GG epidemiologists decided he had failed to report or overlooked a universal health threat, it would probably mean they'd revoke his license, or at best, demote him and move him to a lesser position on a new post. For Varley and other affected stockmen, it would destroy their livelihoods and probably the lives of all of their animals, both those affected and not.

To Varley, he added, "I don't think they've a leg to stand on, actually. I've done autopsies myself on animals with the glitter in their secretions—sorry, there's no impressive-sounding name for it. The glitter is just a by-product from ingesting those little iridescent insects we have around here. From the evidence I've seen, both the insects and their effects are nontoxic. Had I ever had a clue that the insects were harmful, I certainly would have alerted you earlier myself and I certainly would not have allowed your horses to leave Sherwood, much less the station."

"Yeah, well, I suppose I knew that. If anyone is toxic, it's the politicians and officials involved. I may have to put down a few of them myself before this is over."

Jared grunted agreement and signed off.

The Galactic Health Authority contacted him barely two hours later demanding that he submit his records for Varley's animals and any others affected with the "fairy dust" syndrome. He told them about the insects and started to explain about the results of his own autopsies when the official cut in: "An impound order is being issued for all animals in the affected area and any beasts they may have come in contact with. A decontamination team is on its way, and the GHA expects your full cooperation with them in this matter, Dr. Vlast."

The Galactic Government, as ponderously slow as a planet's rotation around its sun when it came to responding to requests for assistance from its citizens, was moving with what was for them lightning speed. Apparently, from their viewpoint, a manufactured public health crisis was much easier to deal with than a real threat.

He commed Varley but got no response. He wanted to warn the rancher, but realized he'd be foolish to leave any sort of a trail implicating either one of them. He also realized, to his surprise, that he had already decided to disobey Varley's orders.

It wasn't until he had made the trip to the surface, located the rancher, and conveyed his message, that he realized just how firmly he intended to resist the role the government was assigning him in this crisis. Varley swore that he would inform the neighbors and they'd take whatever steps they could.

Jared returned to the station. It would be up to him, he realized, to notify any of the ships that had docked at Hood Station that their animals were to be impounded. Including ships' cats. And the next time the *Molly Daise* docked, someone would inform them that their animals must also be impounded. Including Janina's beloved Chessie and her kitten.

ꞏ ꞏ ꞏ

CHESTER ABOARD THE MOLLY DAISE

Three more watches, three more haunted catnaps later, and my rest was disturbed on that fateful occasion when Captain Vesey called Kibble to the bridge. Mother and I were at her heels and under her feet as she hastened to obey her commander. "Looks like we'll be launching a rescue mission," he told her. "But you're the one who will need to go, so I'd like to consult you about whether or not we respond. As you can see, the COB sign, with that cat outline on it, deviates somewhat from the galactic regulation notification. What do you think?"

A dark and drifting ship loomed in the viewport. The *Molly Daise's* running lights illuminated it. On the bow was the familiar glowing paint with the universal COB letters, in addition to a simple black line drawing of a cat sitting upright. The writing was the picture writing from my dream. I was certain that this was the ship containing the cat who had been intruding on my naps.

"I don't recognize it, sir," Kibble told the captain, "but the sign is clear enough, even if someone did add fanciful artwork and the ship does look derelict. No answer to your hails, I presume?"

He shook his head. "None. It's quiet as a tomb. You've not had to do this before, Janina. Perhaps we should just notify the Galactic Guard of its position and give it a miss."

"Sir, by the time the Guard reached it, a cat survivor might have died slowly from lack of oxygen. I've not done it but I have been *trained* to do it. Being a Cat Person isn't all food dishes and litter boxes, you know."

"I know. Do you want to take backup?"

"Hmmm—well, they say in training to take your own ship's cat to help locate the survivor or—well, what would have been the survivor. I was issued a cat-sized adjustable pressure suit and helmet with olfactory amplifiers so the cat could still smell. But only one. They gave me a life-support carrier for the stranded cat. Chester is inexperienced and Chessie is—"

I climbed her trouser leg. "Me! Me!" I cried. "Let me go! I know what's there! I dreamed it." I knew no one would understand me, but since I was only about ten inches long, exclusive of my tail, I felt I needed to make a great deal of noise to get noticed and I might as well give them a real piece of my mind.

"No, Chester, you're too young," Mother said, since of course she *did* understand. I could tell however that she didn't really want to go. Once she'd returned to her ship after her ordeal dirtside on Sherwood, she never wanted to leave it again. Still she protested, "*I* am the *Molly Daise*'s official cat. I am the one who must go."

I ignored her and continued to climb Kibble.

"I think you have a volunteer," Captain Vesey told her, laughing.

"I don't know. He's just a baby, sir."

"Yes, but he's learning and is nimble and fast on his feet, whereas our Chessie is getting on in years. He's smaller too, and you never know when that might come in handy in this sort of situation."

He's also been dreaming with the cat on the ship, you aggravating people, I thought at them. *Now let's get out there and see what that cat has to say for himself.*

I knew I had won when Kibble picked me up and carried me with her to the shuttle bay. On the way she picked up a packet of my favorite fishie treats, a large bag of cat food, an old-fashioned rattling can opener, and a bizarre-shaped object that turned out, to my disgust, to be a suit and helmet meant for me.

She put it on me, leaving off only the helmet, saying, "You have to, Chester. I have to, too. We can't live in space or in a ship with depleted oxygen without our survival suits." While she readied the shuttle, I tried to get used to the suit. Under normal circumstances I would have expressed my displeasure in graphic and disruptive ways that she would find convincing, to say the least, but I desperately wanted—for reasons I did not understand—to accompany her on this mission. The mission included the stupid suit, so instead of spending my time protesting, I practiced moving in it. It was surprisingly flexible, though I couldn't manage much of a tail lash in it.

And there was always that packet of fishie treats Kibble carried with us. Perhaps they were to be my reward for a mission accomplished? I could hope.

Kibble picked me up and tried to stick me in her pouch but I slipped out of her grasp. This was the first time I'd ridden in a small craft in open space and I wanted to see.

"No, Chester, don't stand on the instruments," she scolded when I jumped onto the control panel to look through the viewport at the stars and the derelict ship. I jumped back onto her lap but the slipperiness of our suits dumped me off onto the deck. I tried to wash my paw to show that I didn't care, that the fall was only part of my master plan, but I got only a tongueful of odorless, tasteless shipsuit.

Once more she lifted me, and this time I allowed her to put me in the pouch on the front of her suit, but kept my front paws on the opening and stuck my head out to watch.

Having fixed the ship and stars in my mind, I turned my attention to Kibble's hands, which moved over the controls with a bit of hesitation but seemed to be doing the right thing. I hadn't known she could fly, but then lots of humans on Sherwood seemed to be able to, and as I watched her, I realized suddenly why everyone got in such a lather over me romping across the control panels. Graphs shifted and changed colors and made the shuttle move and make noises with the merest touch on her part, more sensitive than a baby mouse under Mother's paws. *That* was good to know.

The derelict ship was very close to ours, held in place by the *Molly Daise's* tractor beam.

"Initiate docking procedure," Indu's voice told her. "Breaking and Entering Docking Protocol engaged."

Resuming my pouch-perch topside, I saw the side of the derelict slide open, leaving a great gaping dark square hole, like an open mouth waiting to eat us. And for just a moment I saw, as if beneath a ship-shaped veil, the pyramid vessel I had dreamed during my last nap. Then the veil fell back and our shuttle—quite stupidly, I thought—sailed into the open maw.

I must have given an involuntary hiss because Kibble put a hand on my neck and said, "Shhh, Chester, it's okay. We can't very well rescue the other cat if we don't board his ship, can we?"

It seemed to me that with all of their clever little tricks and technologies, the humans might have come up with some strategy less risky to limb and tail, and I gave her a withering look to convey this attitude, but she was staring ahead and missed the whole thing.

I began to wonder why I had been so keen to come on this mission. That package of fishie treats looked increasingly appealing, and all this excitement had worn me out. I was ready for another nap, just as she seemed about ready to go. Maybe I would just curl up inside the pouch and—

"Time to work, Chester," Kibble said. "Let's hook you up and put on your helmet and go see if we can save the other cat. I'm counting on you to help me find him, so try to behave yourself for a change."

For a change? Why, I had bored myself to snores trying to "behave" according to what these people wanted until I could find my boy! I hadn't demanded adoration for my concessions, but a little credit would have been nice.

I soon realized I had underestimated Kibble's cunning and cruelty. She had made sure my paws and claws were encased in the padded shipsuit before forcing the horrible helmet over my head. I knew what it was—she had already put one on her own head, just like it, except that mine had two pointy triangles at the top. Once the helmet was over my head, my flattened ears popped up into the triangular places. A soothing hiss of oxygen filled my nostrils from the hose attaching our suits even before she locked the helmet in place, but I couldn't help trying to paw the thing off, for fear I'd smother.

"Chester, settle down. Trust me, little one, you don't want to be cut off from my hose. Now then, we're going to leave the shuttle and go hunt for the other cat. I've my gravity boots to keep me grounded, but you will be floating in zero g once we get outside. *Please* don't try to run away, baby cat. If this hose comes apart, you may not have enough oxygen in your suit to last until I can hook us back up."

I heard her quite well in spite of the helmet, and I could still smell the inside of the shuttle as well, though her scent was cut off by her shipsuit. The noise of the *Molly Daise*'s bridge on an open channel buzzed in the background. The shuttle's hatch opened and Kibble picked me up and carried me out. Once she let go of me, I was airborne!

This time it did not frighten me. After my recent dance across the buttons that controlled the gravity on the *Molly Daise*, once Kibble and Mother got over being angry, we had flying lessons in the training chamber. Mother said that no kit of hers was going to be afraid of weightlessness.

I meowed loudly and tumbled over three times in midair as my voice filled my own quite sensitive ears trapped in their pointy helmeted casings. "Other cat? Where are you?"

You seek my wisdom and protection, my son? a deep voice inquired in my head.

We seek your furry tail so we can save you and get us all out of this rat warren! I replied, not bothering to use words of feline language at this point. Our actual spoken vocabulary is diminished if we can't use the eloquence of our bodies for punctuation, extended explication, and emphasis.

"Have you got the scent, Chester? Have you?" Kibble asked. From the pouch, she pulled the can opener and the bag of fishie treats.

That was easy, I thought, using my front paws for propulsion and my tail as a rudder as I dived toward the treats in her hand. I knocked them out of her hand and into free-fall, but I couldn't retrieve them because I had nothing with which to grab them, as I discovered when my faceplate hit the package and sent it soaring upward out of my reach. I'd forgotten about the wretched helmet. I wailed at the injustice of it, the awful cruelty of her taunting me with treats. But she, oblivious, snatched the treats out of the air and rattled a can opener in her other hand. Now I understood: the sound was a lure for the stranded cat.

"Kitty kitty?" she called. *Rattle rattle.*

Hark! Do mine ears detect the sound of the sacred sistrum of sustenance? the other cat asked. At the same time, my amplified ears heard a *miau*, faint, as if far away.

No, it's just a can opener, I told the cat.

Yes, that. And is there—perchance—a can or container of some sort for it to work its magic upon? I have had no food for weeks, months, years even!

Should I tell him about the fishie treats? I wondered, as their significance to Kibble became clear to me. Alas, they were not for me but a bribe for him. I was sure of it. Otherwise, why would she have withheld them from me aboard the shuttle when she *knew* I loved them? They should by rights be *my* fishie treats. The strange cat claimed to be starving, and he might fool Kibble with his piteous complaints, but I am a cat. I know what starving means when we speak of it to someone with food. It means we want that food and will say whatever it takes to get it. His lies would not work on another cat. On the other hand, there were lots more fishie treats back on the *Molly Daise,* and if we collected this old feline and returned to a crew grateful to be on its way and proud of Kibble and me for completing our mission, I could probably cadge so many treats I wouldn't be able to follow Mother into the tighter service passages for a while.

I'll share if you'll guide me to you, I told him.

The passage will lead you to no one else, he replied.

So I led us forward.

However, a short distance beyond the docking bay, we met a blank bulkhead with no way a human could go but back the way she came.

What passage?

Then I saw a ramp running along one side of the large corridor from the deck to what was debatably the overhead. Swimming toward it, I saw a hole in the bulkhead, just big enough for a cat.

You'll have to come out, I told the other cat. *My human can't get in to bring you the food.*

You can bring it.

No, I can't. I can't carry it.

Find a way. And be certain, young one, that there is enough left to assuage the hunger of a famished elder when you reach me.

I then engaged in one of the charades I found it necessary to play with most humans in order to convey the simplest instructions. I dived for the treat packet again, bumping Kibble's hand, but she had been watching me, and this time she held onto the prize.

Shaking her head inside the helmet, which moved very little, she said, "No, Chester. The treats are for the other cat."

To emphasize his hunger and helplessness, the wily elder mewed pathetically from within the cat-sized passage, which magnified his voice and sent it echoing through the chamber where we stood wasting time.

I pawed at the food again, then started up, swam toward the hole, pushed off the bulkhead with my back paws, and repeated my assault on the fishie treats.

"That isn't going to work, Chester. The poor lost cat doubtlessly has found an air pocket to hide in—some ships even have an on-board lifepod for the cat. This one is very odd, I must say. Once you located him, I was hoping to get close enough to use the treats to lure him into the life pouch. It will allow him to survive the airless conditions inside the rest of the ship. If he is too far for me to reach, by the time he comes out, he'll have suffocated, and if you go farther than the hose will reach, little one, you too will die."

I didn't like the sound of that. It was good that although she had no telepathic link with either Mother or me, Kibble always treated us with courtesy and explained everything aloud as she would to another human.

It was also fortunate that the other cat was telepathic with me and understood what she said.

Humans! I don't suppose she checked the oxygen levels before she left her craft? Neither of you have need of that clumsy attire. If you lose your tether it is of no consequence. Bring me the fishie treats. Bring me the fishie treats. You will bring me the fishie treats nyow . . .

I was willing to do this, but I couldn't think how, with my teeth behind glass and my claws in gloves. Of course, according to the COB, I could take my helmet off. *He* would not be the one gasping for air if it were less wholesome than he claimed. So I said, with what I liked to think was considerable cunning, *If there is oxygen enough for us to remove our helmets, then there is oxygen enough for you to come out of your hole and fetch the treats yourself.*

I am weak from hunger and injured.

Then crawl out of your hole and fetch the treats and Kibble will tuck you into her pouch.

I knew this old cat was trying to trick me. I wasn't sure how or why, but he did not sound injured any more than he sounded hungry and he certainly didn't sound frightened. He was a sham all the way, I was sure of it.

He said nothing, and for long moments I thought perhaps I had been wrong and he had perished of hunger while I argued. However, after a bit, a slim triangular tawny face with very large pointed ears and very large amber eyes appeared. The eyes glittered in the glow of Kibble's helmet lamp. The face was followed by a short-furred, gold-bronze body with a whip of a tail. The lean and quite alien-looking cat looked like an animated statue of an ancient feline hero. I noticed that there were silver hairs among the gold at his muzzle and next to his ears.

"*Molly Daise,* our new passenger just came out of his hole," Kibble said into her com. "He looks healthy and seems to be having no problem breathing."

"Have you checked your O_2 levels, Janina?" the captain asked.

"Uh—no. We're suited up, though."

"If you click the second button on your suit's wrist monitor three times and hold," Indu told her, "a menu will appear in the window. One of the submenus will be marked ENV for Environmental Control. One of *its* submenus will be atmospheric conditions—three more clicks, same button. One more click on its submenu under 'cab' for cabin. Three more will take you to O_2, and if you click that once the level will show up on the screen. If that's okay, click on the other gases and make sure there's nothing toxic."

"O_2 level is in the middle of the gauge," Kibble told her after following the lengthy instructions, "and the COB seems to be healthy."

"Check the temperature. Though if the cat on board can tolerate it, it's probably fine for you and Chester as well."

What a ponderous and primitive procedure, the skinny-faced ship's cat said. *Did I not say the atmosphere is wholesome?*

You did not, not exactly, I said. *And I am very valuable, and Kibble is sworn to look after me so she can't take any chances, can she? Besides, she can't take your word for it. She can't hear your words.*

You could convey them unto her.

No, I can't.

Have you no link with her?

Nothing but this hose I was telling you about, I said, wagging it as a dog would his tail.

Kibble said, "Thanks, Indu. That will make this much easier. They've changed the way you read these since I trained for this sort of mission. Come here, Chester."

She pulled off her helmet and gloves and plucked me from the air, then removed my helmet and peeled off the stupid suit—and the hose that attached us. Now I was truly free.

Once she'd done that, Kibble opened the packet of fishie treats and shook it, sending their aroma throughout and making me salivate. The other cat was not unaffected. Quick as a wink he shot out of his hole, grabbed the packet in—well, I thought it was his teeth—and darted back into the hole.

"No, kitty, come back!" Kibble cried.

Halt, you treat thief! I commanded him, growling ferociously. He had miscalculated, I thought. *Now* I was free to track him into his lair and reclaim the fishie treats. They rightfully belonged to the feline crew members of the *Molly Daise.* He couldn't just take my—our—treats and run.

Pshaw-Ra extracts his tribute and retires to his chamber where he will deal doom to all who dare intrude.

Wrong! I cried, cat-paddling through the twisting cat-sized corridor. Even then I was beginning to wonder about the ship's derelict status. Low light of undetermined origin illuminated the catwalk beneath—well, usually beneath—my paws, and I could see the tunnels spiraling out in widening triangulations behind me. *Those fishie treats are not tribute. They're mine! Kibble only gave you some to get you to come out so we could rescue you. So either come out and get rescued or, preferably, give me back the fishie treats.*

Foolish kitten, Pshaw-Ra the Mariner never relinquishes the prizes that fall into his paws.

They didn't fall into your paws. You filched them! Under false pretenses too. You sent that pathetic dream pretending you were scared of running out of air, but this ship isn't in trouble, is it? And neither are you.

I was beginning to feel peckish, he argued, and I heard crunching noises and smelled the seductive fragrance of tender juicy fishie treats as they surrendered to his teeth and dissolved into deliciousness in his mouth. *If you'll cease your complaints, I will grant you a morsel or two.*

I hesitated. I wanted to address again the question of who should be granting whom morsels, but he had the upper paw and the treats smelled very enticing, so I swam onward—more cautiously.

Once I slowed my pace—or rather, my float—I noticed my surroundings. The picture-writing featuring seated cats was scrawled all over the walls. Pshaw-Ra was evidently a doodler, I decided, and one who liked depicting himself in his graffiti.

He was also well stocked with live food, I soon realized. Shiny keka beetles dropped onto the pathway behind me and trooped toward the hole into the larger chamber.

Meanwhile Kibble was rattling the can opener and calling sweetly for Pshaw-Ra to come back. I could feel him laughing at her entreaties. She encouraged me to let him know it was okay, he was safe with us, since I suppose she felt he'd trust another cat to guarantee his safety. Kibble was a good Cat Person, but she didn't know much about feline diplomatic relations. Unfortunately, neither did I at that time.

Then I heard her voice again, but this time she was not calling to me or to the old imposter nibbling my treats in his fortress. I recognized the murmur she used when speaking into a headpiece to the ship. At first her tone seemed oddly joyous, but it quickly erupted into surprise, consternation, and anger. She said, "No," then, "I can't do that," then, "But Captain, he's all alone and Chester is just a baby." Finally, resigned, she said. "Very well, I obey, but under protest."

She called me then. "Chester, come out. We need to leave now."

You are summoned, child. Depart.

No, I said. It wasn't only about treats now. The way he said it, he made it sound like I was Kibble's servant and obeyed her orders like a—I had not been around many but the expression is part of my racial memory—like a dog. It was an insult difficult for any cat to ignore, especially coming from another cat who held the treat bag while an empty-handed human tried to compete.

Very well, then, stay and I will tell you a story.

A story? I like stories. The boy and I used to read stories under his covers with a flashlight. I would lie between his neck and shoulder and he would whisper the words to me, but I saw them in his mind.

So can you do with me.

"Chester! Chester come, hurry. We have to abort the mission and return to the ship."

She sounded tearful, which was strange. Part of me wanted to go to her and see why she was so sad, but another part was still angry with her for parting me from Jubal. Let her wait. Let the *Molly Daise* wait. What was their hurry? Pshaw-Ra's ship was locked in our tractor beam and going nowhere.

It all began in ancient times on old Earth . . . Pshaw-Ra began. Good. A long story. I drifted closer and saw him just ahead, snuggled into the nose cone of his peculiar cabin, curled up and relaxed. The fishie treats were scattered in front of him, mine for the taking. I snatched up one and ate it, then composed myself, paws and tail tucked as I floated near the ceiling, settling in to listen and enjoy myself.

⸱ ⸱ ⸱

Janina was delighted to hear that Jared had a message for her but puzzled that the captain had felt it couldn't wait until she returned to relay it. When she heard the content of the recording, though, her heart sank as fast as it had risen. "Chester!" she called. "Chester, come back."

But though she called and rattled the can opener, and called again, he didn't come. She tried to keep her voice cheerful and enticing as she continued to call. He would of course be busy assisting the other ship's cat in devouring the treats. If only the captain's com had come before the stranded cat snatched them away and Chester had galloped off in pursuit.

She used the pocket torch in her utility kit to find the hole where the cats had disappeared, and leaned forward, calling directly into it. She could hear the sound of cat treats being daintily crunched between rows of sharp white teeth, but no answering mew from either cat or the sound of paws coming toward her. She reached up into the hole, putting her arm in up to the shoulder, thinking she might feel a furry hide she could yank out, a measure she would never take under ordinary circumstances, partially from fear she might injure the cat, but more realistically that even the gentlest cat, cornered and grabbed like that, would lash out at her hand.

But her fingers touched no fur, just a bend in the corridor. Then something prickly crawled over them, and another thing and another. Hard nubby little things. She withdrew her arm as if she'd been burned and found the suit sleeve coated with the iridescent shiny beetles like the one Chester had caught in Jared's office.

She shook her arm, but as she did so, she heard something snap and looked back at the hole. She didn't see it. The wall looked completely solid again. Only the beetles scrambling up and around her testified that there had been a door, or a cat.

She had a small laser saw in her kit but her classes had not covered this sort of situation. "*Molly Daise*, Chester and the victim have disappeared inside the cat hole and somehow it has closed solid. Chester did not respond to my calls and I cannot reach him where he is. Request a team to demolish the bulkhead and retrieve him."

"Request denied, CP. Return to base at once." Indu's voice was one of impersonal command that Janina had seldom heard before, and never directed at her.

"But Chester—"

"Abandon feline per-personnel," Indu continued, her voice faltering.

"Janina," Captain Vesey's voice answered. "Leave him."

"Then I'm staying too!" she said. Abandoning her charge was unthinkable to her.

"Consider this, Jannie," the captain said, using the name Janina had sometimes been called when much, much smaller, and before she had gone to CP school. "You say there is plenty of oxygen, the stranded cat is in no distress that you can see. Leave them the food and water on board the shuttle and come away. We have the derelict's identity code and position. Until the government's order is lifted, both cats may be better off there than here. Now do as you're told. Every second you are breathing the oxygen in that ship may deprive the cats of it later on."

That finally convinced her. Janina replaced her helmet and used the suit's oxygen, her tears steaming up the faceplate of her helmet as she returned to the shuttle, leaving the hatch open while she unloaded the emergency bags of cat food, which floated like lumpy clouds, rising to the ceiling. The packaging, though airtight, could be easily ruptured by a cat's standard equipment. The water situation was a bit trickier, but long ago someone had devised a large bottle with a nipple that cats could use in free-fall to quench their thirst.

There were also the beetles, which she saw everywhere now, it seemed. There were even some inside the shuttle. The cats seemed to like those, so they would be additional food for Chester and the other ship's cat. She looked back one last time to where she thought the hole had been, then reboarded the shuttle and returned to the *Molly Daise*, leaving the cats, at least temporarily, to their fate.

ɼ ɼ ɼ

Chessie ran to Janina, looking for Chester. When she realized he was gone, she cried and cried for him, making Janina cry again too.

But the import of Jared's message was even worse than she'd thought.

Jared had not been specific in the brief transmission she'd received on board the seeming derelict, but Captain Vesey had since received further orders from the GG and the GHA elaborating on the state of the perceived emergency.

The glittering matter in the mucosal secretions of the wild pintos shipped off planet had been deemed to be a harbinger of a possible galaxywide epidemic that threatened all livestock and pets aboard ships. All animals exhibiting the symptoms and any they had come in contact with were to be impounded for quarantine and possibly destroyed, depending on further findings.

"But the glittery spit is just a by-product of them eating those shiny beetles!" Janina protested after reading the full edict.

Captain Vesey shrugged. "They apparently think the beetles carry some disease."

"They can't kill Chessie and all the other ships' cats based on an unsubstantiated theory!" Janina said. "They can't!"

"Of course they can," Indu said. "And there's nothing we can do about it."

Jubal scarcely believed what he was seeing as the *Ranzo* threaded its way into the traffic jam over the city that was called the Hub of the Universe.

The skies of Galipolis were almost hidden from the ground by the fleets of ships, shuttles, trackers, and aircars taking off, landing, hovering while waiting to land, coming and going. The *Ranzo* was required to wait an entire week to enter orbit, and then had to orbit an additional two weeks before it was given permission to dock.

All of this was because of the horrible impound order. Too late, they had received the notice that ships would not be permitted to come and go as usual from Galipolis. Each one had to submit to a search. Its animals were to be impounded before any ship underwent a thorough sterile cleaning. Only then would the ship be able to go about its business.

It was taking a perilously long time. Adding to the general confusion, fuel transports were often dispatched from the city and its space stations—also overrun with traffic—to supply ships, so they could continue their wait. Jubal did not envy the transport skippers, who had to pick through the traffic between them and their target vessels.

When the *Ranzo* finally did dock, while the crew waited to disembark, the port authorities boarded the ship. The first thing they did was to snatch Hadley from his favorite nap place on Sosi's bunk and stuff him into a carrier. Then one of them took off with him. Hadley mewed plaintively from the carrier and Sosi ran after him. The hazmat-suited woman carrying him looked down at Sosi through her face screen, and gave her a piece of paper. "This is the receipt for your cat. Don't lose it. It has his number on it so he can be returned to you when the time comes, or, in the event that we are unable to return him, you'll be reimbursed for loss of his services."

Sosi clutched the paper and gulped back sobs to tell the woman, "He's not used to carriers. He's a good cat and likes to be held in your arms when he goes somewhere." But she was talking to the back of the hazmat suit, and another suit stepped between her and Hadley's captor.

"What's going to happen to him out there?" she asked, and turned to Jubal, who had left his other duties when he heard Hadley's meow and Sosi's wail. "Jubal, what if they're mean to him? Nobody has ever been mean to him. He won't know what's happening!"

Even though Sosi hadn't been especially friendly or nice to him before, Jubal's heart went out to her, because her grief and fear for Hadley was so much what he felt for Chester.

He put his arm around her as he had so often done with Mom when she was upset over something Dad had done, and said staunchly, "We won't let them."

"They're from the government, Jubal," she said, shaking off his arm. "Just what do you think a couple of kids can do?"

That was a good question. He said, "I dunno, but my folks always say the squeaky wheel gets the grease. We're going to be in port awhile, right?"

"A little while."

"It must say on the receipt where they're taking him. For all I know, Chester will be there too. So we go and watch them."

"They might run us off."

"They can try. But we're just a couple of little kids. They can't shoot us or anything. If we play it right, they'll end up letting us see what's happening to shut us up. And we won't be the only ones watching. Cats like Hadley and Chester are worth a lot of credits, and their crews are going to be really worried about them. I'm going to talk to Beulah and see if she can help."

Beulah had by then gleaned more information about the massive impound and had a roster of ships in port. A guy in a hazmat suit was buzzing around her com station, supposedly looking for beetles, but the way she was smiling at him and the flirtatious gleam off his faceplate made Jubal think he was maybe taking a little longer than necessary at this part of the task. Beulah was kind of pretty, for an older woman, with curly red hair in a ponytail, dark brown eyes, and freckles. He guessed she might be a little younger than his mom, but then, Mom sometimes complained when she was trying to look nice before Pop came home, that life on the farm had messed up her looks.

"Hey, hotshot," Beulah said to Jubal. "Hi, Sosi."

"We need to talk to you about something," Jubal told her.

"Yeah, I thought you would. Dr. Mbele here and I have just been discussing Hadley and Chester. He said he'd try to look out for them."

Sosi glowered but Jubal gave him a tremulous smile and said, "Gosh, thanks, Dr. Mbele, sir. Hadley is a wonderful cat and Sosi's had him since he was a kitten. I helped Chester get born and took him back to his ship. Please don't let anything happen to them, *please*."

"I cannot promise," Mbele said. "But this lady has given me her personal link, and I will do all I can to make sure that your Hadley is given every chance." He gave Beulah a little salute and left.

"I have some news about Chester's ship, Jubal," his friend said. "I guess you could say it's good news and bad news. The good news is that Chester didn't get impounded when the ship docked, although they did take his mother the Duchess. The crew is up in arms over that."

"So he wasn't infected?" Jubal asked. Odd, since this supposed contagious disease thing seemed to be all about the beetles, and he knew Chester loved to eat the shiny bugs.

"Chester, uh, left the ship, voluntarily."

"He spaced himself?" Jubal had a momentary vision of his poor kitten in despair over their separation stepping out the airlock. No, that was nuts. Cats didn't do that kind of thing. Chester might have gone *looking* for him and made a mistake, of course . . .

"No, he and the CP went on a rescue mission, and both Chester and the cat stranded aboard the derelict evidently decided to stay there. Apparently the cats had lots of food, water, and air, and they got locked in a special cat hatch that kept the Cat Person away from the animals. Since Chester likes to eat the beetles, and the derelict was full of them, he's not likely to go hungry.

"The GHA is blaming the beetles for this so-called epidemic. Chester's captain figured the little guy probably had a better chance of surviving staying where he was. As long as GHA doesn't pick up the derelict, the cats can take their chances with the bugs. And even though the *Molly Daise* had the derelict in its tractor beam and marked its coordinates and registration code, once they released it, they couldn't locate it again."

Jubal didn't know what to think. Chester hadn't been impounded. Good. Chessie had. Bad. Chester was on a mysterious ship with some stray cat. Bad. The ship had some life support for the cats. Good. Nobody could find the ship. Bad and good, depending on how the plague thing turned out.

"You think you could patch me through to my cousin?" he asked Beulah more calmly than he meant to. "I'd like to hear about it myself."

"I'll see what I can do," Beulah said, and hailed the *Molly Daise*.

It was a simple fact that you couldn't say anything the GG might consider "subversive" on the com channels, and Jubal had a feeling that the GG wouldn't like what he had in mind.

He would tell Janina he wanted to meet with her to hear more about how she'd lost Chester. That was the main reason, of course, but he actually hoped to convince her to give him the coordinates and registration number of the ship Chester was on. Then if he could contrive somehow for the *Ranzo* to come anywhere near that ship, Chester would know it and they'd get back together again. If that happened, he wasn't going to let the GG or anybody else take Chester away again.

The whole deal with the beetles sounded as phony as something his dad would dream up. Jubal didn't see how the bugs could do any more harm than beetles usually did. All the cats and kittens ate them, and except for the glittery residue, seemed unaffected.

When Janina came on the com screen, her eyes were red and her face a little puffy. She blinked a lot when she looked at him. "I'm surprised to see you here, young man," she said.

He bit his tongue against an angry retort. Chessie had been impounded and Janina was upset as it was. He knew too well what she was feeling to yell at her now, even if he hadn't wanted something from her.

"I had to try to find you," he said in a rush. "I thought maybe you'd let me help you take care of Chester and his mom."

"Your timing isn't very good," she said. "Is your mother with you?"

"No," Jubal admitted. "My father brought me to the station. He was trying to help me get in touch with you. But something happened to him and he didn't board before we took off."

"It's all kind of pointless now, isn't it?" she said glumly. "You heard what happened to Chester?"

"Some of it. I want to talk to you about it. Is there somewhere in Galipolis we can meet in person?"

"There's a fountain in the center of the city," Beulah offered. "It's famous. Anyone can direct you to it."

"That will do," Janina said, but seemed uncertain.

"Look, if you want to, you can bring a friend. This is Sosi," he said, pulling the girl forward. "She's Captain Loloma's daughter.

They just took her cat Hadley. She's, uh, she's the CP on the *Ranzo*. She's coming too."

He looked at Sosi, half expecting that she would ruin it by disagreeing since it wasn't her idea, but she nodded gravely. She still *hoped* there was something they could do, even if she didn't quite believe it.

"I will speak to Captain Vesey and the others," Janina promised.

r r r

As soon as the *Ranzo*'s crew was cleared to disembark, with Captain Loloma's permission, he and Sosi set out for the fountain. It was a good thing Sosi was with him, because she'd been to Galipolis several times before and was used to its size, its crowded marketplaces, its glittering shop windows and crowded walkways, the artificial light the people needed during the day because the ground was so overshadowed by the air traffic.

Although six space stations serviced the planet, the dirtside port was still a favorite destination for space travelers.

Sosi pointed out the fountain from five blocks away, as tall as many of the surrounding buildings. Its central geyser shot into the air so high it threatened to wash the underside of the lowest-flying shuttlecraft, then the waters cascaded down the central structure, tumbling from one shining precipice to the next. Smaller geysers danced and glittered around it.

Janina and three crewmates, one woman and two men, looked tiny beside the massive fountain. All of them still wore their shipsuits, as did he and Sosi.

Jubal gave them a short wave as he and Sosi approached. Janina's crewmates wore sad expressions that turned hard when they saw him. He said, "This is Sosi. Her ship's cat Hadley was impounded too." The other crew members—the slender sandy-haired woman, the tall white-haired and bearded man, and the shorter red-haired man—regarded his shipmate with more sympathetic expressions.

"What did you need from Janina, son?" the white-haired man asked.

Jubal hesitated, gulped, and cleared his throat. He wanted to talk to her alone about Chester, but for the rest of his plan, he figured they'd need all the allies they could get. He decided to start with that part. "I couldn't say this on the com," he said, "but I think this whole thing with taking our cats and other animals stinks and we need to do something. I have an idea. I was hoping you would all know other people who would help too."

He explained his plan, and to his surprise the adults all seemed to think it was a reasonable thing to do and agreed to help. When they'd talked it over a little, Janina gave him the information about Chester, her voice threatening to break when she described how it had happened. Janina's crewmates seemed a lot more sympathetic now than over the com screen at the vet clinic when they'd made him let Chester go.

He didn't know what to make of what she'd told him about Chester and the derelict. He chewed on it as he and Sosi headed back toward the ship. Her mood had improved a lot since the meeting, and she pulled him toward the marketplace, a skip in her step. "Look at that blue material, Jube!" she cried. "See the silver on the edge?"

"What would you do with something like that?" he asked, genuinely puzzled. Crew members rarely dressed up or wore anything but shipsuits.

"I'd make a princess drape over my bunk," she said. "It would be gorgeous!"

He shrugged. She wound her way through the crowd toward the coveted cloth, and he was following her, when through the babble of the crowd he heard a familiar voice haggling in the booth directly behind him.

"Pop?"

CHAPTER 15

When the *Grania* received the impound notice, Ponty's stock actually went up. "Get your test tubes bubbling, boyo," Mavis told him. "Once the government gets through with the galaxy's livestock, there's going to be a big market for uninfected cats with blue bloodlines."

Doc followed her into the room and hopped up on the console, pretending to use it for a washstand as he carefully groomed his long luxurious gray-striped coat.

First his chest, then his paws, then his ears and whiskers, his shoulders.

"What's this all about, Mavis?"

"Making us rich, mostly," she said, stroking Doc's head, which messed up his bathing schedule so that he had to wash that part next. "Every ship docking at Galport has to surrender its critters to be tested."

Doc's ears flicked forward a fraction.

"You know as well as I do they're not going to bother following up to see which ones are sick or get sick, they'll just put 'em all down. There will be a lot of berths open for expensive ship cats then. We'll be able to name our own price."

Doc sprang to Ponty's shoulder, clinging with all claws. *Save me, boss. I'm too young to die.* Ponty thought he was imagining it, of course. Cats could make themselves understood without words, even ones inside your head. That kind of thing just told him he'd been working too hard. He felt the kitten trembling against his neck, though, so he wasn't imagining that the little fellow was afraid.

"How about this guy, Mavis? You gonna let them take him?"

She looked sad and shrugged. "He's not exactly legal to begin with. Not exactly on the manifest or anything. What the GG don't know won't hurt 'em."

"Hide him?"

She gave him a pitying look back over her shoulder as she strode from the cabin. "And they'd better not find him either."

Doc mewed into his ear again, and although the sound that came out was standard feline issue, the thought that came into Ponty's mind in a nasal little cat voice was in GSL—Galactic Standard Language: *Save me.* Meanwhile, the kitten clung to his neck with sharp baby cat claws that threatened to open a jugular.

"Pipe down," he told the cat aloud. "If I'm gonna hide you, you need to keep your mouth shut or they'll find you. Keep still too."

I'll be as quiet as a—you know, the kitten promised, but Ponty wasn't sure he could trust him. Cats had been known to lie— especially about when they were last fed. He'd learned that from Chessie's and Git's litters. There wasn't anything wrong with a good fib, of course, but he liked to be the one telling it.

None of the kitten's usual haunts would work. The crew would know about those places. They could turn the little guy in to the GG goons and Mavis would never know.

He tried the bottom of a tool bag, but the kitten popped its head back up, wrinkled his little pink nose and said, *Smells bad.*

The ship's intercom blurted that the impound team had arrived to search the ship for beetles and infected animals. Mavis made sure to warn her crew that the team was armed with bioheat detectors and other more lethal weapons.

Time had run out. The only hope for Doc was that nobody would, well, rat him out.

The kitten would make an unlikely spot of bioheat in any clothing or bag where he might be hidden, so Ponty took the cat to his quarters, where he put on his civvies—the jeans and plaid shirt he'd been wearing under his shipsuit when he left home, and the black leather jacket he'd kept in the carrier. The jacket had an interior pocket that was handy for a lot of things. It fit up close under his arm and was, he judged, the right size for the kitten.

He picked the cat up and tucked it in the pocket.

Hey, I wasn't done with my bath yet!

"Yeah, well, if you don't want to be done for, you'll take a nap and be quiet about it until I tell you it's okay, got it?"

This is a good place, the kitten said as it curled into the pocket. A deep purr throbbed against Ponty's side.

"Cut that out, Doc," he whispered to his own armpit. "They'll hear you from the bridge if you keep purring like that."

Sorry. I'm happy.

"Enjoy it while you can, fuzz face."

Boss?

"What?"

You don't have to say words to me. I can understand you. You're my person, boss. I can read you like a cargo manifest.

Mavis was always looking at cargo manifests—of other ships, making her shopping lists for her heists. The kitten liked to get between her and her paperwork.

Like this? Ponty thought experimentally.

You got it.

Well, I'll be spaced. Do you do this with Mavis too?

No. She's nice to me. She likes me. I like to keep it that way. But you're my boss.

Ponty was pretty sure now that the kitten was lying. He didn't actually know much about cats, but he did know that most of them considered themselves their own bosses. The kitten's story stank worse than an unemptied litter box, but the important thing now was to keep the cat safe from the goons and therefore himself safe from the wrath of Mavis.

He strolled right past the goons and their equipment, down the gangway and into Galport, then into the streets of Galipolis.

▾ ▾ ▾

The old man looked around at the sound of Jubal's voice, then grinned down at him as if they had agreed to meet there. "They treating you okay on the *Ranzo*?" he asked.

No hug, no hi, no "How's your mom?"

"Up till now, yeah. At least they honored my contract, even if you didn't honor yours."

"Couldn't help it, son. I was, as they say, unavoidably detained."

"The law?"

"Some old—friends. Find your cat?"

Jubal said, "No. And now Hadley and Chessie and the other ship cats have been impounded. They're probably going to kill them."

"I know. Tough luck about that," his father said, sounding only a little sad. Jubal recognized the credit signs in Pop's eyes.

"I get it. You're going to make money off this, aren't you?" He narrowed his eyes suspiciously at his father. "You didn't cause the impound order, did you?"

"Mercy, no! What do you take me for, boy?" he asked. Jubal didn't answer.

But just then Sosi ran back, clutching her cloth. Seeing Jubal's dad, she stopped in her tracks and looked from Jubal to his dad and back again.

"Ponty," she said to his father. Of course. Pop had probably spent more time on the *Ranzo* and ships like her than he ever had at home. "Ponty, they took Hadley away. You can help, can't you? Or you know somebody who can help? When they arrested my daddy you made them let him go . . ."

"That was a matter of knowing someone, sweet cakes," Pop said, kneeling to talk to the girl. "I don't think there's anything I can do about the kitties they arrested, but I'll see to it you have your pick of the litter of the new kitties as soon as they're born."

For a smart guy, Pop really didn't get it about cats, did he? They weren't interchangeable. Jubal felt like yelling at him, but Sosi for once made herself useful and went him one better. Her lower lip trembled, her eyes watered up and began streaming, then she let out a loud *Bawwww* that would have made one of the cows back home proud. Then she leaped onto his old man. Throwing her arms around his neck while the blue cloth was still in her hands, she nearly strangled him crying, "I want *Had*ley, Ponty. I don't want them to h-h-h-hurt h-him! Please make them give him back. I don't want a new kitty. I want *mine*."

Under other circumstances Jubal would have been tickled to see his old man speechless for a change, but this was serious. Ponty patted Sosi and said, "There there, there there, I'll see what I can do. Maybe I know someone who can let me rescue one cat . . ."

"But Pop, they took Chessie too, and what about the oth—"

The old man shot him a warning look. Then, to Jubal's amazement, he pulled the side of his leather jacket out from under the sobbing Sosi and pointed under his left arm. The tips of two gray-striped ears with delicate pink insides tufted with fine soft white hairs poked up from a pocket inside the jacket. The ears tilted back and the sleepy white-mustachioed face of Doc, Chessie's foster kitten, rose slowly, eyes slitted. Finding nothing interesting to look at, the kitten shut his eyes again and burrowed his face back into the pocket.

How'd you find him? Jubal mouthed. But his father shook his head over the top of Sosi's and pulled the jacket back together in front again.

For just a moment Jubal felt more lighthearted than he had in a long time. His pop was actually on their side. And then, from the other side of the jacket, something blurted and Pop dislodged Sosi enough to answer it.

"Ponty, you'd better make yourself scarce and hide my cat better than you hid his box, food, and toys. The goons found them and they are looking for you."

The old man mumbled something into the com, took off the jacket and gave it to his son, who put it on. Not a good fit. The collar slid over his shoulder on the side where Doc was hidden, and Doc mewed in protest and started to try to climb out.

"Ow," Jubal said. Sosi, delighted when she spotted the kitten, bounced up and down, and when they told her to hush up and act natural, she bit down on her fist to keep from squealing with excitement.

"If you want me to save your furry tail, you'd better behave yourself and stay still," Pop said to the jacket's bulge. "It's okay, I'll be right back and I'll find a better place to hide you." Then, "Okay, okay, I'll find you something to eat too."

He looked up at Jubal's face, shook his head in mock disgust and said, "Cats!" then strode back into the market, turning back once to say, "Stay put. I'll be right back."

He was gone a long time. Jubal stood there in the hot leather jacket as the kitten settled and resettled himself inside the pocket, mewing when his claws caught in the lining, and sometimes in Jubal. Sosi, trying to help, wrapped her blue cloth around Jubal's shoulders three times, but it still dragged on the ground. It did hide most of the jacket, however.

When Pop returned, he was wearing the long loose robe and head cloth of a Khafistani merchant, from which he produced a large bag.

"What took you so long?" Jubal asked.

"I had to have a pocket put in, didn't I? For the merchandise? Give us a hug now."

It was awkward and Jubal got scratched pretty bad during the transfer, but by the time Pop stood away, Doc was in the robe, the jacket was in the bag, and the contents of a smaller bag of dried fish, which had been in the larger bag, was in the kitten.

Jubal looked after them wonderingly. He thought the old man was for once really committed to taking a side regardless of profit. He'd gone to a lot of trouble for Doc, and now he'd be in a lot more trouble if anybody found out.

Not that Jubal would tell. He had other plans.

Beulah had been the one to suggest getting the press on their side. Before becoming a com officer, she'd been a comcaster for one of the big Galactic networks. For the most part, the news these people reported was local and was so stale by the time it made its way through the relays to the outlying worlds that it wasn't worth bothering about. That was what the GG said anyway.

Also, the popular press, as it was called, was mostly only popular with the people affected by the news it reported. Folks on Sherwood didn't care any more about what happened on Galipolis than Galipolitans cared what happened on Sherwood, unless somehow or other it affected prices or taxes or some other pangalactic issue.

The GG kept people informed about that kind of thing. Most of the people on the colony planets and those traveling through space were somehow or other working for the GG. If something they didn't like was happening, they usually found it more trouble than it was worth to say or do anything about it.

Galipolis didn't depend on ships' cats to keep the crew and cargo safe, nor on livestock for a livelihood, but if animals on the other planets were destroyed, it would mean less fresh meat, maybe even less produce, and Beulah said city folks could get almost as attached to their pets as Jubal was to Chester.

What they needed, she said, was a story. The GG doing something unpopular wasn't news, but maybe a group of people whose beloved animals had been impounded trying to save them—or at least trying to make sure they weren't unnecessarily sacrificed— was more the kind of thing the press would latch onto. They would report it to Galipolitans at large, and either the movement—and the pressure on the GG to do the right thing—would gather momentum, or the city people would sneer at the unsophisticated critter lovers. But there'd be attention paid in either case.

Janina and her crewmates had gone to rally crews from other nongovernment-affiliated ships. They were all meeting back at the fountain in two more hours, and Beulah would alert some of her old friends at the networks about their cause.

Meanwhile, Jubal and Sosi trailed an impound team from one of the ships to the quarantine area inside what looked like a large office building. Nobody paid any attention to a couple of kids. Why should they care if the officers in the florries were carrying containers full of beetles and a couple of squalling cats?

"You kids looking for something?" a uniformed security guard asked them.

"Who? Us?" Jubal and Sosi said, each opening their eyes as widely as they could to look innocent and harmless and much too young to cause any problem.

The guard nodded curtly.

"We're looking for my dad—stepdad, actually," Jubal said. "Dr. Mbele?"

"The epidemiologist?"

"Yeah, I think that's what they call it," Jubal said, in case it was a trick question.

"You think he'd want you bothering him at work?"

"No, sir, but it's mighty important. My mama said I was to tell him personal."

"Couldn't she com him?"

"No sir, she—"

"She lost her voice," Sosi said. "She took sick with a sore throat and lost her voice."

The guard grunted and picked up the com behind his desk.

"Get ready to run," Jubal told Sosi from behind his hand. But meanwhile he was watching the lift, trying to tell where it was depositing the impound team and their cargo, looking to see if there was a map of the building on display to help people find the right department.

The guard said, "Dr. Mbele hasn't returned from his mission. I can tell him you kids were here and have him call home."

"Can't we wait?" Jubal asked.

"Not allowed," the guard said. "They're bringing diseased animals in here from all over the galaxy. You kids might catch something worse than a sore throat."

"What's wrong with the animals?" Sosi asked.

"They don't know, but whatever it is, it spreads fast and is hard to detect. That's all I was told about it."

"That's too bad," Jubal said. "What are they going to do?"

"Test 'em."

"Like ask them questions?" Sosi asked in her brightest little-girl voice.

"No, honey," the man said. "Take samples, see what's making them sick."

"Oh. Does Daddy do that?"

"Yes, he does."

"Where? Here?"

The man sighed a deep put-upon sigh. "Of course not. Up in the lab."

"Where's that?" Jubal asked.

The man looked trapped. He didn't want to be mean to the kids of one of the scientists, but he probably wasn't supposed to be chitchatting with them either. "If I show you on my computer, will you go back home and wait like I told you?"

"You can do that?" Sosi asked, clapping her hands.

"I'm not supposed to, but of course I can. You'll see it if you come in at a better time, career day maybe, when your daddy can bring you to work with him."

He was going to get fired for this for sure, Jubal thought, feeling sorry for the man, who kindly showed them a layout of the building, pinpointed Mbele's laboratory, then showed them the scientists at work in the lab on his security camera. He shut it off when it picked up the yowls of the cats and the protests of the other animals.

"Are the kitties sick?" Sosi asked, overdoing it now.

The guard, having bent over backward to avoid appearing officious or unkind, belatedly seemed to realize that the current circumstances called for just such an attitude. He pushed them back into the corridor and said, "That remains to be seen. You run along now and I'll tell Dr. Mbele he needs to call home. You'd better be there to talk for your mama."

As they skittered out of the building, another team arrived. Mbele was among them, Jubal saw. He wished he could signal the man, but he wasn't sure how far the scientist was prepared to help them anyway, even for Beulah's sake. Then he did a double take. He recognized someone else too: Dr. Vlast, the vet from Hood Station. How had he gotten here so fast? Of course, he'd come on a GG transport! It would have been granted priority landing and would have escaped the giant traffic jam. The vet could have come all the way from Hood Station during the time the *Ranzo* had been waiting to land.

Dr. Vlast was surrounded by government types. He looked busy and preoccupied and not a bit happy about being there. He didn't see Jubal and Jubal didn't try to get his attention as the group moved into the building.

At the fountain, Jubal was deeply disappointed to see that Janina, her crewmates, and Beulah had been joined by only a half dozen other people. None of the media people Beulah knew were there yet. "A fuel transport collided with a cargo vessel over Galisouth," Beulah told them. "That's the story everyone is after. We'll have to wait for a slower news day."

"Hadley may not have that long," Sosi said.

Janina looked like she was going to start crying. Jubal said, "On the way out of the building, we saw your vet friend Vlast."

She looked startled, then hopeful, then glum again. "They'll have forced him to come," she said. "That's what they've done historically anyway—traded the vets around so the resident vet can return to what clients are left without having them angry with him. I wish I could contact him. He's bound to be miserable about all this."

"Why can't you?" Jubal asked. "We can show you where he is."

CHAPTER 17

When the children showed her the building, Janina entered and the guard stood to intercept her. "Sorry, miss, only authorized personnel beyond this point."

"I'm looking for my brother," she said. "Dr. Jared Vlast of Hood Space Station."

The lift opened and a herd of hazmat-suited personnel lumbered out of it and toward the outer door. The smell of urine, feces, and fear overlaid with antiseptic spilled down the shaft and through the lift's open door behind them. A small portion of that smell would be Chessie's. Janina couldn't bear it.

"I can take a message," the guard said.

"Could you tell him now?" she asked, her voice trembling a little. "I haven't seen him in weeks and my ship is scheduled for departure. Tell him Janina is here, please."

"You'll have to wait outside," the guard said. "Sorry, those are the rules."

"I—I'll be there. By the door," she replied, and retreated to the not entirely fresh air outside, trembling with her own boldness, with anticipation at perhaps seeing Jared again, and with anguish at the thought of her beautiful, gentle Chessie trapped at the source of the stench.

But she stood staring at the reflective tint of the doors, wishing she could see more of the inside. Jubal had drawn their little group a rough sketch of the building's layout. The lab was on the fourth floor, he said.

Imagining the lab's location made her picture what might be happening to the cats within it, and she shook her head to dislodge all of her pitiful fancies of what those poor animals might be enduring.

The doors retracted, and there, looking weary and red around the eyes, was Jared. She wished she had had the time or the spirit to dress up a bit before this, but Jared looked as if he hadn't slept well in days and was in no mood to notice.

She stepped up to meet him and could not resist the urge to put her arms around him and hug him, since he looked as miserable as she felt. To her surprise, he held her even closer and brought his hand up to the back of her head to keep it against his shoulder.

"I've seen Chessie," he told her. "She's fine. I'll not let anyone hurt her if I can help it, Jannie. I promise."

"But if there's an epidemic . . ." she said.

"There is no epidemic—no more than the glitter effect you and I have already observed in the secretions of animals who eat the beetles, as your little Chester so clearly demonstrated to us back at the clinic. This is all about ranching rivalry and politics. Varley told me all about it before I ever received any directives from the GHS."

He went on to tell her how the import of the wild pintos had upset the balance of power between Varley's friend and the relative of a GHS official, causing the relative to claim, falsely, that the glittery secretions were the early sign of an epidemic so the horses would be impounded.

"But that's madness!" she protested. "What about the colonists who will be ruined, the innocent animals who will be destroyed? Surely our government does not condone such corruption and cruelty!"

"Not openly, of course," he said sadly. He had released her but retained a hard grip on both of her hands. He was clearly angry.

"Sorry to disillusion you, but the welfare of animals and those who raise them is a very low priority with most officials."

"Dr. Vlast," the guard said from the doorway. "You're needed back in the laboratory, sir."

"Coming," Jared said over his shoulder. "I'll try to see you again," he told her. "I'll leave a message with the *Molly Daise* when I'll be free again. I'll do my best to save Chessie, no matter what."

But that was very cold comfort to Janina. She loved Chessie very much, but the thought of all of the other innocent creatures being destroyed over political game-playing sickened her.

Jared was back inside the building before she remembered she had wanted to tell him about the derelict ship and its strange feline inhabitant and the seeming abduction of Chester.

CHESTER ABOARD THE PYRAMID SHIP

Pshaw-Ra launched into his story and I was hooked. I sat with my tail curled around my paws and my eyes half shut, ears tilted forward, as he spoke.

"Long ago, when there was One Sun and One Sky, our feline kind was worshipped by a clever and industrious race of two-leggeds. We all lived in a hot country along a flowing river, the only such place for hundreds of miles. The rest of the country was desert and pretty much useless, but where we lived it was lush and fertile and teeming with prey for us and game for our followers. For our purposes, it was the world, the only world, and we were content.

"Then the two-leggeds got distracted from paying us homage and waged war on one another instead. Persians, Hittites, Greeks, Romans, yada yada yada, they all came and took over our poor country. The last race to descend upon us were the Diggers, who disinterred our ancestors, both feline and human, and carried them from the tombs where they were supposed to find eternal rest into foreign places where their mummies could be defiled and turned into litter.

"After many years, the descendants of the original two-leggeds recognized that the error of their ways, the adulation of less worthy beings and goals, had led to their downfall. They begged our forgiveness and once more paid us homage. This did not make them any more popular with their less enlightened enemies. At last our two-leggeds and our illustrious selves were banished from the sight of the One Sun in a vessel that took us to a new world. Or so those who inherited our old land believed. The truth was, our race— yours and mine—had long ago dwelt beyond the One Sun. It was our ancient wisdom that made the Two Lands great.

"To the surprise and delight of our followers, the new world was far from being a punishment. It was wondrous, an entire planet we might call our own, with a climate lush and fertile as our riverine lands had been. The game in our new home was, for the most part, imported along with our worthy selves, but there were also a few indigenous life-forms, just small ones, that neither our two-leggeds nor their skyborne overlords noticed. One among these species was able to breed with the dung beetles sacred to our people, the ones we brought with us, and from the mating evolved the even more sacred and revered—and delicious, of course—kefer-ka, commonly called the Bug of Becoming among my people."

"Becoming what?" I asked. Pshaw-Ra laid his big pointy ears back a bit and showed his fangs. He didn't like being interrupted and let me know in no uncertain terms that he thought mine a stupid question.

"Becoming One!"

"One what?" I asked. But now I was playing with him. I had a good idea what eating the shiny bugs did, at least for me. It made me one—sort of—with the boy.

He did not answer for some time but started washing his chest and shoulders as if I were not there. Long loving licks from the base of his throat, as high as he could reach, down to his belly, his rough tongue easily smoothing his sleek fur. Hah! I'd like to have seen him do that with a soft fine coat of slightly curly fur such as mine was becoming.

I moved my front paws a fraction forward in the direction of the fishie treats. He didn't notice. Another fraction. From beneath his top whiskers he sent me a baleful glare. "Do not start with me, un-sanctified son of a ship's cat. I am Pshaw-Ra, ancient mariner of the stars, light-bringer to the universe, and I will smack you so hard you'll spin around and swallow your own tail."

I was young but I was already as large as he was. He might be old but he was small and slim, whereas my entire race tended toward substantial size. Fighting with Git's get throughout my land-bound days had made me tough, I believed, and my youth made me quick. Not nearly quick enough, as it turned out. I put my right front paw one claw length forward and found myself knocked two cat lengths back against the bulkhead of Pshaw-Ra's small cabin. My cheek smarted, my whiskers ached, and I was sure my poor little tufted ear was shredded.

I ran for the exit, for the comfort of Kibble, who would take me back to Mother to wash it all better. But the long twisting cat tunnel was dark and full of crawling things. I clawed at the closed opening, crying to be released from my imprisonment with this strange vicious beast who picked on poor little helpless kittens, but no one answered. My sharp ears heard no movement. My sensitive nose detected no smell but the mustiness of the corridor, the odor of Pshaw-Ra, and an intoxicating aroma that reminded me of both salmon and catnip.

If only my boy were out there instead of Kibble, he would have heeded my cries. I scratched until my claws shredded and my paws ached. I cried myself hoarse but no response came until I felt teeth close on the tip of my beautiful tail.

"Monster!" I cried, whirling as fast as I could in the narrow darkness of the corridor. "Fiend! Wild canine in a cat coat! You tricked me! Let me out of here now so I can return to my ship."

"Your ship is far away, son. Did you not hear the cries of your provider? Did you not feel my vessel free itself of the bondage beam? What are you complaining about? You were dissatisfied with the female, the ship, and even the company of your own mother. I took that from your thoughts."

"You did?" I sat back on my haunches and licked my sore paws, my sore face, my poor little ear that had a tiny torn place just above the fluffy tuft adorning its center.

"I can do such things, can read your wishes, intentions, disappointments, and dreads as well as the thoughts you send me," Pshaw-Ra said proudly, blinking his shining gold-coin eyes shut, so that for a nanosecond the darkness was unrelieved. I could tell he expected me to be impressed, but what I had actually meant—as he would have known if he were as good as he claimed—was that I didn't realize he could do it *too*. I'd been reading thoughts—and the thoughts under thoughts—my entire life. "What is the use of my ancient and all-encompassing wisdom without a suitable pupil to receive my teachings? You will do."

Some wise teacher! He had missed the obvious. I didn't want to be there. So I made it easy for him to understand, punctuating each thought with a yowl. "I want out! I want my boy. I want my mother. I want my ship, and I even want Kibble."

"You want a nap. You are getting sleepy. Very sleepy," he said, and his mind-voice became as soft as my fur, his purr so persuasive and soothing that I fell into a deep sleep.

ʼ ʼ ʼ

Jubal, Sosi, Janina, and the *Molly Daise* crew, even the captain, made signs, and with Beulah's help, wrote press releases and flyers demanding that the results of the tests on the impounded animals be made public, along with the supporting data. They drew up a petition and put Sosi in charge of it.

Other crews joined them, and a few disgruntled pet owners, but Galipolis was not agricultural country. The city people who had animals didn't depend on them for a livelihood as folks on Sherwood did, Jubal realized. And of the crews, the ones on GG ships didn't dare protest or they'd lose their jobs. Some crews, like Pop's old friends—even some aboard the *Ranzo*—were disinclined to draw official scrutiny to their existence, much less their opinions.

Even Beulah stayed away. Jubal had been amazed, after all she'd done to help, and when he knew she loved Hadley too, but his redheaded friend shook her head. "Sorry, kid. I've got shopping to do. Give 'em hell for me too," she said.

A cold rain drizzled down on the protesters as they gathered in front of the lab building. Those still clad in shipsuits were protected, but the rain soaked through caps and hair and chilled them from the top down. It made the lettering on their signs run and softened the cardboard so it flopped from the sticks they were stapled to.

People hurried past them, hoods raised to protect their heads from the rain, ignoring the protestors when they tried to press flyers into their hands. Sosi's well-rehearsed tears moved no one— who could tell the tears from the rain?

A Guard transport buzzed them, a few feet over their heads, then returned, and hovered for several minutes, during which time no one walked by, no flyers were handed out, no petitions signed. Just like the rest of the time they'd been there.

The passing transport blew more rain down upon their heads. Moments later coms began beeping, buzzing, and dinging.

Sosi fumbled for hers and said, "Yes, Dad. Okay. Yes. It's not doing any good anyway."

Indu listened to hers then said to the others, "Sorry, folks, but we've been ordered to depart."

"I can't leave yet," Janina told her crewmates.

"Have to," Indu told her. "We've been ordered to vacate our docking berth to make way for the other ships waiting to dock. Shore leaves have been cancelled."

"Then you all go on without me," she said. "As you said on Sherwood, if there's no cat, there's no need for a Cat Person. My place is as near to Chessie as I can get."

White-haired Mick touched her arm. "You can't help her, Kibble. You can't get near her. The government isn't going to risk—"

"They're not risking anything!" she replied hotly. "It's all a sham. Jared told me."

"Jared Vlast, the vet?" Indu asked.

Jubal moved closer to hear them over the traffic and the raindrops.

"Yes, he talked to Mr. Varley just before the orders came down to impound the animals. It's all to appease a member of the board whose nephew didn't want Mr. Varley's friend to have the wild horses we found on Sherwood."

"They can't do that, can they?" Jubal asked.

"Apparently they can," Indu said.

"Even if we could interest someone in launching an investigation, it would take weeks, maybe months, or longer," Mick said. "Chessie could die of old age in that cage before the GG changes its mind."

"What we want doesn't matter," Bennie said bitterly. "Our affection for Chessie, our investment in her, all small potatoes where the GG is concerned."

Jubal threw his sign down in disgust and stalked away from the group.

Sosi ran after him, the clipboard with the soggy petition clutched against her.

"Jubal, where are you going? You have to come back to the ship now."

He ran away from her, not wanting her to see him cry. He couldn't believe how awful everything was. His mom had always led him to believe his old man was a terrible person, and he had pretty much believed her. But Pop was an amateur compared to the GG.

"Psst, kid," a voice said from a market alleyway as Jubal stumbled past. "Wanna buy a hot cat?"

There was the old man in his desert trader disguise, lifting the inner edge of his robe so Doc's whiskered face popped out.

Jubal stepped up to him, covering the opening in the robe with his body, and reached out to give Doc a scritch. The little guy was trembling.

"The part where he understands what's going on by getting into my head is hard on him," Pop said, closing the robe over the kitten again. "Your average cat would be clueless and not give a damn, but he knows what's up and it scares the hell out of him. How did your big protest go?"

"Not so hot. The only attention we got was from the Guard, who told their bosses, who ordered the ships to scram and take us with them."

Pop shrugged. "They're inclined to overreact about stuff like this."

"Yeah," Jubal said, "Especially when it's all a load of cow crap." He told him about Janina's conversation with the vet regarding the origins of the so-called epidemic.

"He got this from Varley, did he? About the broken-color mustangs?" the old man asked, wearing what Jubal's mom called his shifty expression. It was as close as he came to looking guilty.

"Yes, sir."

All his father said was, "Hmmm. Well, you'd best get back to the *Ranzo*."

"Can't I stay with you?"

"No, but can you take Doc to your girlfriend for me? The goons got her cat already so they won't be looking for cats on the *Ranzo*. I have to do a lot of moving around now and it would be all too easy, and inconvenient, for me to get caught with him on me, not to mention unhealthy for him."

But Doc clung to Pop with all four sets of claws and meowed and yowled while presenting his arguments about why he should be allowed to stay. Finally Pop tucked him back into his robe and said with a shrug, "He's prepared to take his chances, and he's still a cat, after all. Can't argue with the damn things." He patted the lump under his robe affectionately and Jubal heard a satisfied purr. "Now you take off before someone wonders where the meows were coming from."

"What will you do?"

His dad grinned through his grizzled whiskers. "Why, what I do best, boy. Stir up trouble."

"So what do you do out here in space, other than convince ships you're in trouble and then kidnap cats who come to save your sorry tail?"

"Have you not guessed? I have a great mission."

"Do tell. And what would that be?"

"Nothing less than universal domination, of course. It's always been the primary mission of our species. I'm surprised you tame cats have allowed yourselves to forget that."

"Watch who you're calling tame, you short-haired nut job," I snarled. "I'll have you know my mother is from an illustrious line of highly respected specialized security personnel for space vessels. Our kind dominate everything it's useful to dominate already. What point is there in controlling more than your own people, your own place, and your own life?"

Pshaw-Ra made a sound like he was starting to spit up a hairball and turned his back, flipping his tail at me as he strolled back up the cat corridor to his cabin. "You truly know nothing of life, catling. Until we achieve universal domination, someone else will always control all other aspects of our lives."

Oh, no. This cat truly was one sun short of a solar system. He had been in space too long and lost it. And I was stuck with him.

Lucky me. Ow! He was the only companion I had and I was the only one he had. I had to keep him talking, not so much to learn his nefarious scheme as to keep from getting bored between naps and snacks. What could it hurt? Either I would acquire the necessary insight to outwit him and escape to another ship, or I would become as crazed as he was, in which case I wouldn't mind how weird his ideas were.

I followed him back to the cabin, grabbed a couple of the remaining fishie treats, and settled down with my front paws tucked under my chest and my tail curled around me. I couldn't help noticing that it really was a wonderful tail. I raised and lowered its tip and addressed Pshaw-Ra. "Okay, so you're going to dominate the universe. How?"

"Why, by introducing the kefer-ka to the unenlightened. Once a cat has partaken of the flesh of the kefer-ka, the mystical properties of the sacred insect enter the eater's bloodline. The offspring of those who ingest the kefer-ka thereby obtain the power to understand the thoughts of other species. They will also, in many cases, be able to begin universal domination by enthralling at least one susceptible member of the currently dominant species, those who have also partaken of the kefer-ka, either directly or through their food chain."

"You mean anyone who eats the shiny bugs, directly or indirectly—like by eating something else that ate them—becomes a part of your scheme?"

"If you must oversimplify, yes."

"And this person us bug-eaters or sons of bug-eaters are supposed to enthrall, how does it happen for them?"

"That human will come to understand your heart and mind, and you will understand his in a profound bond between the two of you. In most cases the bond will be love. Its intensity will range from affection to adoration but will, for the most part, allow the clever cat to bend the human to his or her will."

"Well, then, you can let me out at the next ship. I've eaten the bug, as has my mother before me. I don't know if the boy has or not, but he loves me. I need to find him if I'm going to get back to dominating him or whatever, because your scheme does not work beyond a certain distance."

"Ah, but you have other uses. Since the time when most of our attendants were taken to other planets, our feline civilization, once flourishing, is now diminishing. The purity of our bloodlines may prove our undoing. We require an infusion of genetic material from an unaffiliated breed whose superb qualities may be enhanced by our own."

Breeding and mousing, mousing and breeding. Was that all life was about? It seemed everyone who claimed to want me, with the exception of the boy, only did so because of the vermin I could catch or the kittens I could produce. What about *this* kitten? I wanted to ask them. Aren't you missing a step here? Shouldn't you be paying proper attention to how amazing I am, to what I am doing and what I want right now, before you skip straight to the next generation? I didn't even feel any particular urge to breed yet. Hsst!

"We are all mere links in the great chain of feline divinity," Pshaw-Ra said, then licked his shoulder. "Except me, of course. I'm actually rather special."

"So are we headed back there, to your planet, so you can introduce me to the ladies?" I asked.

"All in good time, my son, all in good time. You are my first acolyte, the first worthy of being recruited, as you alone of all of the ships' cats I've encountered have benefited from the gifts of the kefer-ka. On our great journey we shall encounter other ships with other cats, and these we will draw unto us, recruiting the best, brightest, and most beautiful to join our ranks."

"Like you recruited me?"

"Preferably with less mewling and yowling," Pshaw-Ra said. "But for now, we sleep, we dream, and in our dreams we travel, seeking the minds of others of our kind and drawing them to us."

We would draw them to us as he had drawn me—and Kibble—
to him, trying to save him. I just felt so betrayed, so violated, so
used. So sleepy, suddenly. Nestling my head into the cradle of my
own paws, I fell into a deep sleep.

I don't know how long I slept before I dreamed of the ship. I became aware of it as a distant dot. As it grew larger, Pshaw-Ra entered my dream. "Do you sense a cat? I don't sense a cat. What
kind of ship is that with no cat? I thought all of your ships had cats
now, but this one has no cat."

He was right. There was something empty and sterile about the
ship and the funny thing was, although I did not find a cat in my
dream, I suddenly saw a young human sitting on her bunk weep-
ing, hugging a pillow to her and stroking it with her hand. The
ship had no cat, but it had a Cat Person.

The dream Pshaw-Ra spat in disgust. "Useless!" he said, sitting
down to wash beneath his dream tail.

"Not really," I told him. "That girl needs a cat. Your ship says
that we—or at least you—are here. If the ship sees us, and she
comes to rescue us, she will probably bring more fishie treats, just
as Janina did. That would be good, wouldn't it?"

"You do not fool me, catling. You wish her to come so you may
escape on her vessel. I was not born yesterday, you know. I am ancient and wise to all manner of subterfuge."

I thought the ship would probably stop anyway, and intended to
do exactly as he suspected and hitch a ride back to it with the girl.
But the dream ended with the ship gliding past our pointy pyramid
vessel.

"Hey! That's not the custom!" I said. "They're supposed to stop
when they see the Cat on Board sign, whether they have a cat or
not."

It became evident to us both over the course of our naps, our
waking moments, our meals, our snoozes, our snacks, our rest pe-
riods, our games (he wasn't as intriguing to chase as my own tail
but his moves were somewhat less predictable), and our sleeps,

that the custom had changed. More of the sterile, cheerless, catless ships passed us and none slowed, engaged us in their tractor beams, or made any attempt to see if we were indeed aboard and adrift as advertised.

Pshaw-Ra was perplexed. "Are you somehow warning them away?" he demanded. "Because this has never happened to me before. The ships always stop and try to save me, but I hide while they try to find me. They sometimes leave behind offerings of food, and the kefer-ka return with them to their ships."

"So that's how you spread the bugs," I said. "But I haven't warned anybody. How could I when there's no other cat on board?"

But then the day came when another ship approached. Its course seemed in opposition to the ones we'd been encountering. It had a cat on board. This time when Pshaw-Ra entered into his dream state to board the ship, I easily entered into it with him. I could not understand how I was able to do this, until we entered into the dream mind of the other cat and saw his world. Then I understood that I had an inherent connection that must have given me an advantage. Across his dish was inscribed his name: SPACE JOCKEY. My sire.

The dish looked as if it had just been filled, crunchy nuggets of the Barque Cat fleet's favorite mealtime treat mounding gently in the middle. In another corner of the room a sparkly pond of clear, fresh (for a spaceship) water shimmered with the very slight vibration of the ship's propulsion system, beckoning, beckoning. A comfy, fluffy bed lay empty. In the dream, I looked out from the shadows. Above me was the rectangular berth of the CP, in front of me a barricade of cat toys.

I won't let them take me, my sire was thinking. I was unsure whether he was dreaming that he was hiding or whether he actually was and I was picking up his thoughts rather than his dreams. But I could feel his fury and his fear. *After all I've done for them, how can they treat me like this? They think I don't know, but I overheard them on the com to Galipolis. Impound, they said. My orderly argued against it, but he is of very low rank, despite the fact that he is my only human voice among the crew. No more valuable kittens, he said, and then the captain told him that my offspring were being impounded too, and my entire harem of cosmic queens. They think we're infected with something. They want to "test" us. But my orderly asked if they would then return us, and the captain shook his head. "Not likely, Freeman," he said. "If he's not infected when they take him to the lab, after the contact with the contaminated beasts, he will be."*

Nobody knows this ship like I do. As soon as someone opens this door, I will hide where they'll never find me. I'll miss my regular feedings but I can live on those delicious shiny bugs. There seem to be more since the last station. Besides, if I eat them all up, then my ship will be clean of them and the impound people won't bother us. Yes, that's what I'll do. As soon as someone opens this door. Then I'll hide and they'll never find me until I'm ready.

Then Space Jockey and his ship faded into my old nightmare of the field behind the barn on Sherwood and the wild canine carrying Git in his mouth.

"Another one passed us by without attempting to board," Pshaw-Ra observed aloud, interrupting my sleep.

"Just as well since they'd have to turn us over for impound with the rest of the ships' cats," I told him, surprised to find that he had not picked this up for himself. "You mean you didn't get that? I thought you read everyone and knew everything."

"Of course I did," he said, stretching. "I was testing you."

"Sure you were," I replied. "We're going to be out here for an eternity all by ourselves if this keeps up. I think universal domination may take a bit longer than you planned."

"You've fraternized with humans far more than I have. What is this impound like?"

"I think it's fatal," I said. "At least, my sire seems to think so. My mother has always said he is a very brash and bold cat, a fighter, but he was frightened. Was going into hiding. Impound must be a very bad thing. I think it's got to do with what I overheard the vet and Kibble talking about—a disease. I showed them that what worried them came just from eating the shiny bugs—the kefer-ka, as you call them. But someone seems to have decided those are dangerous too and is trying to impound them as well."

"Hmmm," Pshaw-Ra said, finishing his stretch. "What a nuisance. I had forgotten how troublesome humans can be."

"Don't you have any humans where you come from?"

"Only a few, the ones who were too devoted to us to leave when the rest of their people were resettled on other worlds. Ours recognized that they would be unable to lead full and satisfying lives without us and stayed put. Many of us were worried when the majority of the people and a lot of the cats were taken away, but in truth it served as a selection process. Only the most intelligent, discerning, sensitive, and loyal humans remained with us, and those served us well. We for our part dealt with them generously, allowing them to stroke our fur, granting them purrs on occasion, and permitting audiences at the ends of our naps."

"It doesn't sound much different from what we do," I said.

"Ah, but our attendants never dreamt of trying to impound us. They submitted to us in all things. Eventually."

I yawned. Submission took all the fun out of things, in my experience. When things submitted, it usually meant they were dead. Gone was the chase, the bounce and the pounce, the leap, the catch, the wrestling it to the floor. Submissive things didn't initiate games, bring unexpected treats, or open new doors. I was surprised that Pshaw-Ra set so much store by it.

"You are very very young," he told me, answering the thought I had not shared with him. "One day you will learn that you can enjoy nothing if you do not control it enough to guarantee that it does not betray you."

Being in that ship with that old cat and his warnings was so boring that I slept a great deal, feeling my tail and fur grow longer and my life shrink to the size of that small cabin and corridor. Ships came with anxious cats who knew something bad was about to happen to them. Ships went, empty, sterile, sad, and catless.

I suggested we enter no more dreams. The men who impounded other cats might come for us too if we brought ourselves to their attention. Pshaw-Ra reset our course for his own world. We might as well enjoy shore leave while the rest of the universe went mad. Dispirited by the increasingly catless void of space, I slept.

And unbidden, when I had all but given up hope, my boy came to me at last.

CHAPTER 19

Jubal spent the first day out of Galipolis fuming and frustrated. Sosi burst into tears in the middle of chores and would not be distracted. Her grief for Hadley was noisy and angry, and it made him feel worse than ever about Chester, not to mention Chessie, the kittens, and the rest of the poor impounded animals.

He was also bitterly disappointed that Pop had not chosen to honor his contract with the *Ranzo*, but had gone off doing whatever it was that Pop did when he thought no one was looking. At least now he'd have Doc riding herd on him, if he didn't find the kitten inconvenient and abandon him somewhere or give him up to the GG goons. Jubal didn't see how he could, but then, you never knew with the old man. Meanwhile, Pop had what Jubal wished he still had: someone to keep him company, to do stuff with him, read with him, help him figure things out, as well as all the regular cat things like sleeping beside him and purring, licking his face and hands sometimes.

When Jubal had finished his chores, he threw himself onto his bunk and fell asleep.

He awoke—or thought he did—when he felt paws land on the end of his bunk and walk across his legs. Hadley used to do that sometimes, but Hadley was gone. And then, as he came more fully awake, he knew that these were not Hadley paws marching across his calves. The cat that belonged to those paws was lighter and stepped more quickly than Hadley. The feel of this cat, although he weighed a ton compared to what he had before, was much more, wonderfully more, familiar.

"Chester?" Jubal said, rolling carefully onto his back and opening his eyes. There was no cat there, not physically. But he felt Chester's presence more strongly than he ever had since they'd been forced apart.

"Prrt," Chester's voice said clearly, and the invisible paws leaped from his legs and onto the cabin floor, trotting to the door.

Jubal followed and opened the door. Trying to understand what was happening, why he was suddenly aware of the cat as he had not been for so many weeks, he had a terrible thought. Had Chester been impounded and killed? Was this a cat ghost returning to say good-bye?

A claw through the lower leg of his shipsuit trousers goaded him forward. He had the sense that there wasn't much time. The paws padded up the carpeted corridor, and periodic nudges—mental ones and seemingly physical ones—led him to the *Ranzo*'s bridge. The crew was tired after the exhausting inspection and enforced shore leave, reloading the ship and threading it back through the heavy traffic orbiting the planet and circling the city. Once the course was set and the *Ranzo* was back in space, the bridge crew could doze at their duty stations. The first officer and navigator sat with their heads thrown back against the backs of their chairs, snoring. Beulah cradled her head in her arms and leaned across her console, her back rising and falling slightly with her breathing.

The invisible cat feet hopped across the console, and a cat shadow was outlined against the forward viewscreen. Jubal saw it then. It was very small, in the distance, another ship.

He touched the zoom control and the ship shot forward, into his face. A derelict, drifting and dark, but the COB sign, along with the outline of a sitting cat, was outlined against it.

You want me to save that cat, Chester? Is that why you're here?

It was. Emphatically. And in a rush, Janina's story of losing Chester on a strange derelict came back to Jubal. Before he could reach up to touch the silky cool fur that brushed his cheek, the cat shadow leaped through the viewport, into the derelict, and shrank as the zoom reversed.

Beulah had awakened and was staring at him.

"What is it, Jubal?"

"Chester. He's on that derelict out there, Beulah. He wants me to come and get him."

"Jubal, you can't—"

"No, really. He is. Janina lost him there. There's another cat."

"We'd just have to give him up again, Jubal. He's better off out there."

"No. No, he's not. He wants us to come and get him."

"You can't know that, honey."

"But I do. I *do*. Please, Beulah. Please help us. There's got to be a way for us to do it. Please. We have to try. He'll starve to death if we just leave him."

"The GG goons will take him off to that lab if you don't leave him," Beulah said with a sleepy sigh that actually reminded him a little of a cat waking up.

"I've gotta go, Beulah. He knows I'm here. He came to get me."

"Where is he?" Sosi asked.

"Not you too!" Beulah said.

"Hadley came. I felt him jump up on my bed," Sosi said.

"It was Chester," Jubal told her. "He came looking for me."

"I don't think so. Where is he? I'm sure it was Hadley."

"He went back to his spaceship." Jubal pointed. The ship was nearer their position now.

"How?"

Jubal shrugged. "I was telling Beulah I need to go get him or at least take him more food."

"I'm going too."

By now Captain Loloma had awakened too, and he waved his hands for them to calm down. "Whoa. I'll have no mutiny aboard this vessel. Understood?"

"Daddy, look. There's a Cat on Board sign."

"Honey, we'd just have to give that cat up too if we rescued it."

"But we can't just let it starve, Daddy. It's already isolated on its ship. Can't we just take it some food and water?"

"It may have run out of oxygen," her father said, not unkindly. "It would just upset you again. No more cats."

"Captain, the cat came to the kids in a dream," Beulah said. "Jubal thinks the cat he lost is on board. There *is* some corroborative evidence from the *Molly Daise*'s CP, Janina."

"A dream?" To Jubal's surprise, the captain did not dismiss this as nonsense. He rubbed his chin with one hand, considering, and gave his daughter a look Jubal didn't understand but that seemed to indicate that the two of them placed more than the ordinary emphasis on dreams.

Sosi nodded gravely and put her hand on his sleeve.

"Yes, sir," Jubal said, backing her up. "We both felt paws land on our bed. And in the dream Chester had me follow him to the bridge to show me the ship, then he jumped through the viewscreen and back aboard the derelict."

"Well, you could just go see if the cats are all right, I guess," the captain said. "Beulah, you go."

"Begging your pardon, sir, but he's my cat," Jubal said. "I need to go too."

"Me too," Sosi said. "*I'm* the Cat Person. It's my job."

"I cannot ask my com officer to babysit you two on an away mission."

"It's okay, sir. They'll be a lot more trouble if we don't let them go," Beulah said. "I'll take responsibility. Besides, Jubal will come in handy if I have any difficulty. He's very good with repair and maintenance."

The captain waved his assent with a couple of back flips of his fingers, then woke up the navigator to have her alter the course to intercept the derelict and capture it in the tractor beam.

Meanwhile, Beulah, Sosi, and Jubal, after scouring the stores for unopened bags of Hadley's favorite kibble, some treats, and sippy containers of water, plus an extra tank of it, scrambled to the shuttle and into their survival suits and grav boots. Hauling the cat provisions on board, they awaited the command from the bridge.

For Jubal, except for the dream and the fact that there were three of them instead of just Janina and Chester, so far the whole incident echoed what Janina had told him about her mission to the ship.

"It looks normal on the outside," he told Beulah, "but Janina says that once you leave the shuttle bay, it's a lot smaller than it looks, and funny shaped."

＊ ＊ ＊

It was different taking the shuttle from the ship to the derelict, scarier, blacker, the stars more distant than simply going from a space station to a planet and back again. Beulah avoided the tractor beam on the way out, entering it only to access the hatch to the docking bay.

"Normally we would bring the derelict in close and use accordion tube to connect the hatches," she told Sosi and Jubal, "since we'd worry that the bay on the other ship might be damaged. But according to what Janina told you kids, it's safe enough. Besides, the captain doesn't want us recontaminated. It's going to take several good trips as it is to repay the cost of that hosing down they gave us in Galipolis."

"*They* took my cat and *we* have to pay *them*?" Sosi demanded indignantly.

Jubal quelled his excitement at the prospect of seeing Chester again long enough to flash on what would be happening to his neighbors—and Mom too—back on Sherwood. "Oh, that's not the worst of it. On Sherwood they'll be impounding or killing outright all the animals the farmers and ranchers need to make a living—trillions of credits worth, and maybe burning the crops as well. And expecting the owners to pay for being ruined."

"That's so not fair!" Sosi protested as the derelict's hatch opened smoothly and the shuttle settled down in the darkness with a bump. The running lights illuminated the smallest docking bay Jubal had seen on what had appeared to be a full-sized ship. One other shuttle was docked there, small and triangular-shaped, gleaming like gold in their lights. Beulah tested the air quality outside. "We don't need the helmets. There's plenty of O_2 so your Chester is probably still alive, Jubal."

"Yeah, I know," he said, surprised that she'd doubted it when he and Sosi had both told her they'd just seen him—sort of.

Beulah had them wrap the cat supplies in a cargo net and they pushed the bundle out ahead of them, where it floated like a bubble while they clumped onto the deck in their gravity boots. Jubal kept back a packet of treats for Chester, to show him how glad he was to see him.

Jubal was the first one out. Grabbing the net with one finger of his glove, he pulled it behind him and up the corridor until, as Janina had said, he met a blank wall. "Chester?" he asked, and mentally called, *Hey, buddy, it's me. Where are you?*

CHESTER ABOARD THE PYRAMID SHIP

I knew it was him, of course. I'd drawn him to us, hadn't I? But I couldn't answer just then. It didn't suit *my* scheme for domination, not of the universe, but of the cat door.

I pretended to sleep. Pshaw-Ra hissed at me, "Silly catling, the boy and his friends are here. With food. Will you not greet them?"

I yawned. "Not right now. He abandoned me to the vet. Let him stew. I'm sleeping. It's your ship. You go get the food."

He waved his sinuous tail with a purr of satisfaction. "My teachings have already taken root in a mind fertilized with betrayal and disappointment."

I opened one eye and looked annoyed. "Look, I lured them here to replenish our supplies but it was hard work and I'm tired, so could you please do what you must do quietly?"

He finally did what I was waiting for. Pretending to stretch, he placed his front paws among the hieroglyphics. One pressed the symbol for cat, the other a triangular-shaped symbol, probably signifying the ship, I guessed. From down the corridor came a slight hiss, one I heard only because I was sleeping with my ear on the deck.

Pshaw-Ra sauntered down the corridor until he was out of view, around one of the twists, then he picked up speed. I heard the patty-pat of his paws turn to thuds as he galloped toward the opening and the food. The old faker was more worried than he'd appeared when fresh supplies hadn't been forthcoming from passing ships. Although I had not been able to go back into the hold through the cat hatch since I joined Pshaw-Ra, my host had apparently made raids while I was sleeping to avail himself of the supplies Kibble had brought. That was the only explanation I could think of, because when I awakened from my naps and dreams, the food dishes had been filled—though I had no idea how Pshaw-Ra could have done it—and a little fountain trickled fresh water down into a trough along one wall. It tasted like the water on the *Molly Daise*. For fresher food we had the kefer-ka. I was not witness to any of his supply trips, so this was the first time I observed him making his exit. Before, he'd been as quiet as a mouse. Oh, a mouse! I could have really gone for one right then, but this ship had none, and besides, I had a more urgent mission.

Pshaw-Ra would be close to the opening now. I crept into the corridor, slinking down it as if stalking prey. When I beheld my host's lean shanks and twitching tail as he teased my boy from the opening in the wall, I flung myself forward, knocked him away from the hatch, tail over ears, and leaped straight through until I floated over Jubal's head.

He reached up and pulled me down. "Chester!"

It took you long enough, I said, my whole being vibrating with the force of my purrs. He started to pull off his gloves to pet me, but he was not alone. A woman and a girl were there too, the girl stamping her gravity boots with frustration as Pshaw-Ra eluded her grasp.

"Jubal, no," the woman said. "I know you want to pet him, but decontaminating your suit will be easier than decontaminating you. If we do this smart, Captain Loloma may let us return to bring them more supplies. He might even agree to tow their vessel out of the way of the GG, somewhere we can find them again and check on them. But we can't cause trouble."

"No trouble," my boy told her. "Sorry, Beulah, but if Chester can't come with us, I'll stay here with him and his friend. I'm not leaving him again."

"You can't do that!" the woman said. "You'd exhaust their oxygen and water supplies and there's no food for you here."

"I don't care. I don't want to go back where they treat anybody with four legs like they're disposable. As valuable as Chessie is, they took her, and Hadley too. And it's all a big lie!"

Mother? They were going to kill Mother? The whole situation, as I read it in Jubal's mind, was wrong. Just wrong. My mother and our kind had worked in partnership with humans, and now were to be destroyed for no more than a convenient ruse to assure the dominance of one human over another.

"Come back, kitty!" the girl — Sosi, according to Jubal — cried. I looked away from Jubal's face as Pshaw-Ra's tail disappeared through the cat hatch.

CHAPTER 20

"Can't you just release them when nobody's looking?" Janina pleaded with Jared. He looked tired and as ill as the healthy animals in his charge were supposed to be. She knew he was under tremendous stress from the conflict between his duty and his inclinations. He and a vet tech were on duty that night in the central laboratory, where the Barque Cats as well as the dogs of some of the more prominent citizens were kept. The farm animals had gone to a separate facility, the house pets who were not valuable working animals to another. Jared broke security by meeting her outside the building again while the guard slept at his station.

Jared shook his head. "It would do no good. They'd only round them up again and maybe kill them on sight as health hazards to the general populace." He ran a hand through his hair, which was in need of washing and cutting. "By the government's definition, all of the animals in custody are contaminated by this terrible threat they've invented. They just haven't decided how much of a threat it's supposed to be. Every minute, I'm afraid some overly cautious pencil pusher will decide to destroy the animals just to be on the 'safe' side. I'm arguing against it and so are many others, because after all, so far no one has found anything to indicate the fairy dust effect is harmful to anyone.

"Of course, the more aggressively scientific among us want to sacrifice a few animals for further analysis, but I've been able to keep them from doing it since I've been here, so far, at least, and some of my colleagues have done the same thing at their new duty stations. I have a few allies here, but there are also some who are very eager to please the officials who started this mess. I can only hope that there are other officials who depend on their animals for a living or just love them and don't want them threatened. Some-one has to come to their senses and expose the rotten root of this madness and end it."

Janina was silent, clinging to his arm, conveying her support through her touch.

After a long moment Jared added, "Chessie is fine. I think she exerts a calming influence on the other cats, in fact—at least when I'm around—because she knows me and trusts me. I talk to her and she rubs against the wire of her cage."

"Cage?" Janina asked, her voice breaking to think of her beauti-ful, intelligent, resourceful friend caged.

"Banks and banks of them, I'm afraid," Jared said. "I'm sorry, Jannie."

They parted, and Janina walked away. The sidewalks had little traffic at this hour, since Galipolis theoretically had a proper night and day, though you could hardly tell with the sky so full of traffic all the time. The buildings were all connected by sky bridges, and had docking bays for flitters on their upper levels, so mostly only heavier, more industrial traffic used the roads, especially at night. The swooping, circling, orbiting lights from ships and shuttles waiting to dock was so heavy that it obscured the real stars and cast writhing shadows, black against darkened surfaces of streets, build-ings, and alleyways. This time of night, before the street sweeping sucker-trucks began their morning rounds, the gutters were full of debris. Hard to understand how it got there since notices against littering were posted everywhere and the penalties were heavy. On previous trips she had sometimes encountered people walking a dog, or an entire pack of dogs, and in residential districts cats had often watched at the windows or from the tops of fences, or darted across roads. Now there were no animals in evidence, of course. They would all be in cages somewhere.

She continued her walk, though her feet were sore from the uncarpeted sidewalks and streets, which were much harder to walk on than the plusher amenities of the *Molly Daise*. Indu's cousin Chandra had agreed to put Janina up in her tiny fourth-floor flat. It was a walk-up because the lift was broken. The arrangement was only intended to be temporary. Jared had suggested that he speak to his superiors about hiring her to help in the lab. But her position as a ship's CP, and the fact that she had been spotted during the protests, was against her.

There was no work for an "animal handler" elsewhere at the moment either. Should worse come to worst, she'd need to start over, find some other low-paying job here in the city or be out on the streets. Galipolis was not Sherwood. For that matter, by now Sherwood wouldn't be much like Sherwood either, with no animals and all of the farms and ranches closed down.

Formerly prosperous or at least surviving landowners and agricultural workers would be packing their own bags, looking for unaccustomed work elsewhere.

She did not think she could bear it, that Chessie and the other glorious, useful, beautiful ships' cats, and all of the gentle, trusting animals who had been reared in love and friendship, should be destroyed, murdered. The way things looked, the GHA might as well put her down too, along with a lot of other people.

Suddenly, as she passed a darkened alleyway, someone grabbed her arm, yanked hard and pulled her off balance. She tried to resist but was taken too much by surprise to remember any of the self-defense moves she'd been taught by the *Molly*'s senior crew members. Her assailant twirled her around, and she ended up with her back against the tall front of the man whose arm held her slight form firmly in place.

"Psst, look sharp, Kibble," he whispered into her ear. "If I were as bad as some of the company I keep, I'd say you would make a good victim about now, what with that hangdog expression and slumping posture."

She twisted, kicked, and tried to fight, expecting at any time he would pull a knife or a gun and beat, rob, or rape her—probably all three—when her flailing hands sent her elbow back to his chest.

"*Meyeh!*" came a protest from the vicinity of his chest.

"Hey, careful there, lady," the man said, releasing her. She started to run, but two things stopped her. One, she recognized him as the man who had accosted her at Hood Station just before Chessie was kidnapped. And two, he had stopped paying any attention to her at all. He'd opened his robe, and a pair of golden eyes peered up at him.

"You okay, little buddy?" the man asked in a soft husky voice as his big finger stroked between the shining eyes.

"Meep," the kitten replied, and began rumbling loudly enough to be heard above the traffic circling the city.

"You're the catnapper!" she accused him. "How come everyone else had to give up their cats and you were able to keep this poor kitten?"

He shrugged. "Other people play by the rules or aren't as good at breaking them as I am. And you gotta agree this little guy is better off with me than he would be in that lab with your boyfriend."

"What?"

"Jubal is my kid. He told me what your sweetie told you about this whole fiasco."

"But the kitten?"

"Never mind him. He and I are pals and none of your concern. But what I want to know, lady, is what are you and that vet going to do now to end this before this little guy's mother and—"

"His what?"

"Oops," the man said, tucking the kitten back inside his robe. "What I meant to say was, with all the cats in the blinkin' universe locked up there, this guy's mother must be among them."

"She is!" Janina accused. "That's one of Chessie's kittens, isn't it?"

The man hesitated only slightly before saying, "You caught me. If I help you help Chessie and the others, you won't try to take him back, will you?"

Suddenly finding a worthy target for her pent-up frustration, fear, and anger, Janina said, "I'm not promising you anything! You started this whole thing by burning down Jared's clinic and stealing Chessie. You nearly killed her, and now she can't have any more kittens. I think you stole the entire litter, including the one you have now. If you can help Chessie, and me and Jared, you will anyway because otherwise you and the little one will be caught and he'll be killed with the others. So stop wasting time and tell me what's on your mind."

"You're not as dumb as you look, Kibble, though you don't know the half of it," he said. "Glad to know you're on the ball. I need you to be smart and look lively. I also need you to help me talk to your boyfriend."

r r r

Jubal stood his ground, watching truculently as Beulah herded Sosi back to the shuttle.

But suddenly Chester's full weight settled onto his shoulder, just before they both fell to the deck as the ship accelerated. So much for the *Ranzo*'s tractor beam, he thought. They were on their own.

Chester bounded up the carpeted ramp to the cat hole. Jubal felt elated when he realized he could see, through Chester's eyes, into the dark corridor, all the way up the twisted passage to the tiny cabin where the skinny, short-haired, tawny-colored cat—*Pshaw-Ra*, Chester supplied the name—pawed at the controls. They looked like raised carvings of ancient hieroglyphics. The skinny cat dabbed them with his paws and bumped them with his nose in a methodical manner.

Chester asked, "What are you doing, Pshaw-Ra?"

"Leaving, of course," the other cat replied without looking at him.

"But why?"

"The humans are attempting to foil my plot for universal domination," Pshaw-Ra replied. "I must intervene before all is lost to their ignorance and superstition."

Jubal asked Chester, *What plot? Who's he calling ignorant and superstitious?*

Chester didn't answer, but instead asked Pshaw-Ra, "How do you plan to do that, exactly?"

"By stopping the foolish two-leggeds from destroying our kind and the kefer-ka. Tell our guests to make themselves comfortable. They'll be with us until I have need of them."

"I don't think they're going to like that," Chester told him, but Jubal, who had despaired that anything could be done to help the impound situation, gathered that Pshaw-Ra intended to do something about it. Furthermore, both Pshaw-Ra and Chester seemed to believe he actually could.

It's about time someone tried to do something to stop this horse manure, Jubal told Chester. *I think I've got it figured out, Chester. Pshaw-Ra is a superior alien being in cat form, isn't he? But he's a cat too and he doesn't like what's happening to the other cats?*

He thinks he's superior, Chester agreed. *But he's not exactly an alien. He's got a ship he can fly himself and does some cool telepathic tricks. But he says all cats could be like him—as if that would be a good thing.*

You think he can pull it off? Can he save Chessie and the other cats?

I have no idea. He thinks so. But then, he thinks a lot of himself. Did you bring any fishie treats with you, perchance?

Chester left Pshaw-Ra still working the controls of the ship with all four paws, his nose, and certain impossible maneuvers with his tail. The ship's cat-tain made no attempt to stop him from rejoining his boy.

Leaping from the cat hatch to land heavily on Jubal's shoulder, Chester licked the fingers that scratched his fur and took a couple of long swipes at his chest fur for good measure.

Jubal dug into his pocket for the treats. They weren't Chester's favorites, but he accepted them after a preliminary sniff, eating them from Jubal's hand.

Once the treats restored his strength, he gave greater consideration to Jubal's question. Could Pshaw-Ra do what all of those cat-less ships full of people had been unable to do?

Finally he came to the conclusion, which he shared with Jubal, that probably Pshaw-Ra did know something that would help. It would only be fair if he did, in Chester's opinion, because the skinny cat and something called the kefer-ka—Jubal picked up the image of one of the shiny beetles—had created the basis for the panic to begin with.

If he flies his own ship and tricks people into bringing him supplies, he must be a pretty smart kitty, Jubal replied. He thought he was being encouraging but realized his mistake when Chester bristled, jealous that the boy he considered his offered praise of the other cat. *Not as handsome as you, of course, and nowhere near as nice, definitely less fluffy, and he doesn't look nearly as soft, but still, really smart. I don't suppose he ever mentioned what his plan might be?*

Before Chester could respond, footsteps came running down the corridor from the shuttle bay. "Jubal, Beulah says to tell you we're stuck," Sosi said. "The docking bay hatch won't open and the *Ranzo* has disappeared from the sensors."

"It's okay, Sosi," Jubal said, not knowing for sure if it was but thinking it was a good idea to help his crewmates see their predicament in a positive light—as he, despite Chester's reservations, was beginning to do. "Chester's buddy, the short-haired cat, is a superior sort of alien being named Pshaw-Ra. He, uh—watches over cats, and he's going to do something to try to help the impounded cats now. I think he may need us and the shuttle to do it."

"You are so full of it, Jubal," Sosi began, then seeing his serious expression, asked, "Really? You're not kidding?"

"I'd never kid about something like that and neither would Chester."

"How do you know?"

"Because he and I talk," Jubal said. He'd never told Sosi the nature of his bond with Chester, but now seemed like a good time.

"Hadley talks. He says 'meow,' 'yow,' 'rrrowl,' 'prrrt,' and a lot of other stuff."

"No, I mean, Chester and I can understand each other's words and hear and see what's happening in each other's lives. We've been able to since he was a baby kitten."

"No, you haven't!" she scoffed. "That's just silly. Sure you can tell what a kitty means by his expression and how he holds his tail and ears and stuff, but even the smartest, best bred ships' cats don't talk Standard."

"I didn't say they did. Chester doesn't actually speak in human words—his vocal cords wouldn't handle it. But you don't need language to read thoughts. It's experience, you know? You can think something in one language or another, but what you mean is always in there in the thought, regardless."

"Well, Beulah doesn't need words right now to say what she means either, but she's saying a lot of them and they aren't fit for my delicate childlike ears. So you and the cats had better fill her in before she tries to blast our way out of here."

ↄ ↄ ↄ

The GHA inspection team took Klinger's farm by surprise. As the nephew and namesake of GHA head councilman P. B. Klinger,

Secretary of Agriculture, Phillip B. Klinger considered himself immune from harassment by what he considered his uncle's agency.

And yet, when Phil and his latest bride dismounted following their morning ride, there was the team of white-suited, clipboard-wielding technobureaucrats, claiming they'd come to inspect his stock. They actually called his expensive, beautifully bred horses "stock."

"Mr. Klinger," said the older of the two men, a rugged-looking and, judging from the latest Mrs. Klinger's reaction to him, handsome fellow. He possessed a deep authoritative voice. "It's come to our attention that there's been an oversight in my predecessor's coverage of this area. While your neighbors have all had their stock and homes inspected for the target pathogen, your property does not seem to have undergone similar scrutiny."

"I had my own vet look at my horses and other beasts," Klinger told him. "He found no irregularities. Evidently my precautions —"

The younger white-suited man cleared his throat. "Sorry, sir, but that is precisely why the GHA has temporarily cross-posted its veterinary practitioners. The fear is that doctors might not deal conservatively enough with their usual clients to adequately address a threat of this magnitude."

"We think it highly unlikely, with the pathogen so pervasive in the surrounding properties," the older man said, "that your animals would have been spared, Mr. Klinger. We'll need to test all of them—"

"I just told you, they've been tested—"

"—again," the older man finished.

"This is an outrage," Klinger said. "I'll have you know my uncle is the head of the GHA council. He'll have your jobs for this."

"On the contrary, sir," the younger man replied. "Animals with these symptoms have been impounded throughout the galaxy. Your uncle surely would be the last to want favoritism to a relative's stock that could possibly lead to further contamination. The impound transport will be along momentarily, so if you'll have your employees stable your horses and round up any other animals living on the farm . . ."

"I don't believe this," Klinger said. "I'm putting in a call to my uncle now. He'll straighten you out."

"As you say, sir. But in the meantime, we need to begin inspecting the stock," the older fellow said.

"I don't think so, Mister—" Klinger looked at name tags. "—Pointer."

The older man looked at the other two in dismay. He gave Klinger a wounded look. "Frankly, Mr. Klinger, I am surprised at your attitude."

He didn't elaborate, but Klinger knew what he meant. Even though his uncle had impounded his neighbor's horses at his own suggestion that there was something wrong with them, he had not expected that he would be identified as the origin of the information. The matter was supposed to be between his uncle and himself. Actually, it was essential to the credibility of the report and to his uncle's image as an impartial defender of public health that a family member's involvement not be revealed. No, his uncle wouldn't have told even his closest associates about the connection, though all they needed to do was look at the names and do the math.

"What do you mean by that?" he challenged Pointer finally.

"Simply that a man with such close ties to the GHA surely must be aware of the vital nature of our mission in protecting the health and welfare of the universe at large, and this farming community in particular. All of your neighbors have submitted to impounds, despite protests that we were ruining them. Economic concerns cannot be allowed to overrule the need to protect the public. Of course, it's upsetting to lose land that's been in your family for generations, or have to see valuable beasts taken for possible slaughter, but we need to protect the people."

Klinger thought about the offers he'd made his adjacent neighbors for their land at a fraction of its value. They had been resentful, but hadn't turned him down yet. Had they reported him?

The younger man spoke again. "We can bring in the Guard to assist us if necessary, Mr. Klinger, but I don't think you'd want that."

Klinger's lips tightened. His uncle would kill him if he got into trouble with the law over this.

His new bride clung to his arm but said with a smile, "Of course not. We know you're just doing your job, but all of our animals are as healthy as can be."

"All of the other animals appear to be on the surface too, ma'am, but on further investigation, we've found an alien substance in their bodily fluids. The GHA says that we must impound all animals pending our investigation of the long-term effects of the suspected pathogen."

She looked back at the beautiful bay mare Klinger had given her as a wedding present. She was a horsewoman first and foremost. Her husband was not as bad as everyone said he was, or so she wanted to believe, but the horses were absolutely splendid, and she couldn't bear that anything would happen to them. She squeezed Klinger's arm warningly. She was very beautiful, from a family of powerful lawmakers herself, and furthermore she had—on the advice of and with the support of her relatives—not signed the prenuptial agreement. "Why don't I show you around the stables while Philly takes care of a little family business?"

CHAPTER 21

Chessie sat up on her haunches, watching the door. It was time for Jared to come, perhaps bearing Kibble's reassuring scent on his clothing again. But when the door swung open, a strange woman, tall and lean, with short white hair and a stern expression, walked through instead. Chessie craned her neck a little to the side to see if Jared was coming in behind the woman, but he was not.

She kept a sharp eye on the door for a long time after, but Jared never appeared. Only a little discouraged, because even the best and most reliable humans tended to have irregular habits, she spread herself as far as she could across the floor of her cage, laid her head on its side against her outstretched paws and tried to sleep.

She had been very worried indeed before the first time Jared appeared in this place. Since she had come, some of the other cats were carried off by humans who took them through the Other Door, the one no cat in his or her right mind wanted to be on the other side of, and never returned. The caged cats had heard few cries, but the smell of fear and death leaked through that door like the stench of rotting rat flesh.

Overhead lights flickered all the time. This was of no particular consequence to ships' cats, who cared nothing for dirtside definitions of day and night. The food was of far lower quality than Chessie was used to, and nothing fresh was available, except for the occasional beetle that crawled into a cage. The efforts the laboratory people made to collect and confine the beetles were largely unsuccessful.

The sanitary conditions were appalling. The incarcerated cats were not provided with proper boxes but instead were given paper on which to deposit their excrement and urine. The smell was unappetizing, especially so close to one's food and water dishes.

Jared had been making it his business to see to it that papers were changed often, so the cages were in a constant rotation of being freshened. It was a comfort. Even those in the lab who seemed to have a liking for her species had difficulty tolerating the stink—which should have told them how much more awful it was to the cats who sat in the middle of it all.

Then there was the cat-cacophony of the hundreds of voices protesting their fate.

"What will become of me?" a young female, as well bred as Chessie herself and heavy with kittens, cried incessantly. "Will they spare my young?"

"Hah! I knew no good would come of helping humans," an old tom said bitterly. "I thought my shipmates were different but they turned me over quick enough, didn't they?"

"My girl won't know what to do without me," cried a male by the name of Hadley. "What if rats bite her? What if she has bad dreams? Who will knead her middle with his paws to wake her up, and then, when she has forgotten all about her dreams while she feeds him, who will purr her back to sleep?"

"Who will keep the mice out of the wiring?" another fretted, pawing at the wire of his cage until his paws bled.

"Why are they doing this to us?" wailed Git's kitten, Bat, who had been snatched from his berth before he'd served two months of his contract. "I want ooooowwwwwt!"

Most of the humans had begun wearing devices in their ears that Chessie thought must block out the cries because they ceased responding with either kind words or curses.

Chessie herself said nothing. She was weary and sad, but she had been near death many times already, both as its agent and as one bereft because of it. She had lost children and her friend Git to it. A practical cat as well as an ornamental one, she knew she could not avoid her doom if it chose to take her, so she chose to ignore the situation as much as possible. When she slept, she dreamed of her old life with Janina, between litters, and of the good times when she was a new mother, washing the kittens and watching them play and hearing them being praised for their beauty and liveliness. She was sorry for them because it looked as if they would not grow up to have families of their own or form the kind of friendships she had formed. She certainly did not blame her Kibble for this situation.

When Jared came to the laboratory that first day, although other cats who had been his patients snarled that he had betrayed them and joined the enemy, she welcomed his caresses. Lately she had smelled her Kibble's scent on him, and that comforted her. Kibble had not abandoned her. She believed Jared truly meant it when he said he would get her out of there and back to Kibble, no matter what. But she didn't think he could. She knew too much about humans after all of her years among them.

"Don't worry, old girl," he'd told her that first day while scratching her head. "We'll find some way to get you out of here." The key word in this reassurance was "out," and that made her a little hopeful, a little less resigned, and when she felt panic rising in her, she resisted. She was a very patient cat, as a good hunter had to be. She would wait and watch, wait and watch.

The cats in the cages next to her, at first unable to understand why she was not as agitated as they, eyed her warily. But slowly, as their own exertions wore them down, her calm curling, sleeping, waiting and watching, quieted them, so they followed suit. And their calm quieted the cats in the cages next to theirs.

Chessie knew that dwelling on what you feared but were helpless to change was a waste of time. All that did was make your fur fall out. So when they were more settled, she began telling stories to the other cats, especially the kits. Stories of the bravery and independence of catkind, of the first cat to contact humans, whose tale was told by a human as "The Cat Who Walked By Himself," of Scarlett who went into a burning building over and over again to bring out her kits, sustaining horrible injuries but saving most of her family. She told them (again) of her illustrious ancestor, Tuxedo Thomas, and how he saved his human's ship many times by his cleverness and the quickness of his pounce and paws. And she told them the most ancient stories of all, of the origins of Earth cats, those who guarded the temples of ancient Africa, Asia, and Indochina, those who were worshipped as gods, those who were hunted as the accomplices of supposedly evil people and yet still caught and killed the rats that brought plague to the very humans who had killed their own noble protectors. This was another of those terrible times for their species, but she knew that the qualities that made cats great would keep them from becoming extinct. The truth was, humans could not actually do without them, though cats could do without humans.

Others among the captives had tales too, losing their fear momentarily in the presence of a large appreciative audience. The cats who were in heat and those who were in pursuit sung tales of their ancestors, of their own beauty and prowess as hunters or makers of enchanting offspring. They sang lustily and drove the lab tech humans to take refuge from the caterwauling in headphones and earplugs.

But that day, when Jared did not come, Chessie slept to escape the fear that she had been abandoned to her fate once more. She wanted to trust, but among the stories of her fellow cats were many ancestral tales of human treachery and betrayal. These cats seemed not to have particularly good positions on their ships. They, like Git, seemed to feel that trust was for dogs.

Chessie awakened suddenly, though at first their section of the laboratory seemed quiet. The white-haired woman who'd come in

Jared's stead was gone—along with all but one of the attendants. Light, muffled noises, laughter that made her spine quiver, and the scent of terror leaked around the Other Door. And something else. What?

First she thought it was that something—or someone—was missing again. Who? Who had been taken? She scanned cages as far as she could see, above, below, to the right and left and behind her. She saw no one furry in the corner cage where the cranky old cat had been.

She wanted to howl a warning, but what good would a warning do? The other cats were sleeping, grooming, or murmuring quietly among themselves. She watched and waited, sensing danger so close that her fur stood on end along her ruff and back.

Peering at the Other Door again, she saw that the keka beetles were moving more purposefully now. Earlier they had been scuttling. Now they leaked around the door in several not-entirely-silent unbroken lines.

Under the babble of cat voices, she heard the skittering of the beetles, the whisper of their carapaces against the floor.

Whispering husky and hoarse, and a sigh like an expulsion of breath. "Kefer-kah!" it sounded like. "Kefer-kah! Kefer-*kah!*"

Some of the bugs had apparently mated, for among their ranks were young ones that were very very tiny. Even Chessie's sharp eyes could barely detect them. Their movement was marked by the thinnest filament of motion as they crawled to the cages and up the legs of the tables and the desk where the human slept with his head thrown back and his mouth wide open. A can of liquid sat within the curl of his hand. One tiny suicidal creature made a leap of catlike proportions directly into the open mouth. Another leaped into the can. And then all of the others retreated into the corners of the room, or entered the cages of the bored cats.

Chessie could not imagine why the kekas were doing all of this. If it was instinct, it was a very odd instinct indeed, but they were bugs, not sensible cats, and their buggy agendas were beyond her comprehension.

* * *

Later, while the food dishes were being filled, the white-haired woman approached Chessie's cage. She smelled like death and disinfectant, but Chessie noted with some satisfaction the scratch along one cheek and the red cross-hatching on the woman's wrists.

"So," she said in a purr that seemed ominous to Chessie. "You're a fine fluffy lady, aren't you, my dear? I understand you are a favorite of Dr. Vlast. We're not quite sure what happened to your friend, or why he didn't come to work today. Perhaps he couldn't bear the idea of having to examine you to the degree necessary to determine the nature of your illness. So we'll spare him the pain by doing you before he changes his mind and returns. They've just got to tidy up the last of that other specimen and we'll be right with you."

Chessie puffed to four times her size, her soft fur stiff and straight as quills. She hissed and told the woman off in no uncertain terms. Had the basest crewmen on the *Molly Daise* been able to understand her spitting and growling, they would have found their gentle Duchess could outcurse them. The woman unfortunately was out of her claw reach, but she leapt back anyway, uttering a high-pitched nervous giggle.

"Nice try, you nasty little beast."

When the woman had gone, Chessie slowly deflated, her calm all gone as she huddled shaking in one back corner, pushing into the wire as hard as she could for safety. She felt a lick on her left ear. The young mother in the next cage purred comfortingly, the purr fluttering occasionally with her own fear. "Tell me again that story," the younger cat said. "The one about the place where anyone who killed a cat was put to death."

* * *

CHESTER ABOARD THE PYRAMID SHIP

I don't see how we can do the other animals any good by landing and getting you and Pshaw-Ra captured too, Jubal said, stroking me. I could not seem to get close enough or be petted quickly or thoroughly enough to suit me. I flipped my tail, impatient with Jubal's distraction from his main job of keeping my fluff patted smoothly to my form.

I hadn't the slightest desire to talk about Pshaw-Ra while I was getting caught up on the long weeks without my boy, but clearly the matter of the captive cats was causing agitation among the humans.

To Jubal's own memories of Hadley's capture and the cold forbidding fortress now holding my mother and most of our spacefaring kind, I added my memory of Space Jockey, my notoriously cocky sire, trembling in his fur coat as his ship cruised into port toward the fate that he sensed awaited him. I jumped down from Jubal's lap and padded up the ramp and into the cat corridor in search of the ship's captain. I supposed I'd have to cope with this before Jubal—for whom I had waited all these weeks—would give me the undivided attention I deserved for as long as I desired. It wasn't fair, but there it was.

Pshaw-Ra was as enigmatic as ever when I queried him. "I need not land to command," he said loftily. "But I do require images of the place where the unfortunate felines are being held and under what conditions."

I showed him the building my boy showed me, the building Jubal and the others had stood in front of yowling at the tops of their voices and scratching to go in while groups of people in white coveralls and masks carried cats inside. I showed him what the boy remembered of the building plans the guard had shared with him, but Pshaw-Ra was not satisfied and was hardly paying attention.

"Stupid of those cats to get caugbt in the first place," he remarked. He had stopped fiddling with controls and sat cleaning his claws. "But then, they've been captives all their lives, I suppose, cozying up to humans, afraid to meet their greater destiny. I'm not sure such devolved cats, with such a slavelike mentality, will be of any use to my grand plan."

"What are you on about?" I growled. "The humans didn't want to surrender the cats, and the cats didn't want to go."

"Nevertheless, they were surrendered and they did go," Pshaw-Ra said, smirking through his whiskers. His ears were angled back and his eyes narrowed. "Thus delaying my plan." His tail smacked the deck in annoyance.

"They were carried in cages," I pointed out, reminding him of that part of the boy's image. But though I thought I was being patient with him, my voice came out in a growl and my fur stood up in a huff. That way, even though I was still young enough to be smaller than he under normal circumstances, I was at least as big, probably bigger. I felt enormous. "So, do you really have some idea how to help them or do I have to—" I jumped on top of him, biting and clawing as I'd been wanting to do ever since I met the smug creature.

The fight ended before it began. My claws unhooked, my mouth opened so my teeth let go of the chunk of fur they were ready to yank off him, and I floated up as if back in zero g, then abruptly dropped onto the very spot from which I'd launched my attack. I hunched there glaring at him. What kind of a trick had he played on me? He cheated. Otherwise I could have walloped him at least a little.

"Foolish catling, how do you think you can stand against me? You can achieve nothing without my gracious acquiescence. Do you know how to control my vessel? I think not. Do you know how to release the shuttle? Even if you did, with the mother ship so distant and the target planet still out of range, you and your human companions would perish before you arrived. Confront your fate, catling. You are at my mercy. You and your plodding, inelegant human companions as well."

"Stop waggling your rear and hunt if you're going to, Pshaw-Ra.

Jubal says they're probably murdering cats while you sit here grooming your bung hole."

"The information he provided me was inadequate. I need more details if I am to deploy my resources to the best advantage."

I checked with my boy but he had already told me everything he could about the building. *We couldn't get past the lobby, Chester. They weren't about to let us up there so we could tell people what they were doing.*

When this was conveyed to Pshaw-Ra, he said, "Well then, if the human captors will not allow humans inside, no doubt they would be well pleased to acquire another of our noble race to humiliate and degrade. This presents an opportunity for you to prove your worthiness, catling."

"You mean I should go in there on purpose?" I asked.

Before I could continue my own protests, Jubal sent such a forcible one it made my poor little head ache. *No! Chester, no way are you going in there. They've got your mother and Hadley already. I just got you back and I'm not going to let them make a science experiment out of you. You're not going. Period. Just forget it.*

I relayed his sentiments to Pshaw-Ra.

"I thought you said you were not a slave. Yet if this human boy forbids you to do a thing that will free our kind from what he at least considers a dreadful fate, you just curl up and purr and say, 'Yes, master'? You are a disgrace."

"Jubal is scared I'll be hurt because he loves me. If you cared about anyone but yourself, you'd understand that. In fact, if you have this great plan to free everybody, why am I the one who's supposed to crawl tamely into the cage? Put the cat where the chatter is, Pshaw-Ra."

"Foolish spawn of a tame pussycat, you think I fear to go among those puny humans?"

"You bet your slinky tail I do," I said, lashing my own fluffy appendage.

"I simply thought you would want to be on the scene to rescue your mother and be praised by your human. That sort of thing seems to matter to you."

I glared, tired of his catty remarks about my relationships. He was just jealous.

"Don't be ridiculous," he said, catching that last thought. "I am not jealous of your extended childhood attachment to your mother, and certainly not of your unnatural bond with that oafish child."

"Take that back," I said.

"You are so easily distracted," he said lazily. "I suppose I had better come along and supervise or you will botch everything. Now then, this is the plan . . ."

No! Jubal said, when Pshaw-Ra had spoken. *No way, Chester. I am not turning you over to those goons. Or the skinny cat either.*

Wait till you get to know him like I do, I suggested. *You'll change your mind and beg them to take him. You think he's so smart. This is the kind of scheme he devises—ones that involve getting* my *tail stepped on.*

Why would a cat even think up something like that?

He says because of his plan for universal domination, I replied, licking my paw and inspecting the result. *So far it isn't really working out for him. But he says we are approaching Galipolis now and I'm supposed to tell you to tell the others to put us in cages as if we're your captives.*

Only one problem with that, Jubal said. *We don't happen to have any cages with us. I bet every cage in the cosmos is already in that lab.*

I told Pshaw-Ra the bad news. He was still in the cabin, apparently preparing for landing. "Useless!" he complained. "These people are utterly useless. Very well, then. I will be landing on the roof of the building in question. Once we are there, one of your humans must go to the evildoers and request the loan of a cage so that they may surrender two more cats for degradation and persecution."

"If not death," I said, liking this plan less all the time.

"If there is death, it will not be ours."

"How are we going to prevent it if they want to kill us?" I asked. "Once we get out of the cages, will you get yourself wet and grow into a lion like some sort of dehydrated food packet?"

He then said those words truly aggravating to the young of any species: "That, my son, is for me to know and you—and them—to find out."

Maybe I wouldn't wait for the humans to kill Pshaw-Ra. Maybe I'd rip his ears off myself.

Chessie screamed and snarled when the hazmat-suited lab assistant, protected by his gauntlets and helmet, scooped her out of her cage and deposited her in another one.

The cage smelled like terror. The urine and fur had been cleaned from its surfaces, but not the fear of the cats who had preceded her into the cage.

The man who carried her cage bore it swiftly toward the door, eager to get rid of the maddened animal inside.

The other cats, alert and in full voice, protested at the tops of their lungs. The cry of her foster kitten Bat was among them, "Mama, *no!*"

She knew when the door opened that she would never see them again, and then it swung wide and in an instant she was on the other side, in That Place. It smelled bad, worse than inside the cage room. It felt bad. The light was too bright, the walls swallowed her protests. The man deposited her cage on a metal table and turned away. She thought he was leaving her there alone. Then something came at her through the wires of her cage and stabbed her sharply, like a very long claw. When she whirled to slap it away, she saw the man withdrawing a syringe, the kind Jared used to give her vaccines and antibiotics.

"That should calm you down, old girl," he said, not unkindly.

She shuddered, and her legs collapsed under her.

She didn't close her eyes, however, didn't sleep, just lost the ability to control her own movements.

Vaguely she was aware of the whispering of the shiny bugs from the edges of the room. She caught a whiff of the old cat who had preceded her. When the man opened the cage door and pulled her out, she couldn't so much as bite him. Her head was too heavy for her to raise it. When he lifted her, it drooped and she could see her tail dangling like a length of old rope. She had soiled it, though she had not felt her bowels and bladder releasing.

The man left her lying there helpless while he ducked out the door and called, "She's quiet, Doc."

The white-haired woman, wearing a suit and a mask, but not a helmet, entered. "You can leave, Weeks. I'll take it from here," she said.

Chessie didn't see the man go. She was staring up at the woman, though her vision kept blurring. One moment the woman was just standing there. The next she was holding some horrible metal thing with teeth. The woman grabbed her front paws with her free hand and flipped her onto her back. The toothed thing sprang to life, buzzing like a swarm of angry insects, as the woman lowered it toward her belly.

It touched her, cold, hard, and pinched and pulled, followed by a sensation of openness, bareness. Fluffs of fur drifted up from the toothy buzzer.

"Maybe I'll shave you all over, cat. No one will recognize you without all that fuzz."

Chessie could not even cry.

CHESTER TO THE RESCUE

"I control the kefer-ka, instructing them in their destiny, guiding them to their tasks," Pshaw-Ra bragged as he settled his vessel onto the roof of the laboratory building. Even though it could look like an ordinary ship, the pyramid craft was actually so small that it slipped easily through the tangled traffic over Galipolis. The biggest part of it was the shuttle bay, which seemed to be much larger than its actual capacity, just big enough to dock one ordinary shuttle and its own little cat-sized one. I wasn't sure how he managed it, but Pshaw-Ra had expanded on the natural feline ability to appear larger than usual when necessary, extending it to his vessel. Was he as brilliant as he thought or merely crazy? Brilliant would be best, under the circumstances.

My boy and his companions were gone long enough for me to enjoy a refreshing nap. When they returned, bearing one cage among them, they appeared both concerned and oddly smug.

Jubal was shaking and his mind roiled with fear and frustration. He had the most to lose, namely me. To amend that, he had the most to lose *other* than me, and of course Pshaw-Ra.

This is not a good idea, Chester, he said, scooping me up and cuddling me to his chest. I felt his heart beating hard. It seemed to be raining warm drops, even though we were still inside the ship. I turned in his arms, put my paws on his collarbones and licked the salty drops from his chin and cheeks. *Dr. Vlast isn't there anymore. I asked for Dr. Mbele but he wasn't there either. It's some lady vet instead. She acted like she was too busy to loan us the cage, but her assistant wouldn't do it. He said he wasn't authorized to accept animals from anyone other than the designated GHA agents. They had a really silly argument about it, and in the end she had to come down and bring us the cage herself. The guard couldn't let us in or leave his post. She looked kinda mean. I think maybe she's a dog doctor they assigned to cats. You'd better stay here.*

As Pshaw-Ra received this intelligence, his eyes slitted with calculation and he marched straight into the open cage, where he sat down, waiting.

But then, he was crazy. Definitely crazy. And I didn't want to leave Jubal. I'd just got him back. It wasn't fair. Pshaw-Ra didn't care about anyone else so he had nothing to lose, but I had to think of my boy, didn't I, if not my own tail? "Since it's your grand scheme, Pshaw-Ra, just go by yourself."

He yawned and gave me a withering glance. "I could, of course, but at some point I'll need two-legged minions for the heavy lifting parts of my plan. Your connection with the boy would be useful in summoning them. But if you don't wish to keep all felinekind as we know it from doom and destruction, please don't let me inter-rupt your touching reunion. I'm sure your mother will forgive you with her dying breath. And without my protection, of course, you're left with these useless humans who will be forced by their evil overlords to submit you to meet your own death. Unless, of course, we end their evil dominion here and now."

In favor of his own evil dominion, no doubt.

But I knew I could not stay behind. With the cage into which Pshaw-Ra had so blithely settled himself, Jubal and the others had brought the stink of fear—and it smelled like my mother's. *She* had been imprisoned in this cage.

Stick me in there, Jubal, I told the boy. I'm sure to everyone else it sounded as if I said "mew," but Jubal had heard me, and through me, most of my discussion with Pshaw-Ra.

Jubal sniffed and wiped his nose on the arm of his suit. *I knew cats were good at guilt trips but I didn't know it worked on other cats,* he complained, the tears still falling so hard he petted them into my fur as he deposited me next to Pshaw-Ra. The poor boy could hardly breathe, he was so choked up with worry for my sake and grief at the prospect of losing me—again—but he said bravely, *I'll be with you as far as the lobby. If you change your mind, let me know and I'll let you out. Then run like crazy.*

Pshaw-Ra yawned again. It was meant to show his disdain, but watching his tail switch I realized he was actually using it to dis-guise his own nerves. "Oh, really. Such histrionics. Spare me."

"Just shut up," I told him. "Or I really will let you go alone!"

His eyes widened earnestly as he looked at me. "You must trust me, catling. I have a plan. I really do. It is in motion even now."

"Oh, goody. I can't wait to see what happens," I said, lifting my leg and cleaning under my tail. At that inopportune moment Jubal lifted the cage, toppling me into Pshaw-Ra and rolling both of us to the back of the cage. I thought it was fear making my skin crawl, then I saw Pshaw-Ra's bronze coat ripple like wind blowing across the sand dunes in one of Jubal's books. We were sharing our fur with guests. The kefer-ka were using us as transport and concealment.

Jubal carried us out of the vessel and onto the roof.

The woman Beulah led us, her back straight and her red curls bouncing as she walked down the steps, Jubal carrying our cages in the middle, the girl Sosi bringing up the rear. All of the humans were afraid. I knew that if they were caught they would be in a lot of trouble with the authorities, probably whether or not our mission succeeded. They didn't care about that too much—at least, Jubal didn't—but they were worried about the captive cats.

We emerged from the stairwell into a broad, bland corridor of white walls and, to the right of us, a bank of double metal doors. Beulah pushed a button and a lift came to pick us up.

"Let's not go to the lobby," Jubal said. "We should stop at the fourth floor instead. That's where the cats are."

"We don't have the pass codes, Jubal," Beulah told him. "We won't be able to get in to see them without the pass codes."

"Can't we just take the stairs, then?" Sosi asked. "I want to see Hadley." And with that she bolted past Beulah and the lift, through the exit to the staircase, and clattered down flight after flight, with Jubal right behind her, shaking us up thoroughly.

It would be faster and easier if you'd just let us out to run down the steps, I told Jubal.

But by then we had bounced to our destination and he was helping Sosi push through the heavy door from the stairs to the fourth-floor corridor.

Sosi raced through ahead of us and pounded her fist on the double doors opposite the stairwell. There was a little box with a flickering red light to the right of the door.

Beulah pushed through the stairway door behind us and pointed to the box. "Stop! Kids, we can't get in there without proper codes either."

Leave this to me, Pshaw-Ra said, ignoring her. *It would be most useful to have our two-legged assistants lurking nearby to aid us. I will send forth the kefer-ka to smooth our pathway . . .*

I felt my skin crawl again and pounced toward the line of movement departing the cage, but I was too slow. A string of something extremely tiny in a line half the width of one of my whiskers zipped across the pristine surface of the floor and up the wall to the electronic latch.

Before I had a chance to see what marvelous thing they were going to do, Sosi banged on the door with her skinny fists and in her shrill little-girl voice hollered, "Cat delivery!"

The door slid back far enough to allow us to see a harried-looking man in a white suit.

"You again?" he asked, and said to Beulah in a rather angry voice, "I told you to leave them with the guard in the lobby. How did you get past him?"

"We didn't. We're not there yet. We docked our shuttle on the roof. We figured it would be faster to just drop them off."

"Can I see the other kitties?" Sosi asked, trying to push around the man. "I want to see the kitties!" She was doing okay until one of the cats began yowling especially loud. "Hadley!" she cried, and nearly knocked the man over trying to push past him.

"Easy, kiddo," he said.

"Hadley is in good hands with this gentleman, Sosi," Beulah said, pulling on the girl and patting her shoulder.

A mother cat would have boxed her ears for endangering the whole litter. But I could hardly blame her. I could hear her friend crying out to her, "Girl! Come and get me! I want to come home! Get me owwwt!" In a few more minutes that would be me, probably.

From behind the man a woman's strident voice called, "How am I supposed to work with all this racket? That damn cat is waking up already. She scratched me!"

Her footsteps clicked up behind the man and she peered over his shoulder. Her left hand clutched a tissue to her right forearm. In spite of her own disinfectant stench and the scents of all of the other cats, I smelled my mother on her. Had I been out of the cage, I'd have scratched her up one side and down the other myself.

"Steady, catling," Pshaw-Ra cautioned. Easy enough for him to say. It wasn't *his* mother that woman was doing terrible things to — or trying to. Reading me, he replied, "Already the diversion created by our entrance has delayed this creature from harming your mother the queen. How do you like my plan so far?"

"Terrific," I replied. "I hope you've worked out the part where someone diverts the woman from harming us."

"All will be revealed in due time," he said sagely. Of course "all" would be revealed in due time. "All" inevitably *was*, sooner or later. It didn't take a sage to tell anybody that. I only had to worry about what "all" would consist of, vis-à-vis my own personal tail.

"You again!" the woman was saying, as if my boy and his shipmates were some troublesome spot that would not fade from her upholstery. "Weeks, call security and have these people removed — preferably to a holding facility."

"Doctor, please," Beulah said in a reasonable tone. "We docked on the roof and were on our way down when it occurred to us it would be faster — and involve less chance of infection — if we simply brought the cats to the lab ourselves. Besides, they know us and it comforts them to have us near longer."

"I can't tell you how moved I am by that," the woman said with a sneer worthy of Pshaw-Ra himself. She had to shout over the cats in the banks of cages behind her, though. "Too bad your presence hasn't settled *them* down. Now leave before we're forced to sedate every single specimen and have you jailed for obstruction of a GHA investigation. Weeks, pick up that cage and log in these cats."

He picked up our cage and, as he carried us to the towering structure of cages, the door slid closed with a soft *snick* behind us, separating us from Jubal, Beulah, and Sosi.

My fur was erect, and quite involuntarily I began yowling in response to the pathetic cries of the assembled cats.

Don't worry, buddy, Jubal's presence beyond the door reassured me. *We won't be far.*

A lot of good that would do!

"Lookit here, Fluffy. Fresh meat!" an angry old tom called out to a crony.

"Guess they weren't the ones that got away after all, eh, Socks?" his friend replied.

"Maybe the woman will take them ahead of us. Hey, there, you new cats! You can go ahead of me. Think nothing of it. I don't mind a bit."

I smacked Pshaw-Ra into the wire of the cage, furious that he had talked me into this. We were as helpless as everyone else. Pshaw-Ra still outweighed me, but I rode him clawing and spitting over and over from one side of the cage to the other and from back to front.

"Stop it!" he said finally, laying on his side, his paw raised within a whisker width of my nose. "Why's your tail in such a twist all of a sudden? This is all according to my master plan."

"Weeks, bring that cage here," the woman said. When she peered in at us, I saw that her nose was damp, which is not a sign of health in humans. Her eyes were red and her pale face blotchy. She poked at Pshaw-Ra with the end of a pencil. "What kind of cat are you, anyway?" she asked, though she didn't expect him to answer.

He did, however, sit up as nonchalantly as if I had decided not to rip his throat out, and pretended to play with the end of the pencil.

"Weeks," she said, "bring out that fuzzball in the other room and clean the place up. All that fur of hers is bringing on my allergies. This fellow is a far more interesting specimen. He has a wild look about him, don't you think?"

Pshaw-Ra gazed adoringly up at her and purred loud enough to rattle the cage.

"He seems to like you, Doc," Weeks remarked.

I had thought, momentarily, that perhaps she had taken a liking to Pshaw-Ra as well. They had a lot in common, both being insufferable and all. But her smile was not kindly as she looked down at him. "Oh, I think we can fix that," she said.

Pshaw-Ra gazed at her as if she were wonderful and held one front paw up, as if he couldn't wait to leap into her lap.

"We're out of cages," Weeks said. "We've no place to put the kitten."

"Stick him in there," she said, motioning toward a half-empty cage. "It won't hurt them to double up. They're all here for the same thing."

"So you concluded definitely that the Duchess isn't infected?" Weeks asked hopefully. "Because I'm sure you wouldn't want to put this little guy in with an infected cat."

"Weeks, look at this arrangement, will you? If any of these beasts came in here clean, they won't be by now. You don't think the GHA can risk returning them to their ships and homes do you?"

"Well—yeah," Weeks said. "If they're healthy, why not?"

The female rolled her eyes.

Weeks stooped and looked into our cage, noting Pshaw-Ra's attempts to ingratiate himself with the doctor. "These guys look friendly enough. You want to hold the one with the big ears, while I park the kitten and go get the Duchess?"

She gave him a withering look. "Of course not. Do I look like I want to be scratched again? Give the other cat more sedation and carry her out yourself. Then I can sedate this one while he's still securely caged."

Pshaw-Ra squeezed his eyes at her, lovingly. Not that he did love her, but he was trying to confuse her. She did not soften, however, even though a look like that was usually good for an extra feeding on shipboard.

Weeks took me from the cage and stuck me into one that smelled like my mother. Even though I knew she was in no position to help me, it comforted me. After a while Weeks returned with her, sleepy and reeking and matted, lying bonelessly in the impersonal padded arms of his suit. "There you go, old girl. You've got company," he said, shoving her in beside me, which wasn't all that easy, as her paws, tail, and head were still floppy. My poor beautiful mother! What had they done to her? I began washing her ears and face and bit the mats and snarls from her long silky fur, which was wet in places with blood—but not her blood. As I had already noted, my gentle mother left her mark on the woman who was now carrying Pshaw-Ra into her lair.

Mother was not unscathed, however. She was filthy and a strip of bare pink flesh gleamed in the midst of her creamy belly fur. I bathed her bare patch and cleaned her up. By the time I finished her bath, Mother was stirring, and purring, though she hadn't opened her eyes.

When she did, she lifted her head, licked my ear, and said, "Son, I had hoped you'd escaped this madness. I can't think why our people have allowed this to happen to us."

I didn't answer. She knew as well as I did that the cat-serving humans were not as dominant as the cat-impounding humans. "Don't get your ruff in a tuft, Mother," I told her. "Pshaw-Ra has a plan to release everyone."

"I don't see how anyone can do that," she said, her ears flattened slightly against her head to show her consternation. "Even if we did escape, the scientists would just round us up and bring us back. Even if we made it back to our ships, they'd probably make our people give us up again."

"All I know is he has a plan and he is also captain of his own ship."

"You mean he is the captain's cat."

"No, I mean he is the captain and the ship has controls a cat can work. Very paw-friendly. Cats run things where he's from."

Weeks had been going from cage to cage, filling dishes and emptying the filthy papers that served each of the occupants for toilets. He pulled the paper out of each cage, scraping the contents into little jars and labeling the jars. He spoke to each cat in turn as he worked, and when he got to us he said, "You two seem to be getting on well."

I gave him my best innocent kitten expression and rubbed my cheek against his hand. No mutinous plotting going on here, Mr. Weeks! We are good kitties!

CHAPTER 23

Jared was showing Mrs. Klinger the "fairy dust" in her bay mare's saliva when her husband entered the stable, followed by Ponty strutting officiously at his heels, and Janina, carrying a clipboard and wearing a grim expression. "Oh, Philly," Mrs. Klinger cried. "Dr. Vlast says Leaf is infected! Tell them they can't put her down. She's mine!"

"Nobody's going to be put down," Klinger said. "Uncle Phil says it's just been determined that the fairy dust syndrome isn't dangerous after all. The impounded animals are all going to be released, so you see, there's no reason whatsoever for you to impound ours."

"You understand, sir, we have to follow procedure," Jared said. "The proper entries must be made in the data banks, and the decision to release the animals must come through the proper channels. Otherwise it would look like favoritism, and you wouldn't want that."

"Look," Klinger said, "be reasonable. My animals have remained unimpounded all this time with no harm to themselves or others, and now it seems there's no threat after all. Can't you just return to headquarters and get the orders before you upset my wife further?"

Ponty gave him a "there's nothing we can do" shrug and shake of the head. "If it's any comfort, sir, you have a lot of company. All over the galaxy this epidemic scare has been a nightmare, the potential ruin of generations of careful breeding, the burning of farmland—"

"And the deprivation of countless ships of the services of the Barque Cats," Janina added.

"Of course," Ponty said, as if he'd suddenly thought of a loophole, "I suppose if you personally made the journey to Galipolis to confer with your uncle when he signs the documents ending the necessity for these measures, we could allow your stock to remain here pending further orders."

"That's reasonable!" Mrs. Klinger said, looking imploringly at her new husband. "Oh, Philly, do it. Leaf is coming into season. I don't want her disturbed."

"Fine," Klinger said at last. His voice sounded smooth, but Janina noticed that he was perspiring.

Jared's com buzzed. He checked it and looked up. "We need to return to Galipolis now, Mr. Klinger."

"If you'll just step this way, sir," Ponty said firmly.

"I can follow you in my own craft."

"That won't be necessary, sir, since we're all going to the same place anyway," Ponty replied. "I'm sure you can catch a ride back with the teams that will be dispersed to release your neighbors' animals from impound."

"Very well, then," he conceded when his wife made little shooing motions at him.

Janina wasn't sure what had passed between the councilman and his nephew on the com, but she thought it odd that the councilman had single-handedly reversed the decision to impound animals because of the supposed epidemic. Of course, according to Jared, vets and animal owners all over the galaxy had been protesting to the council that the fairy dust syndrome was just an odd side effect of the ingestion of the beetles, but no one had paid attention so far, least of all Councilman Klinger.

Her heart lightened as she strapped herself in, Jared in the seat beside her, while Ponty piloted the GHA craft Jared had commandeered.

The small ship had two compartments—the bridge and a section normally reserved for passengers. The latter had been converted into a cage for carrying suspect animals, so the councilman's nephew sat behind a grid of heavy black wire in a hastily reinstalled passenger seat. Before take-off, Philly Klinger had grabbed his personal entertainment system and was goggled and earplugged, his body moving slightly to music only he could hear.

"You really think this will turn things around?" Jared asked Ponty. Poor Jared looked so haggard and frazzled. Janina reached over to him and with one hand began massaging the back of his neck. He let out a grunt of sheer relief as the tension in his neck muscles was released, and let his head droop forward so her fingers could find the tight spots more easily,

"Yeah, I think so," Ponty replied.

"It'll be a miracle if it does," Jared told him. "My reports to the GHA and those of every honest vet I've talked to have consistently failed to show any harmful side effects connected with animals ingesting the bugs. The GHA has basically called us incompetent and dangerous for 'failing to recognize and properly contain this sinister invasive organism.' What sinister invasive organism, I ask you?

"What I think—and others agree with me—is that the beetles are nothing more than a latent emergence of a native species from one of the terraformed planets, one that's either lain dormant until now or that mutated and merged with some of the imported species and entered the food chain of free range animals via the grasses and grains they ingest. Very few of the impounded animals I've examined have any signs of illness whatsoever. And I've examined as many as thoroughly as I can without being invasive myself.

"The ones that are sick are mostly sick from the stress of being snatched from their homes and stuck into cages in close quarters with other unfamiliar animals. Of course, I've been dealing with the Barque Cats, who are exceptionally well cared for and a hearty species anyway. But if one of them were ill with something contagious, we could lose them all even without the idiocy of the GHA."

Ponty had one hand on the controls as the other fished inside a flight bag between his seat and Janina's. The bag moved with far more agitation than the slight twiddling of the man's fingers seemed likely to cause. Abruptly he snatched his hand out and yelled, "Ouch, you little savage!"

Janina withdrew her hand from Jared's neck and leaned down to look inside the bag. A grave furry face with a slanted white mustache and huge golden eyes looked up at her.

She reached down to pick him up, and he humped his back and curled his tail to be petted, but Ponty said, "Better not—Klinger back there might take off the gaming goggles. I need to keep Doc a secret."

Jared was staring at the three of them—Ponty, the kitten, and Janina—evidently trying to understand what was happening.

"Jared," Ponty said, "I don't want to confuse the issue after all your fine arguments and research and such, but there might be this one little *teensy* side effect I maybe ought to tell you about, just among us friends . . ."

Janina wanted to throttle the man. He'd been holding something back! She should have known it. She had gone along with Ponty's plan simply because it was the only one anybody had proposed that showed signs of working. It didn't mean she trusted him. Knowing that he was Jubal's father, she realized he had to be the person who kidnapped Chessie and probably set fire to the clinic to cover his tracks.

"How could you?" she demanded, keeping her voice low so as not to disturb their passenger. "Do you mean there *is* a real threat, and you know about it but you've *still* let Jared stake his reputation to participate in your charade?"

"I didn't say it was a threat, young lady," Ponty replied smoothly, with a hint of amusement in his tone. "I said it was a side effect. And it might not be. I have to ask you something. Have any of the Duchess's previous kittens developed psychic bonds with certain people?"

"Psychic *what?*" she asked. "You're saying Chester can read someone's thoughts? Jubal's?"

"That's about right," he said. "Any of Chessie's previous kittens done that sort of thing?"

She shook her head, then amended it. "Not that I know of. No. I'm certain somehow I'd have known."

"You don't have that kind of link with her?"

Janina loved Chessie very much, but she had no idea what the cat was actually thinking, aside from what she could understand from Chessie's body language. Janina felt a little cheated. She was the Cat Person, Chessie's Cat Person. If Chessie had psychic kittens, she should have been the first to know about them—perhaps bond with one herself. On the other hand, even she couldn't have cared more for a feline friend than Jubal cared about Chester. It hurt to think of how the boy must be feeling now that Chester had been lost to the derelict ship and its peculiar COB.

Jared took a more scientific approach. "You're just taking this on faith about your son and the kitten, aren't you? Is it possible he was misleading you to reinforce his position? Besides, one connection like that wouldn't mean that all of the exposed cats or even all of Chessie's kittens—"

Ponty shook his head. "You can't kid a kidder, Doc. Besides, it's not just the two of them. There's this little guy." He pointed into the box. "Though, technically speaking, and just between you and me, he isn't one of the Duchess's line. She adopted him. But he's adopted me, for some reason." He tipped his head backward, toward the passenger section. "How do you think I learned how to catch a rat?"

✂ ✂ ✂

Dr. Agneta Wren, DVM, regarded with disdain the creature who should have been cowering before her. He stared at her with huge yellow eyes, coiled and uncoiled his tawny snakelike tail and purred aggressively. The others in the cages had an injured innocence in their stares, as if they couldn't believe what was happening to them. Of course, the ones she examined had turned into the nasty, hissing, scratching furies she knew them to be before she immobilized them, but this one was different. He was clearly behaving in a shamelessly obsequious manner because he wanted something. Loose, probably.

"Purr all you want, beast. You're about to become dogmeat," she told him. She had no time for evasive feline antics. She had been able to perform only one autopsy, and that was spectacularly inconclusive. Her colleague, the absent Dr. Vlast, had performed exactly zero autopsies since he arrived, and had no findings whatsoever. She wondered if he'd been sacked for slacking off. He was a troublemaker. He refused a direct order to sacrifice a few of the animals for testing, and she suspected that under his instigation other relocated practitioners had done the same. He had failed to contain the specimen beetles, which she spotted scuttling along the walls of the laboratory. His conduct was unprofessional and unscientific, and it would serve the man right if his decision had sacrificed his license and career.

The tawny cat's big yellow eyes gazed up at her, no doubt plotting his next move. She had a feeling that if she dropped her own gaze, he'd spring at her quicker than a striking snake, ripping her flesh and biting her as that other cat had done so many years ago.

Her mother, also a veterinarian, had been much too kindhearted, and took in all sorts of strays without considering her main responsibility, the welfare of her own child. That last feral cat had seemed tame enough, purred and accepted the milk from her cereal bowl, followed her around and allowed her to touch his fur with her uncoordinated childish hands.

But a year later, when he was lying on her bed as she started to get dressed, he waited until her shirt was over her head and attacked her with tooth and claw. Surgery had repaired the worst of the outer scars but she still bore internal ones.

Until lately, focusing her career chiefly on horses and other useful animals, she had even stopped the nightmares. But as she looked into the urine-colored eyes of the devious, cunning beast before her, the old claw marks began to throb. She knew that as soon as she closed her eyes again the nightmares would return.

She had the needle poised, and broke eye contact long enough to grab the cat's ruff and pin his struggling haunches.

The door from the cage room burst open then and Weeks rushed in. His face was stricken and his voice not quite steady as he said, "Dr. Wren, I have something I need to show you."

"Not now. Can't you see I'm busy?"

"I know, and I wouldn't interrupt, but it's important. I think I've been infected, and you might be too."

She lowered the needle but didn't release her grip on the cat, who hunkered under her hand, though she could feel his muscles tensed to spring. "What makes you think that?"

"The fairy dust effect. I've got it too. I took a specimen. Look!"

He held out a specimen jar with a lump of shiny yellow phlegm in it. "I've had a cold, but since I had to work a double shift today, I haven't been back to my quarters to pick up my cough medicine." He hacked, turning his head.

"Cover your mouth, for goodness' sake, Weeks, and set the specimen down over there." She shook her head. This whole assignment had been so badly mismanaged. They were impounding millions of large useful animals all over the galaxy, where her expertise would be truly useful, and they assigned her to temporary duty testing a bunch of cats. And on top of that she had to fill in for colleagues who were not up to the job, and make do with one lame assistant—at least on this watch.

She pointed at a counter, and Weeks set the specimen down. "You do know how to prepare a slide, don't you?" she asked.

"Uh . . ." his voice trailed off and he shook his head.

"Where *do* they find these people?" she muttered to herself.

"You need another cat to work on?" Weeks asked.

"Of course not. I haven't finished with—" She looked back to her hand, now empty. The cat was nowhere to be seen.

Just then the com buzzed and pandemonium erupted in the cat room.

CHAPTER 24

The latch on our cage clicked. I looked up from my own bath, having finished Mother's, to see a line of the tiniest kefer-ka extending from the latch in all directions to the other cages.

I watched the latch as carefully as I had once watched the larger, juicier kefer-ka. I couldn't see very well so I stuck my nose through the wire and tried to look around the front of the cage.

The smaller kefer-ka crawled into the round lock, clicking faintly. Two of their larger kin tried to pull the lock free. I pulled my nose back, changed position, and stuck a paw out, giving the lock a tap that pulled the heavier bottom part away from the catch. With a nudge of my head, the door swung open.

Both humans were still in the other room with Pshaw-Ra, I thought. However, as I looked down from my cage I saw a blur of gold fur.

"Stir yourself, catling. We must free these others now. Do to their cages what you did to your own. I will do likewise."

"So we get them loose. Then where do we go? You and I can return to your ship, but how about the others?"

"All part of my master plan, catling. We take them with us, of course."

"How? Have you noticed that there are more cats here than would fit into your vessel? Don't tell me it's expandable!"

I jumped to the floor and released the locks on two of the lower cages. The inhabitants, a white mother and three unweaned kittens in one cage, a solitary female with black and brown markings in the other, looked at me wide-eyed, then, at Pshaw-Ra's instructions, left their cages to help release other cats on the lower two levels.

I had to hand it to the old fellow. He had something. Under ordinary circumstances, the feline thing to do would have been to let those strange cats fend for themselves and hightail it out of there.

Somehow, he was herding the cats. I couldn't imagine how—or why—but I was impressed by the strength of his personality and will. Cats do *not* like to be herded.

The younger, smarter, more flexible cats could free themselves as I had, with a little instruction. The youngest kittens were too small to help, and the mothers-to-be had lost agility, as had the very old or those who had been hurt during the capture. So I left the lower two tiers in the paws of others who had escaped their own cages, and scaled the wire to the upper tiers to assist our shiny insect liberators.

Semiliberators. It took a feline paw to finish off the lock, and this I provided. From the outside it was a snap, literally. I had the advantage over other kittens because I had observed closely what the beetles were doing and knew what was required of me to complete the task. I had the advantage over older cats because I was younger and lighter, and could climb the tiers of cages without pulling them down on me and everyone else.

So it was leap, leap, leap, wait for the beetles to click the lock, then tap it and leap to the next tier, click, tap, unclaw the wire (no mean feat for paws), let go, free-fall, twist in midair, land on my paws and start the process again. All in less time than it takes to tell, mind you, because our captors were only temporarily detained in the other room.

On the final assault, however, I ran into a small problem. The larger beetles had begun dying from the strain of forcing open the locks. There were none left to release the last cat in the fourth row, a burly orange one-eyed tom who prowled his cage yowling furiously like one of our larger wild cousins. His legs were thick and his paws too massive to poke through the heavy mesh and free himself.

So there was I, hanging by three paws, while the tiny kefer-ka click-clicked but the lock did not snap open. The larger beetles had twisted the lower, heavier part of each of the other locks to free it from its catch, but I couldn't make the lock twist with the swipe of a paw. Still, I had to try. The old fellow was frantic, yowling abuse at me and pleading, "Don't leave me, get me owwwt of here, don't leave me, don't leave me, don't you dare leave me."

Pshaw-Ra had snaked open the laboratory door and driven our formerly captive comrades to the steps. I heard my boy's voice soothing them, along with Sosi's.

"Want me to come up and show you how it's done, little brother?" a voice called from the floor. I looked down to see Bat, his dapper black and white spots as tidy as ever, staring up at me with wide inquisitive eyes, tail flicking back and forth, ready for action.

I didn't answer but hooked most of my paw over the back of the twisty part of the lock, keeping my dewclaw in front. I tried to put pressure with it, to twist, as I had seen Jubal do to some of the latches on the farm. But he had a strong practiced thumb, not an untried dewclaw, and though it almost worked, my poor claw hadn't the necessary strength.

The cages all around were empty and the last of the tails were disappearing through the door still held open by Pshaw-Ra.

I heard the tower of cages clatter as below me the wire was caught, held, and released three times before my milk brother leaped up. His claws grazed me and I shifted my grip to the upper part of the cage.

The entire edifice, empty of stabilizing cat bodies, rocked, tipped, and crashed to the floor. I leaped clear and so did Bat. The old cat screamed as his cage fell and smashed. Many tiny kefer-ka lost their lives in that fall, but the lock broke open and the old cat climbed out of his cell, unhurt.

It took very little time and made a satisfying amount of noise. The door of doom swung open and stopped, stuck in place by the toppled cages. The white-haired woman barked orders and cursed, but to my surprise I heard Weeks's voice ask, "All clear now?"

And Bat replied in his thought voice, with an inner purr of satisfaction, *That's the last of us, Weeksy. You're not bad for a lab rat.*

✦ ✦ ✦

Because they were in a GHA vessel, Jared, Ponty, Janina, and their passenger had priority landing privileges and were on the ground when other vessels continued to orbit.

Jared rose and opened the wire partition to the passenger door, tapping Klinger on the shoulder. Ponty said he was going to let them lead because the kitten, Doc, was raising a fuss and insisted on being carried in the underarm pouch Ponty had rigged for him.

"Poor little feller," he told Janina. "He's worried about his foster mama and those other kitties."

"Because they're caged?" she asked.

"He knew about that before. No, something's upset them, and we're still a little too far to figure out what. They're in a real lather, from what he can tell."

They hopped a flitter to GHA headquarters and Klinger got out ahead of the others. Ponty hung back and avoided contact with their former passenger. Janina knew that Ponty didn't want Klinger to discover the increasingly agitated kitten and suspect that he was less than he claimed. She feared that would become clear soon enough.

There was a com on the front door of the GHA building to signal the guard inside. Klinger stepped confidently up to the com, pressed the button and said, "Mr. Phillip Klinger and, er, party—to see Councilman Klinger."

The guard came to the door and checked ID. "Councilman

Klinger has returned to his office in the Klinger Building to conduct private business, Mr. Klinger," he said deferentially.

"Very well, then," Klinger said, sounding relieved, "we'll meet him there."

While this was playing out, Ponty cornered Janina and turned her so their backs were to the guard and Klinger. "Take the little fellow with you, hon," he told her. "I have to beard an old lion in his den. Doc understands I'm coming back for him but he's real anxious to get to where the other cats are."

Janina tucked the kitten inside the kitten pocket in her own uniform jacket. All Cat Persons' uniforms featured two such large deep pockets, one on each side, for carrying kittens who needed extra contact or care. Perhaps Doc smelled the vestiges of his foster mother on her clothing, because he settled warm and purring against her side, a sensation she always found calming.

She sneaked a hand inside her jacket to touch his fur.

Leaving Ponty behind, she, Jared, and Klinger climbed back into the flitter and flew at street level along the few city blocks to the fountain and then the Klinger Building, which was to her surprise the building where the laboratory was located.

They had to overfly it to reach the authorized vehicle docks in the rear.

A small vessel sat on the roof. Janina recognized it, although it was no longer disguised as a derelict. She had caught a glimpse of the pyramid ship as she'd pulled clear of it after being forced to leave Chester behind.

Now it seemed that somehow Chester and the strange short-haired tawny cat had come here—perhaps captured and brought into custody?

In her pocket, she felt the kitten shift and sit up. He pawed her side. She patted him through her jacket and wished she were the one who had the psychic connection so she could warn him to stay still. It didn't seem to be necessary, though. His little body felt as taut as the string of a violin—didn't they call those catgut? Horrible thought. But though he was stiffly alert, he didn't mew or try to climb out of her pocket.

"No one is supposed to dock there," Klinger said, pointing at it as they flew over on their way to the building's private docking bays. "And that is not a GG vessel. It will have to be moved."

Jared nodded absently and docked.

Klinger used his passkey on the lift and they took it to the fifth floor, where the councilman had his private offices.

Jared had been there before, once, when he'd attempted to present his arguments to the elder Klinger after he first arrived, but the councilman had not had the time to see him.

The office had no receptionist except for the com. "Uncle Phil, it's me," Philly Klinger said. "I'm here with the investigators I told you about."

Jared turned away from the com screen, gave Janina a conspiratorial glance, and jerked his head back to the entrance. "Tech Mauer," he said formally, extracting the envelope containing the smears they'd taken at Klinger's farm, "please take these to the fourth-floor laboratory for further testing."

His eyes dropped to the bulge in her jacket. He didn't expect the kitten to behave much longer either.

"Aye aye, Dr. Vlast," Janina said with the sort of salute hardly anyone ever used on a civilian ship these days except for formal occasions. She was fairly certain there would be a video com recording their movements and conversations, however, and she wanted to make everything look official and aboveboard.

Before she had taken three steps, the door opened and Jared and Philly Klinger were admitted to the councilman's inner sanctum. As if he knew the coast was clear, the kitten in her pocket hooked his claws into her uniform shirt and pulled himself up and out, then raced past the lifts, to the exit she assumed led to the stairway. He clawed at the door and mewed but she bent down to stroke him and said, "No, little one. You can't be loose in this building. Come with me now."

She pressed the button for the lift and waited. And waited. And waited longer still, trying to coax the kitten to return to her all the while. He danced out of range every time she tried to grab him. Then she heard the sound of feet running in the stairwell, followed by something that sounded almost like the patter of raindrops, except that it was going up.

The kitten pawed at the door, turning his head to look at her, cuing her to open it, but she didn't. She had no idea what was happening on the stairs, but this little fellow didn't need to be in the middle of it. She continued trying to catch him but he zipped under her hand just as she was about to grab him. This cat might not be psychic, as Ponty claimed, but he almost seemed able to teleport.

Beneath her, in spite of what she was sure was considerable soundproofing, she heard raised voices and then more clearly, voices from the staircase following the pattering.

The lift dropped from the fourth floor to the first, then suddenly dipped down to docking level.

The kitten suddenly sprang onto her shoulder and then walked down her chest and burrowed back into her pocket. She decided she was never going to catch the lift and returned to the staircase exit. The voices and the pattering had begun to fade. As soon as she opened the door, the kitten, getting his own way at last, leaped from her pocket and landed sprawling at her feet, then raced up the stairs ahead of her, never looking back.

Jubal breathed a sigh of relief as Chester, Pshaw-Ra, and Bat dashed into the stairwell to join the reverse cataract of felines flowing up the steps to the roof. Chester didn't follow the other two stragglers, but with a graceful leap and a rather painful last minute drag of claws, landed on Jubal's shoulder. Beulah guarded the stairs leading down, deflecting any confused cats away from it. Sosi and Hadley had returned to the roof and Pshaw-Ra's vessel.

The cats were free of the lab, but how would they escape the roof? Jubal had no idea. Earlier Sosi had asked, "Can cats count? Do you think the skinny cat—"

"Pshaw-Ra," Jubal said. "That's his name."

She'd wrinkled her nose. "Funny name. Do you think he has room in his little ship for all of the kitties? Maybe once we get the shuttle out?"

"I think if we packed his ship and the shuttle both with all these cats, there'd be no room to navigate and nothing to breathe or eat. I don't know what he has in mind."

Chester, exhausted from his exertions, was content to sleep wrapped around Jubal's neck as he climbed to the roof. It was covered in cats.

"Clear a path, Jubal," Beulah told him. "I'm going to fly the shuttle out of the docking bay."

But before she did, Sosi came scuttling out, looking very much like a cat who had swallowed a particularly tasty canary.

"What?" Jubal asked. He knew she was dying for him to ask.

She knelt down and stroked the coat of the nearest cat, who happened to be Bat. "Don't worry, kitty. I called Daddy to come and get us. They were already entering orbit. They followed the tracking sensor in our shuttle."

"But, Sosi, they'll just make us give the cats back again," Jubal said. "There's no place we can go or way to hide them."

Chester stretched and yawned, kneaded Jubal's shoulder and said, *Pshaw-Ra says he has a master plan. I think I believe him now.*

Cats leaped over each other to escape the path of the shuttle Beulah was very carefully flying out of the open hatch. She hovered overhead. Cats scattered beneath her and she set the craft down beside the pyramid vessel.

In a moment more Beulah appeared at the shuttle's hatch, calling, "Here, kitty kitty." Some were reluctant, but most, raised on ships and having ridden in shuttles all of their lives until recently, were heartened by the familiar smells.

Hadley was the first one in, even though Sosi remained on the roof shooing cats toward the shuttle. Soon furry, whiskered faces were peering through all the viewports.

"I think we have a load now," Beulah said.

Jubal glanced nervously at the door from the lower part of the building. Any minute now the security guard, at least, or maybe a whole squad of the Galactic goons, would come thundering up with weapons ready to recapture the cats and drag him, Sosi, and Beulah off to jail.

When he looked back at the shuttle, he saw that Beulah was no longer at its entrance and the shuttle was now several feet off the rooftop, ascending slowly at first, then more quickly.

Another shuttle swiftly replaced it. Captain Loloma himself stepped out onto the roof, narrowly avoiding crunching six tails and two sets of front paws beneath his boots.

"Daddy!" Sosi called, and hopped across cats, saying, "'Scuse me, kitty, 'scuse me, kitty," causing furry pile-ups in her wake as the cats jumped on top of each other to escape her feet.

"Come on, kiddo. You too, Jubal. We're going back to the *Ranzo.*"

"The kitties too, Dad?"

"He can't take them, I'm afraid, Sosi," Jubal told her, saying it before Captain Loloma had to say what he surely must. "He'll get in trouble."

But the captain surprised him. "I've been in trouble before, son," he said. "How do you think I met your father? What they've tried to do to these animals is wrong. Beulah told me this entire epidemic scare was manufactured to enrich some politician's family."

Jubal started to ask how the captain intended for them to escape—where would he take the cats and his ship to be safe from the Galactic goons?

Pshaw-Ra stepped away from his vessel and the furry bodies packed inside. With his tawny tail waving majestically, he daintily stepped forward and looked up at Captain Loloma, fixing him with that brilliant golden gaze of his.

Chester sat up on Jubal's shoulder and interpreted what the sand-colored cat seemed to be trying to laser directly into the captain's brain. *Pshaw-Ra needs you to tell the captain about his master plan,* Chester told him.

The one for universal domination? Jubal asked.

The one where we all escape to his world, Chester said. *He will lead the ship. But we have to make our leap now.*

Bat jumped over several other cats to slap at Jubal's pant leg. Chester interpreted. *Weeks has let Bat know that the goons have arrived below and are sending copters. We have to go now.*

Jubal relayed all of this to the captain so fast his words got tangled, but the argument and questions he expected didn't come.

"We'd better get a move on," Captain Loloma said, but even before he spoke, the rest of the cats were filing into the open hatches of the shuttle as if recalling the shipboard discipline of their lives as Barque Cats.

Sosi entered the *Ranzo*'s shuttle and took a seat. Hadley had to share her lap with three or four other cats, while two more sat on the chair back above her shoulders.

When every cat was packed into a vessel and Pshaw-Ra had returned to his own bridge, Captain Loloma asked, "You coming with us, Jubal?"

But Chester purred into his ear and Jubal shook his head. "No, sir. Pshaw-Ra is saving a berth for me on his ship. He wants someone with thumbs to help the passengers."

⸓ ⸓ ⸓

Since the communications equipment the pyramid ship contained was available only for someone cat-sized, Jubal had no way of maintaining contact with the *Ranzo*'s captain once they were airborne.

True to his word, Pshaw-Ra had somehow managed to convince the other cats to leave a Jubal-sized space nearest the hatch leading into the docking bay where the boy could sit during the journey.

He was crowded into his seat so tightly there was no need for the strap, but he wore it anyway, though cats crouched on his lap, his knees, legs, and feet, huddled against his neck and shoulders, and a kitten perched on his head. Chester allowed this, busying himself on the bridge with Pshaw-Ra.

Although Jubal was sweating under his living cat coat, the feline passengers, bred for space, were well-behaved and calm now that they were on board something with the kind of noises, smells, and air pressures they were used to. Jubal wore his arms out trying to pet everyone.

He was glad of the strap as the ship zigzagged, dodged, and wove as it tried to reach open space beyond the orbiting traffic jam. He was also glad of the sturdy fabric of his shipsuit as cat claws dug into him for support when the ship tilted, climbed, and dived. The kitten flew off his head and landed in the middle of another cat, taking ten strips of Jubal's scalp with him. Blood dripped down his neck and into his eyes, but after the first pain from the raking his head took, he didn't notice.

Because while his body was encased in fur, most of his mind was joined with Chester's as he and Pshaw-Ra guided the ship through the intricacies of the space jam, outmaneuvering and outdistancing the GG attrackers that were hot on their trail moments after they left the empty roof behind.

*T*he pyramid ship was incredibly fast, and they soon broke atmo and were nose and nose with Captain Loloma's shuttle. Through the viewport they saw the *Ranzo* hanging in space, waiting for its captain to dock.

The drawings on Pshaw-Ra's bridge moved, Jubal saw, viewing them through Chester's eyes. As the glyph of the pyramid enclosing a cat moved toward the spaceship-shaped glyph that must represent the *Ranzo*, smaller spaceship-shaped glyphs edged toward the pyramid.

"Engaging mouse hole," Pshaw-Ra told Chester, who told Jubal, who asked, *What's that?*

It's his supersecret hiding device, Chester said.

I figured. But how does it work?

He says it's too technical to explain to kittens and two-leggeds, but basically he can project a mouse hole ahead of him in space and fly through it. He'll make it big enough that it will swallow the Ranzo *and its shuttle too.*

And that works? Like carrying your own wormhole around with you?

Mouse hole, boy. It's a mouse hole. Pshaw-Ra says how else do you think he managed to be found only by those he wanted to find him?

I didn't know he could do those things, Jubal said.

He says he can. There it is!

Through the pyramid's viewport, Chester watched as space parted before them in a spiraling telescope of blackness. It was a little like vids Jubal had seen of the rings of fire that lions and tigers were made to jump through in old-time circuses. Captain Loloma's shuttle passed before the screen and the *Ranzo* opened its docking bay hatch to admit it. As soon as the ship swallowed the shuttle, it disappeared.

Outside the viewport, Jubal saw only whirling darkness.

Through Chester's eyes, he saw that on Pshaw-Ra's bridge the pyramid/cat glyph had passed the *Ranzo's* glyph, preceding it into the belly of a snake glyph. Once the snake glyph swallowed the *Ranzo* as well, it closed its mouth.

The smaller pursuing ship glyphs stopped short of the snake glyph's snout, fell back, turned around, and vanished from the picture.

When they were gone, the pyramid glyph retraced its path back to the *Ranzo* glyph, drew even with it, then blinked out of sight.

All around Jubal, cats' eyes that had been glowing like lasers in the dark suddenly shut as the pyramid's viewport filled with light. The hatch in front of Jubal's cat-covered toes slid open and he was staring out at the *Ranzo's* familiar docking bay.

Suddenly the cats leaped, exploding through the hatch in unison as Sosi's voice rang throughout the bay, calling over the com, "Kittykittykitty, dindin!"

◢ ◢ ◢

Too slow, boss. Doc cried. Ponty saw the empty roof through the eyes of the kitten even before the lift door opened onto the expanse where nothing but clouds of fur wafting on the wind and a distinctive odor remained of the former occupants. *Too slow. All of the cats are gone. Mama-Chessie, Bat, Chester, and your boy. All gone.*

I am the only one! The last cat in the galaxy! The thought mixed ex-ultation at his own specialness with despair and loneliness. Then, *I'm hungry and I have to pee.*

As soon as the lift doors spread a hand's width wide, Ponty jammed his way through and was on the roof, practically teleport-ing himself to Janina's side to relieve her of Doc. Jared Vlast and two council members were right behind him.

I told Bat and Chester I was coming but they didn't wait, Doc cried. He was quivering as Ponty stroked his fur flat. *They said that other cat, the alien one, rescued them and was taking them to a safer place. I want to be rescued too! What kind of food does the safer place have, boss? I think the alien cat was promising catnip trees. He said something about a big mouse hole too.*

It's okay, little guy. You've been rescued already. You and all the other animals. If the cats had waited, they could have been rescued here without having to go someplace else. You don't think your boss would let you down, do you? Ponty couldn't believe he was think-ing like this.

The kitten inserted the top of its head into his palm.

When Ponty had gone to talk to his old friend, Councilor Taymere Zin, Councilor Klinger's chief political rival on the council, Taymere introduced him to a lovely white-haired woman in council robes, Sanina Rose.

While he related to Taymere what amounted to Klinger's con-fession of presenting false evidence leading to the plague scare, Councilor Rose listened intently. He thought she was going to have kittens herself.

Along with many of the council who were less than impressed with Klinger, she was unconvinced of the necessity of the im-pounds and appalled by the repercussions. She insisted on accom-panying him and Taymere to confront Klinger.

But even before they arrived, Doc had been sending Ponty bul-letins about the noises on the fourth floor, then in the staircase, and how Janina did not seem to understand that he needed to go through that door and find those other cats. By the time she did, it was too late. They were all gone.

Ponty was so preoccupied trying to send calming thoughts to Doc that Councilor Rose had to tug on his arm twice. "Come on, Mr. Poindexter, Taymere has people to intimidate here, but you, me, and the vet have commandeered us an attracker. Did I mention I am a captain in the Guard Reserve?"

It couldn't have taken more than a minute from the time they arrived on the roof until they were airborne again, with Councilor Rose directing the pilot, whose name tag said E. HART, to track the shuttles. They were not made for long-distance space travel, so it was inconceivable they could go far from the ship waiting for them beyond the jammed traffic orbiting the planet. Fortunately, the jam wasn't quite as bad as it had been a few days before or the chase could have turned deadly.

The attrackers blared sirens into the coms of the orbiting vessels, forcing them to part before the authorities. Just as they were about to resume their previous courses, Hart blatted his siren signal and the other ships fell back again.

Before long the ship commanded by Councilor Rose had caught up with the other attrackers, passed them, and led the pursuit.

Originally there had been three shuttles, according to the first attrackers to take up the chase.

The sensor screen in front of Hart now showed only two small vessels flying alongside the *Ranzo*. Then suddenly one of the shuttles disappeared from the screen.

"Damn, it docked," Hart said. "The mother ship couldn't go into deep space while the shuttles were still deployed."

"That ship, that's the *Ranzo*," Ponty said. "Hail her. I know the captain and the com officer is an old friend of mine. Once I tell them the cats aren't fugitives anymore, they'll come about."

By the time he'd finished speaking, the *Ranzo* had picked up speed and warped out of com range again. Miraculously, the sensor screen showed that the other small vessel seemed to have no problem keeping pace, even slightly leading the ship.

Doc was too excited to communicate what he was feeling, but spent a lot of time running around the cabin looking out the viewports, peering anxiously at instruments and climbing Ponty, trying to sit on his head.

The *Ranzo* was an old ship, built for the long haul, not a sleek predator like the attrackers, and once more they closed on her quickly.

They were close enough to get a visual on the small vessel, a funny-looking triangular craft that had been barely a blip on the radar as it ran beside the *Ranzo*.

Doc said, *There it is. There's the alien cat's vessel. Chester is there, and the boy too.*

And then, before the hail could be sent, first the smaller vessel and then the *Ranzo* disappeared, seemingly swallowed up in space.

"No!" Ponty cried. "They can't *do* that!"

But they just had.

CHAPTER 27

In the months that followed, the galaxy almost returned to preimpound status. The Klingers were fined most of their holdings to help defray the costs of reparations to other farmers and ranchers. Varley's friend Trudeau ended up with a good part of the Klingers' land. The most recent Mrs. Klinger got what was left and began divorce proceedings against Philly. His councilor uncle was not incarcerated, but the nephew, who took most of the official blame, spent time being reeducated by the Galactic government in one of their holding camps. For a camp, it was extremely expensive, and the expenses came out of the pockets or the sweat of the campers.

Punishing those responsible for the damage didn't diminish what was irreversible. As Jared feared, in some facilities animals sick with ordinarily treatable communicable diseases had been penned side by side with healthy ones, infecting them. Inferior food and water—or in some places, by some officials, profound neglect—had damaged other herds.

Janina, with no cat to tend aboardship, left the *Molly Daise* for full-time employment with Jared, who had all the work he could handle helping rebuild herds and restoring health to sickened or frightened animals. Weeks, the lab tech from the Klinger building, joined them as a full-time vet tech. The man wore a permanently wistful look, as if part of him was always elsewhere. Janina desperately missed Chessie.

But the Barque Cats seemed to be a thing of the past. The beautiful, highly bred ships' cats had vanished into space on that last fateful day and could not be readily replaced in the ships or hearts of their crews. Since many of the pet cats, barn cats, and feral cats dirtside and in space stations had also been impounded, the felines were mostly wary of people. Those who were not had no more experienced cats to train them in their duties. Not all cats liked shipboard life either.

Ponty and Doc rejoined the *Grania*. Ponty found he always needed someone threatening him with death and dismemberment to do his best work, and Mavis fit the bill admirably. Besides, even though Doc had bonded with Ponty, he was still technically Mavis's cat. They kept quiet about their link on shipboard, feeling it was best all the way around if Mavis knew nothing of it.

Older ships from smaller, less prosperous lines started being decommissioned after experiencing accidents that could have been prevented by a resident guardian cat. Even the newer, more expensive vessels that had better technology for detecting air leaks and hull holes weren't worth a damn when it came to catching mice and other vermin.

Meanwhile, Ponty researched, repeatedly comming Janina to ask more about the short-haired cat in the triangular ship and anything she could remember about it.

"There were picture symbols," she told him. "Like the one on the hull with the cat outline over the COB sign. The registration was in picture symbols too—a feather-shaped thing, or maybe it was a carving knife, another cat, a bird. Not Standard." She tried to draw some of them. They looked like hieroglyphics, so he began researching places where those might still be used.

The thing was, they weren't, except by people translating them from museum pieces of great antiquity. Very few of those had survived the disintegration of Earth.

There was one early settlement of Egyptian Revivalists, but it had been disbanded after less than a century and the inhabitants scattered among newer colonies on planets made habitable by upgraded terraforming techniques. He was trying to figure out where it might be when Mavis had a little disagreement with the Galactic Guard over a cargo consignment and decided to retire to Alexandra Station until the law got interested in someone else.

Alexandra Station was a dump, one of the earliest and still most primitive outposts of the GG, manned by surly corrupt staffers who were rejects on punishment duty from elsewhere. The place was dirty, dangerous, and so fraught with safety hazards it was a wonder it remained aloft. But it was far off the frequent flier spaceways and ignored by the Guard, who had noticed an alarming tendency for people in authority to go missing or be taken suddenly dead if they ventured onto Alexandra.

It was just the place for the *Grania* in disgrace.

It also gave Ponty an excuse to stay in his cabin with Doc while the rest of the crew caroused. He was fresh out of charm and amiability. His wife had left him (well, technically he'd done the leaving, but she made it clear he wasn't welcome back), his son was missing, and he was stuck on yet another outlaw ship trying to pull off a trick he was increasingly unsure would work. His searching and researching had been a distraction to keep him from facing the truth. Dung heaps like Alexandra Station were going to be his lot for the rest of his life. It was him and Doc, and in a few years— since cats didn't live long—Doc would be gone too. Actually, as a matter of fact, he didn't feel too great himself. His back ached and he felt a throbbing in his left temple that maybe was the beginning of a stroke?

He lay down, hoping it would go away, and Doc curled up on his chest.

He was too depressed to sleep, which was a good thing because he was awake—or so he thought—when Chester walked into the room, jumped up on the bunk, and with a flip of his black fluffy tail beckoned Ponty and Doc to follow him. The ship was much more deserted than Ponty had ever seen it before. He thought at least a skeleton crew was aboard, but everyone seemed to be off partying or wheeling and dealing at the station.

Chester walked unconcernedly through the ship. Ponty tried to talk to him. "Did you know it was okay to come back now, boy?" he asked aloud, his own voice resonating strangely in his ears, and then asked Doc. *Did he know?*

But Doc seemed preoccupied and didn't reply, just trotted along behind Chester.

Yeah, everything is fine and everybody really misses all you cats and wish you'd come back. Jubal's mother and I miss him too. Is he okay? Doc, dammit, can't you talk to him?

Doc looked over his shoulder then forward again, his tail beckoning like a finger curling in and out—come here.

One minute Ponty was staring at their tails and the next he was on the bridge.

The com screen filled with words, glowing green on a black screen. It had never done that before. Why now?

Chester jumped up to the keyboard, and as the words kept forming, it seemed to Ponty almost as if the cat was writing the message, but cats couldn't do that. Could they?

He looked to Doc again, but Doc just hopped up beside the keyboard and looked over it while Chester's big fluffy paws patted the keys and green letters flowed across the screen.

Some of us are ready to negotiate. The planet of Pshaw-Ra is all that he said it was, more or less, but it is also hot. It's all very well for Pshaw-Ra and his short-furred kind, but we Barque Cats have long fur, and clouds of it rise with the heat as we try to shed ourselves cool.

Mother misses Kibble. Bat misses Weeks. Sol says the place may be a cat sanctuary where we are worshipped and our culture has had a chance to advance, but it's too open for his taste. It reminds him of the field where Git and our sister were killed. He craves the cozy rooms on shipboard. Jubal says that is angoraphobia, but there are no angoras to fear, just us and the short-hairs.

How is Jubal? Ponty tried asking mentally, as he usually did with Doc, but Chester didn't turn around.

Some like it here very much, but some are ready to negotiate. Kibble should come, and Weeks. And the doctor.

Come where? Are you and Jubal ready to come back, Chester boy?

The cat had disappeared, though, and on the screen the last of the flowing letters lingered for a moment: *Some are willing to negotiate.* Then they too disappeared.

Doc jumped down, and Ponty caught a glimpse of another fluffy tail whisking past, then Chester was sitting beside the navigation screen. On it was Alexandra Station, and the nearby moons and planets. One of the planets blinked. As if moving his hand through molasses, Ponty reached forward and clicked the SAVE SCREEN key.

Chester touched noses with Doc, then with a soft breath of fur, rubbed against Ponty's arm. He shouldn't have been able to feel it because he had long sleeves on, but somehow he did. Chester leaped through the viewport and out across space until his form was swallowed by a familiar triangular craft in the distance.

Ponty opened his eyes and found himself in his bunk. Doc sat up on his chest, did a hazardous stretch that threatened Ponty's chin with extended claws, yawned with a curl of bright pink tongue, and started washing. Ponty dropped him to the deck and sat up.

Did I dream that or what? he asked the cat, but Doc yawned again, hopped back up on the bunk and snuggled up in the warm spot.

With his feet firmly on the deck, Ponty headed for the bridge. He walked down the corridor, past shipmates in other cabins playing cards or eating. Mavis was gone and the navigator was asleep at the helm, but Ponty could see something blinking on the screen that should have been blank while they were docked. The com officer was not at his station, but across the screen, in glowing green letters across the black blankness, were the words: *Bring Fishie Treats.*

The evolutionary journey of the Barque Cats continues as the refugee cats seek asylum on Pshaw-Ra's planet, Mau, a world of ancient secrets and advanced science that Pshaw-Ra declares will bring about his goal of feline domination of the universe! Can Jubal and Chester stop the tawny cat's master plan? Do they even want to? Wouldn't cats running the universe actually be a *good* thing? Watch for **CATACOMBS**, the next in the Barque Cats series, coming from Del Rey.

ABOUT THE AUTHORS

ANNE MCCAFFREY, the Hugo Award-winning author of the bestselling *Dragonriders of Pern* novels, is one of science fiction's most popular authors. She lives in a house of her own design, Dragonhold-Underhill, in County Wicklow, Ireland. Visit the author's website at www.annemccaffrey.net.

ELIZABETH ANN SCARBOROUGH, winner of the Nebula Award for her novel *The Healer's War*, is the author of twenty-one solo fantasy novels. She has co-authored fourteen other novels with Anne McCaffrey. She lives on the Olympic Peninsula in Washington State. Visit the author's website at www.eascarborough.com.

ABOUT THE TYPE

This book was set in Electra, a typeface designed for Linotype
by W. A. Dwiggins, the renowned type designer (1880–1956).
Electra is a fluid typeface, avoiding the contrasts of thick and
thin strokes that are prevalent in most modern typefaces.